THE COVENANT of WICKERSHAM HOLLOW

*Thomas A. Bradley*

This book is a work of fiction. Names, characters, places and incidents either are products of the author's imagination or are used fictitiously. Any resemblance to actual events or locals or persons, living or dead, is entirely coincidental.

Copyright © 2015 by Thomas A. Bradley

All rights reserved, including the right to reproduce this book or portions thereof in any form whatsoever. For information contact Thomas A. Bradley at tabradley55@gmail.com.

## Chapter 1
## THE HOUSE (1)

April 17, 2017

It sat silently atop the hill. It drew its breath in the stillness and time shifted. The great white eye of the moon filtered down through the surrounding trees, giving the wispy fingers of mist that crawled along its foundation a silvery glow. Ringed by acres of forested land, the house stood alone in the night and waited. Its windows looked out into the darkness and back into time. It had the luxury of patience because time had no meaning to it.

Within, floorboards creaked under the weight of formless shadows that moved along the walls, leaving swirling motes of dust in their wake. The echo of a baby's cry rose and then fell away in a single tick of the great hall clock that no longer had form. The laughter of many voices mixed with the tinkling of glassware and rattled through the downstairs rooms – a cough of a noise – heard and then gone. The sweet smell of alcohol passed into the acrid, coppery smell of blood.

Unheard footsteps padded deliberately toward the master bedroom. The knob turned and the heavy door swung inward and then closed with a solid, heavy thump. A flicker of a candle flame lit the eye of the window and disappeared, unseen by any but the trees that stood sentinel outside. Muffled cries of fear and despair filtered through the closed bed curtains and – like the candle flame – died away in an instant.

The steps leading down into the dark, dank hollow of its being held their memory. They groaned under the descent of thumping boots no human ear could hear. What walked in those boots held no heart within its chest, but bestowed upon the house a heart that would continue to beat – a heart that would long after pump the blood of malice from which it had taken shape. It would pump its evil and hatred throughout the hollow arteries of it halls and stairwells and vents and chimneys. Its unheard rhythm, *lub-dub, lub-dub, lub-dub*, beat against its walls and ceilings and floors. Its formless chambers expanded with each beat, shaping and reshaping the house – and the time it held within.

Night watched over the house. It saw the flickers in its window-eyes and heard the rustle of its breath along its eaves and gables. It blanketed it in its velvet blackness and held it safe upon the hill.

When the first rays of dawn shed their thin orange lines through the wavering branches of the trees, the house exhaled and settled itself to sleep. And when it did, seventy-seven yards away, hidden in the thick of the forest, an old well, long disused, spat out a plume of dust and shadow from its circular mouth – a sigh of stillness and repose, issued through a stone trachea. And all that stirred or walked within fell into timeless slumber.

\*\*\*

Aroused by some ill-defined foreboding – a remnant thread of a nightmare that clawed at the back of his head and brought sweat to his brow and his heart to a gallop – the old man struggled from his bed and made his way out back. The early morning sky sported no more than the simplest brushstrokes of orange, the sun still well below the tree line. He shambled out to the edge of the porch and turned his gaze northwest. It was there. He couldn't see it for the intervening forestland, but it was there: the old Wickersham place.

"Dadblameit, Walcott, you loathsome old fool!" He slammed his frail fist down on the porch rail. "I shoulda never done it. I shoulda let it rot and crumble all to hell. I shoulda never signed them papers." He shook his head and let out a long, low sigh of self-reproach. "It's all stirred up again. I can feel it; I can–"

A tall column of thick black rose above the trees in the distance and fell silently out of sight again.

The old man wiped a tear from the corner of his eye with a shaky hand, turned and went back into the house. He poured a cup of coffee and worked himself into his seat at the kitchen table.

"I'm sorry; I'm so by God sorry for you folks. But this all has to end. I just can't do it anymore." He hung his head and sobbed.

## Chapter 2
## FRIENDSHIPS DISSOLVE

*October 30, 2017*

**1**

Henry Travis knew in his bones that the time had come around at last. He was as certain of that knowledge as he was in knowing the sun would come up in the morning. The difference was: the sunrise was a bright and cheerful thing. This was dark and foreboding. He pecked the last few sentences out, one finger at a time, dragged the cursor over to the tab that said FILE, found the PRINT button and clicked on it. A second later, the HP Inkjet began spitting out his electronic words onto paper. It was his last chance to try to explain everything. His last chance to try to explain the unexplainable.

Henry gave the contraption on his desk a sour look. He grumbled to everyone that would listen (and most that wouldn't) that computers and electronics were going to be the downfall of society. He told them he loathed sitting in front of a panel of bright light that hurt his eyes, just to be able to type a letter. *I'll take an old manual typewriter to a computer any day of the week and twice on Sundays* he would say. But secretly, in a place where we all keep our private thoughts and opinions, he liked the computer – at least a little bit.

He neatly folded the document and placed it in a rectangular metal box with the same care a mother would place a baby in its crib. For a moment he just sat there and stared at the little pouch that sat on the desk beside his keyboard. Just the thought of what was inside made him shiver. He didn't want to look at it again; he didn't *have to*. What was inside, what it looked like, what it felt like was burned into his memory. But the truth was he did have to look at it. It would not permit him to put it away again *without* seeing it, *without* touching it just one more time. Its draw was too powerful. Opening the flap on the pouch, he dumped the item into the palm of his hand. The touch of it instantly turned his stomach. It was cold – and warm – all at the same time. Its yellowed finish and the netted series of cracks that ran along its surface spoke of its age.

Henry leaned forward and examined it under the globe of the desk lamp. A key of sorts. A key fashioned from a finger bone. He slipped it back in its pouch, dropped it into the box next to a smaller box labeled, *Tommy Vorland*. He locked the lid and shoved it into the lower left hand drawer of his desk. That done, there was nothing to do now but wait. Wait and think. He mentally ticked off all the things he needed to tell his granddaughter about that house.

*That House*! He closed his eyes and seventy years fell away. He was sixteen again. It was a warm July day, 1947, and the seven of them had agreed to meet at their secret spot in French Creek State Park. He had arrived early, as usual, hoping that she would come first and they'd have some time alone before the others arrived. His (never before worn) denims were startlingly blue, still creased and very stiff. The light blue cotton short-sleeved T-shirt he wore was neatly tucked in all the way around.  He sat on a rock on the embankment of a little stream that had managed to break away from the creek and cut its own diagonal through the woods.

The crackling of leaves behind him got him to his feet.  He brushed furiously at the seat of his pants, hoping that any smudge the rock might have made would be dusted off without a trace.  Then he heard her voice and his heart sank.  It was not the *she* he had hoped would be first.

## 2

"Hi Henry."  The girl stood just inside a thicket that marked the boundary of the stream bank.  "Is-is it safe, do you think?"

Henry looked around.  "Yeah, I think so, Janet.  Come on."

Janet Egan was a slip of a girl, thin and wiry.  The yellow cambric top barely bulged at her breast line and fell almost straight down over her narrow hips.  Her dark brown hair was pulled together at the back and held in place by a butterfly hair clip.  It fanned out over her shoulder blades and cascaded down her back.  She stepped out of the brush and found a place on the bank that suited her and sat down, her knees pulled up to her chest.  Henry resumed his spot on the rock.  Now it didn't really matter what his jeans looked like.  The chance of having any privacy had just vanished with Janet's arrival.

"Hey!  Where is everyone?"  The voice came from a few yards downstream.  It was followed by a few expletives as Matt Holloway fought his way through a stand of blackberry. When he emerged, his T-shirt was torn at the shoulder and his arms bore thin crisscrosses of red.

"Goddammit! I always do that. How come I always end up coming out in the wrong place?" He trotted up and sat down between Henry and Janet, slightly closer (but he hoped not noticeably so) to Janet.

"I think it's because your sense of direction is as backwards as-" Henry smiled. "-as your shirt."

Janet giggled. Matt looked down and turned red. He did, indeed, have his shirt on backwards, the tag plastered to the hollow of his throat.

"Shit!" He yanked it off and turned it around.

"Maybe you should get your mother to dress you from now on."

At the sound of Amy Pritchard's voice, Henry's pulse quickened; he felt warm and cold all at the same time. Goosebumps puckered his forearms and a light sweat dampened the strands of black hair that swept across his forehead. He stole a glance at Matt and Janet and wondered if they knew what he was thinking, wondered if they knew what he was feeling.

"And I certainly wouldn't become a tailor or take any job where you were responsible for dressing others. When you have kids, let your wife dress them if you don't want them laughed at." Amy pointed a playful finger at Janet and then winked.

Matt flushed and Janet rolled her eyes.

Everyone in the group knew that Matt had a thing for Janet. Just as they knew that Henry would have walked over hot coals in bare feet with two broken legs for Amy. The couples in question knew everyone knew, and yet, somehow, the wiles of teenage years kept them pretending. Everyone knew because it was impossible for them – for that group – not to know. This knowledge, and everything else that ticked by in the clocks of their minds, came to them whenever they were together. The larger the group, the stronger the mental tie. But even with just two, a link of weak threads could be established: a passing glimpse of a thought-provoked image, or a word spoken to oneself. It was a gift and a curse that none of them had asked for. It was a gift that brought them closer together and pushed them farther apart, like electrons of opposite spin in an eternal dace as neighbors, never being able to touch, only waiting for that day when they would be stripped away, pulled out of orbit. Today was that day.

Amy plopped down on the bank next to Henry, her elbows on her knees and her chin resting on closed fists. Four of them were here now, so talking was not a necessity, but it still felt more normal.

"I agree," said Amy, to a thought that Henry was having.

"I don't know if I do or not," said Matt. "I don't like the idea. We're all friends. We're all best friends and this doesn't feel right at all."

Janet put a hand on Matt's knee. "But you know it is, don't you? Our being together is dangerous. You've seen that. We've all seen that. Yes, we can hear what each of us is thinking and that's pretty cool, but it's the other that isn't, and you know what I'm talking about."

Matt nodded glumly. "We're not bad people. I don't understand how just being together makes bad things happen. Why can't it make good things happen? We all stick up for each other, we're not mean or bullies or perpetually angry people. How can we ... why do bad things happen when we're together?"

"You're hedging," said Amy. "What you really wanted to say is: 'How can we cause bad things to happen.'" I don't know. But whenever we're together ... we do. And you know it. It's us. Somehow ... together, we're like some ... oh, I don't know what."

"Like some kind of wild, charged circuit ... a live wire that's snake-whipping around in all directions just waiting for someone to get just a little too close," said Henry, looking at the cap of light that played across the surface of the stream.

"We should have never gone into that damned house," said Tina Farley, stepping onto the small path that ran above the group. She forgot for a moment about their mental connection and thought: *It was Tommy's fault all this happened. We should have never gone in there with him.*

"It wasn't his fault at all," said Amy, giving Tina a reproachful look. "He didn't force us to go. We all went on our own, for our own reasons. Don't blame Tommy ... or anyone else ... for decisions you make. We all went. That's all there is to it. Nobody's to blame."

Henry stood up and shoved his hands into his pockets. "Besides, Tommy has enough problems without us laying ours on his shoulders, too. From what I hear, he's never going to get out of that booby ... uh ... hospital."

"Yeah," said Matt. "I heard my parents saying that they have him in a straightjacket and keep shooting him up with meds all day long."

"I don't know if that's true or not," said Amy, looking at Henry. "But it's true enough that whatever strength and sanity he had when we went in there went out of him before we came out, like air out of a popped balloon. Whoosh! ... and gone."

Henry turned and faced them, his eyes moist. He kept blinking to keep the waterworks behind the dam of self-control. It wasn't working too well. "Well then," he said, his voice cracked with emotion. "We know why we're here. I guess it'd be easier if we just all do it."

"Are you sure we have to?" asked Matt.

Henry didn't have to answer. Amy did that for him with a series of thoughts.

*McKendrick's drug store. We went in for some snacks and sodas. First the glass cracked on the cold case we were looking through. Then all the bottled waters exploded. Mrs. McKendrick went to clean it up and was electrocuted when the wires of the blower at the bottom all of a sudden ripped themselves out of the fan and wrapped around her ankles. Sitting at the traffic light on our way home from the movies. That old couple pulled up next to us, remember? They asked for directions. As soon as we gave them to them, the old man stomped down on the gas and shot through the red light, right into a passing bus. And the best one was our visit to the retirement community with the pets. Six people who had never had heart conditions died of heart attacks five minutes after we left, and all three dogs we took from the shelter developed rabies and had to be put down. There was also-*

Matt held his hands up. "Okay, okay! I get it. I don't like it, but I get it."

"I don't like it either, Matt. Not one bit." Henry was looking at the ground so the others couldn't see he was crying. "But we can't be together ... ever. We all know it."

## 3

The memory of it all swelled in Henry Travis's heart and left a hollow place in the pit of his stomach as he came back to the here and now. He dabbed at the corners of his eyes and looked at his watch, wondering when Annabel would arrive, wondering if Annabel would ever arrive to listen to him. He wheeled himself back over to his writing desk and closed his eyes. He thought back to that day, the day best friends had to walk away from each other forever. And then he smiled, because – by some miracle – two of them had found each other again and had learned how to be together. But that togetherness came with a price. Together alone – never in public.

He picked up the framed photo of his wife and gave it a kiss. He ran the backs of his fingers across her cheek and could almost feel the softness through the glass.

"God how I miss you, Amy."

His eyes dropped involuntarily to the lower left hand drawer that held the key. By sheer force of will, he drew them back up to the picture of his wife, stared at it for a moment longer and then set it carefully back on top of his desk.

## Chapter 3
## THE VISIT

### 1

Brian Michaels pushed up off the bed and gave his wife, Annabel, a kiss on the forehead. His hand instinctively slid down and cupped her right breast.

"God I love you, Belle. I love making love to you. In fact-" He flipped the sheets back and slid in next to her again. "-How about another go-round?"

Annabel pushed him away with a short laugh. "Enough already. I'm running late as it is. My grandfather's waiting."

Brian blew a raspberry as he wormed himself out the bed for a second time. "Boy, you sure are a killjoy. Wish you didn't have to go. You know what he's going to go on about, don't you?"

Annabel propped herself up on one elbow and rested her head on her fist, a silky spray of coppery-colored hair fanning out across the pillow. She drew the sheet up over her breasts with her other hand to discourage any further delay on Brian's part.

"He loves us, silly. That's all. If he wants to believe in spooks and goblins and ghosts, and thinks that he has to warn us, so what? He's only doing it because he cares."

"I know that. I do." Brian dragged his pants up over his hips and buttoned them, grabbed his shirt off the floor and slid into it. "But really, Belle ... does he honestly believe were going to give up such a fabulous house after spending all that time and money restoring it, just because he thinks it's haunted or something? If he does, he must be really losing it."

Annabel flopped back on her pillow. "I swear to God ... the two of you are cut from the same mold. You're both stupidly stubborn. The least I can do is go hear the man out. He deserves that much. Maybe, just maybe, it doesn't really matter whether or not we believe what he says. Did you ever think of that? Maybe just hearing him out is all he really needs. You know, makes him feel important and part of something we're doing. After all, he helped raise me."

Brian sighed, leaned over and gave Annabel another kiss.

"You're probably right. I guess sometimes I can't see the forest for the trees, either. You know I think he's a great guy. I suppose I just get so caught up in bills and what has to be done and what should be done-" He shrugged. "I guess I just forget sometimes that he's stuck in that house and his life is winding down and ... well, I guess if it were me ... or maybe, when it gets to be me ... guess I'd want to feel useful, too."

Annabel smiled. "Ding, ding, ding. We have comprehension, folks. Now go on. Scoot! You get that sexy ass of yours up to the house and make sure all the renovations are up to spec. I'll see you back here for dinner."

Brian climbed on the bed, swept her up in his arms and gave her a long, hard kiss.

"Love you, Babe. See you for dinner."

## 2

Annabel Michaels had grown up in Wickersham Hollow and knew all the stories. She had told her own versions to her friends and listened to theirs sitting cross-legged in a tent in her grandfather's back yard. Now, on her way to her grandfather's, she was thinking about them again. It was time to bring the ghosts out of the dark and shine the light of reason on them. It was time to chase them away forever

## 3

Henry looked up when Annabel stepped through the door. He had his wheelchair pushed up against the small writing desk that sat in one corner, nestled on an angle between the floor-to-ceiling bookshelves. His left hand was pressed against the side of his glasses, helping to keep them in place. Dropping the pen from his shaking right hand, he wheeled the chair around to face his granddaughter.

"Well," he said, the strength of his voice standing in antithesis to his frail looking body. "You finally condescended to come and listen to the ravings of an old man, have you?"

Annabel walked over, gave him a kiss on the cheek and pulled up a worn, brown leather chair. Leaning forward, she placed her hands on the backs of Henry's. "How have you been, gran'pop? Have you been taking your medicine and getting enough rest?"

The old man pulled away and waved a dismissive hand in front of her face. "Forget the medicine and the rest. You know why I asked you here. No ... why I begged you to come. I'm glad you finally did, especially since I know you've been avoiding this."

Annabel sat back. "Gran'pop, it's just that..." Her eyes darted to the floor. "Well, we've already bought the house; we've spent a modest fortune restoring it. It's a beautiful old place and ... well ... Brian and I are tired of living in an apartment. It's perfect for us. It's-"

"Listen to me," barked Henry. "I know all your reasons for wanting to live there. I do. And if it were any other place, we wouldn't be having this conversation at all. But that place is not right for you. It's not right for anyone. It should have been torn down years ago ... burned to ashes, actually."

Annabel let out an exasperated breath. She was trying not to lose her patience, but it was difficult. The house was perfect for them. Why couldn't he see that? "Gran'pop-"

"Hush! The word came out so harshly that it could have been delivered from the end of a bullwhip. "It's my turn to talk. When I'm done ... well, you'll do whatever you do. I know that. But for God's sake listen to me. Really listen to me. Then-" He held his hands up in an I surrender gesture. "-I'll never mention it again."

Annabel nodded. "Go ahead, gran'pop. No matter what, I know I owe you that much respect. I promise ... I'll really listen to everything you have to say."

"Humph!" Henry rubbed at the patch of gray stubble on his chin and folded his hands on the afghan that was spread across his lap. His head was cocked to one side as he stared off into space. When he looked back at Annabel, a single tear ebbed from the corner of one eye.

"It was just after the war, nineteen forty-seven. I was just sixteen when we went in there. It was the first and the last time I ever set foot on that property." He let his gaze slip down to the wrinkled hands jittering on his lap. "To this day, I've never forgotten it. In fact, sometimes, I still wake up thinking-" His voice trailed off and he wiped at his eyes.

Annabel leaned forward and put a gentle hand on her grandfather's shoulder. "Take your time, gran'pop. It's okay."

The old man patted Annabel's hand, coughed, wiped his eyes, shook his head and dropped his chin on his chest. "I was sixteen. Tommy Vorland was eighteen; he's the only one who could get his hands on a car, stole it from his pop. He drove us up there, along with his sixteen year old girlfriend at the time, Lucy Darrow." Henry smiled. "I say at the time, because Tommy never stuck to just one girl. Tina Farley was also sixteen and her best friend, Amy Pritchard, had just turned fifteen the week before. There was also Matt Holloway and his girlfriend, Janet Egan. Matt and Janet were also fifteen. It was Halloween night. We all wanted to go someplace spooky, where we could do what young folks do when they're away from their parents."

Annabel smiled. "Drink?"

"Of course, drink." He said it as if Annabel had asked if he had to breathe to live. "And more. I fell hard for Amy. Ended up marrying her ... as you well know. What you don't know is that I almost lost her that night." His mouth turned down at the corners, a wistful look briefly clouding his eyes, and then spoke in what was no more than a whisper. "You know, you look just like your grandmother. So beautiful."

"What happened, gran'pop? How did you almost lose gran'ma?" Annabel was genuinely stunned. This was something she'd never heard before.

Her grandfather raised his head and looked right into Annabel's soul.

"The place had been empty for years. There was some scuttlebutt about a group of workers getting killed up there when old Walcott, the absentee owner, had them making some minor repairs to the place. Whether or not that's true, I can't say. What I do know as fact is that, after that, old Walcott put up a big, ten-foot high chain link, barbed wire-topped fence around the whole kit-and-caboodle. And it's been that way ever since. Leastwise, till you went and bought the damned place."

"Yeah," said Annabel, "it was the first thing we had torn down. We couldn't believe that someone had actually spent all that money putting-"

"Will you gosh darn let me finish the telling?" the old man broke in.

Annabel sat back, the look on her face – that of a scolded puppy.

"Tommy Vorland drove us up there. We couldn't drive all the way up because the road was private, but Tommy knew a spot where we could hide the car. From there, we hiked our way up the hill through the woods. About seventy-five yards or so outside the fence was an old abandoned well. It had dried up a long time before, but it led to an old tunnel that led up to the foundation of the house. That's how we planned on getting in."

"How did you know about the tunnel?"

"We were kids; kids find things like that. Hell, I don't know. But stop interrupting me." He shook his head and rolled his eyes. "Now, as I was saying ... everything was going along just fine. We all climbed down the well ... after we lowered the cooler of beer down, of course ... and started making our way through the tunnel. For the first hundred feet or so, the going was easy. But after that, the tunnel narrowed all the way around and we had to walk hunched over. It was damp and dank and moldy and musty. The air was close and heavy. The walls oozed, and the bottom was two inches thick with sludge and water.

"It wasn't until we came to a fork that things started to go ... go..." Henry closed his eyes. "I want to say wrong, but that's not the right word. I remember Matt calling it ... *weird*."

## Chapter 4
## THE TUNNEL

**1**

"...*weird*. I mean, this is really spookier than I thought it would be." Matt Holloway took a step back, shined his flashlight down one of the forks, slid it over to the other and then back again. "It's really getting cold down here. It shouldn't be this cold, should it? I mean, a minute ago ... back there-" He cocked a thumb over his shoulder. "-we were all sweatin' from the humidity."

"Cold-shmold. Who cares about cold?" said Tommy, digging in the pocket of his dungaree jacket and fishing out his Marlboros. Flipping a cigarette toward his mouth and catching it in his teeth, he spoke around the butt as he snapped open his Zippo. "Isn't spooky the whole point of this?"

"I guess so," stammered Matt. "Which way should we go?"

Amy Pritchard was standing next to Tina Farley, who was just in front of Henry. Janet Egan had one hand on her hip and was shining her flashlight down the tunnel behind them, and Lucy Darrow was pressed up against Tommy's back, her hands massaging his hips.

Tommy held his cigarette up and watched the smoke drift off down the left tunnel. "That's our path, ladies and gentlemen. Always follow the breeze." He snatched the flashlight out of Matt's hand, bumped him aside with his shoulder and splashed off into the dark. Lucy did a quick skip and short run to catch up to him. The others looked at each other, shrugged almost in unison, and followed.

When they reached a spot where the tunnel opened up enough for them to stand upright again, they all stretched, hands in the small of their backs. Tommy took a last drag of his cigarette and dropped it into the water that was now ankle deep. It disappeared with a dying pfft!

Ahead of them, the tunnel cut sharply to the left. From where they were standing it was hard to tell, but it looked to Tommy like the water was much deeper at that end.

"I think we're all about to get wet," he said.

"I already am," whispered Lucy in his ear, slipping her hand inside his jeans pocket.

Tommy grabbed her wrist and slowly pulled the hand out. "Hold your horses. There'll be plenty of time for that soon enough. Let's just get out of this damned tunnel, first."

"I agree," echoed Amy. "I'm cold, and my feet are freezing in this water. Let's get out of here."

Tommy moved forward, and with each step the water climbed higher and higher up his legs. "I think we're going to be in up to our waists soon. Anybody wanna turn back?" He shined the flashlight across their faces one by one. No one objected. He turned and plunged forward into the deepening pool.

When they reached the wall at the end where the tunnel turned to the left, they found that it also climbed up at a steep angle. "I think we're making progress," said Tommy, more to himself than anyone else. "And it looks dry up there. That's why the water's so deep. It pools up here at the bottom. Come on everyone, we're almost home. I'm pretty sure that in a few more minutes it'll be party time."

## 2

They turned left, thankful to be out of the water that had risen above their waists. The farther up they went, the steeper it got. Lucy's thighs were burning and Matt was starting to pant heavily. Exercising had never been one of his indulgences. And, although he wasn't what could be considered fat, he did carry a considerable amount of extra weight. Tommy, for his part, was doing surprisingly well, considering how heavily he smoked.

Amy, too, was having no trouble, as she spent most of her time playing field hockey, swimming or backpacking. She was a natural born athlete and loved just about all sports. Tina and Janet were struggling a bit, but both were so glad to be out of the water that they didn't dare complain.

At the top, the grade leveled out and curved away. As he rounded another bend, Tommy came to a dead stop. In front of him was an old oaken door, standing just over four feet high. It was hinged to the left side of the wall with iron castings. A large, wrought iron ring served as a handle. The right side had a slide bolt, but there was no lock.

"I think we just hit pay dirt," said Tommy. "Quick cigarette break ... and then we find out just how much fun we can have in this dump."

"How do you know that door leads into the house?" asked Janet. "It could go anywhere."

Tommy snorted. "Cut me a fuckin' break, would ya? Where the hell else do you think it would go? It has to be the door into the basement."

"No, it doesn't have to be," corrected Amy. "But I think you're right; I think that's exactly where it goes."

"Tommy held his flashlight up under his chin. "Wooo-haaaaaaaa. Vel-come to my castle." He did his best Lugosi imitation, making the word castle sound like cossle.

"You think it's unlocked?" asked Matt, still puffing.

"Guess we'll find out in a minute or two," answered Henry, who was feeling a bit uneasy about the whole thing. Sneaking into the place had sounded fun at first, but now that he was here, he wasn't all that sure he should be. Something in the sleepy dark of his subconscious was telling him it would be better if they all left. And he wanted to listen to it, but that was out of the question, now. If he even *suggested* leaving, the others would surely brand him a chicken. That was the kind of moniker that would lead to all kinds of trouble in school. Good or bad, there was only one way to go. Through the door.

Pushing past Tommy, Henry slid the bolt back, grabbed the ring in both hands and yanked. At first it didn't budge. The dampness of the tunnel had all the wooden joints swollen to capacity. He placed his right foot against the wall and tried again. This time the hinges squealed and the door cracked open.

## Chapter 5
## COFFEE AND A SHILLELAGH

Henry stopped talking and looked up when Emma came in carrying three coffee mugs and a glass of water on a silver tray. Beside the water was a soufflé cup with two yellow pills and a large white one. Annabel jumped up and took the tray from her mother and set it on one of the end tables. Emma walked around the back of Henry's chair, gave him a kiss on the head as she passed, and handed him the water. When he had it steadied, she dumped the pills into his other hand. "Down the hatch, Dad!"

Henry grumbled, tossed his head back and dropped the pills in. They all went down with the first swallow, which made Henry very happy.

Emma handed them each a mug, smiled and then left. Annabel looked at the steaming mug of coffee still sitting on the tray. "You drink two?" she asked.

"Are you crazy?" replied Henry with a smile. "That'd probably make my heart explode. Technically, I'm not even allowed to have this one. But I say: 'what's the point of livin' if you're miserable'. And without my coffee ... I'd be miserable."

"Okay," said Annabel, obviously confused.

"That coffee is for your grandmother. It was a ritual of ours. After I retired we made it a habit to spend thirty minutes in the afternoon together just relaxing. We called it our coffee-resty time. It became one of those beloved habits that are so hard to break. So-" He nodded at the coffee mug on the tray.

Annabel smiled and absently brushed her fingers across her cheeks. "I miss gran'ma. Of course, I can't say my cheeks feel the same way. I think they're happy to be left un-pinched."

Henry let out a short chuckle. "Yeah, she was a touchy-feely kind of gal when it came to her granddaughter. I remember lots-a nights she'd sit up with you playing all kinds of silly games. Some of them she couldn't even pronounce right ... or refused to." Henry winked. "Always called that silly Candy Land game clandyland."

"I remember that, gran'pop. She always used to let me win, too."

"She was crazy about you, Belle, just as she was crazy about your mother." A stern look grew on Henry's face. "You know, when you're father walked out on the two of you, well ... grandma wanted to beat him to death with a stick."

Annabel smiled again.

"I'm not kidding, and it's not a euphemism. Do you ever remember seeing a big old stick we used to keep by the door? You used to play with it sometimes."

"Yeah, I remember that. Wasn't it a real Irish shillelagh?"

"It was. Do you remember looking for it one day and crying because you couldn't find it to play with?"

"Wow, now that you mention it-"

"I had to throw it away. Your grandmother was going to go down to where your father worked and bash his brains in with it. She was one strong-willed woman. O'course, she could have used anything for that, but that damned shillelagh was just too tempting and too convenient."

For the first time since she'd arrived, Annabel really laughed. The image of her grandmother walloping her father over the head, blow after blow, was just too much.

Henry leaned back in his chair. "She was an amazing gal, and I miss her more than I can say." He thumped his chest. "But she's in here, and always will be."

Annabel placed a hand over her heart. "In here, too, gran'pop; in here, too."

Henry nodded, drained what was left of his coffee, cradling the mug with both hands to keep it steady. When he finished, he passed it to Annabel who set it back down on the silver tray.

Henry closed his eyes in thought and settled back in his wheelchair. "*Belle...*"

## Chapter 6
## THE HOUSE (2)

Brian brought the F-150 to a stop, cut the engine and set the parking brake. Leaning back, his hands still resting on the wheel, he took in the view of his new house. The three and a half story Gothic-Victorian blend stood at the top of the hill. Its freshly laid marble steps climbed to a balcony-covered front entrance, spanned on either side by a wraparound veranda. Plumbers and electricians jostled around each other, avoiding masons and plasterers. Most of the work was already done, but Brian and Annabel had decided on some changes at the last minute.

Brian stepped out and walked up to the steps. One of the masons was just finishing pointing the retainer on the left side and looked up. "Um ... I don't think you're supposed to be up here, sir." He knelt there looking at him, mortar in one hand and trowel in the other.

"It's okay. I'm the new owner and architect. I wanted to have a quick look." Brian smiled. "I'll try to stay out of everyone's way."

The mason shook his head. "T'ain't safe up here. Lots-a cords and junk and nails an' other junk that ain't been cleaned up yet ... and... Well, you just shouldn't be here, that's all."

There was something about the last unfinished "and" that piqued his curiosity.

The mason set his mortar and trowel down and stood up. For a moment, he just stood there looking around, and Brian got the distinct feeling he was checking to see if anyone was watching. Whatever the reason, he hesitated a good two minutes or so before stepping forward.

"Why don't we go over here?" He pointed to the end of the building. "Easier to talk quiet-like." He strode away without waiting for Brian and slipped around the corner.

When Brian caught up with him, he was halfway down the side of the house standing against a large walnut tree. He had his hands stuffed inside his white bib-coveralls and was shifting nervously from foot to foot, his eyes darting from side to side.

"Why all the secrecy?" asked Brian

The man yanked his hands from his pockets and patted them up and down. "Shh! Keep your voice down, please. Don't want nobody to see or hear me talkin' t'ya. I'm only doin' it cause I think it's the right thing t'do."

"Well, you certainly have my attention. No doubt about that. What did you leave off? What was that last and?"

"It ain't right up here. Ain't right by a long shot. Things ... things happen here. Odd things. Things that ain't supposed t'happen anywhere." He slid further back around the side of the tree, peered around and then motioned for Brian to follow.

"What are you so afraid of? I don't think anybody ... except maybe your boss ... will care that you're talking to me."

"Sir, I am the boss; leastways, boss of the masons workin' here. But it's more 'an that. Look around. Go ahead. Look at the workmen coming and going. Tell what you see. Go on." He flapped his hands as if shooing a cat off a countertop.

Brian stepped out from behind the tree and stood there watching. It took him a few minutes to catch on. At first, all he saw were workers coming and going – carrying tools or parts or whatever. Nothing seemed odd. But then it struck him. Not a single one of them was talking or whistling or muttering. Their faces were all blank, flat pictures of what living people should be. They had the stoic countenances of animated mannequins. And now that he thought about it, the mason had had the same blank look when he'd first noticed him.

"What's wrong with everyone?" he asked, stepping back around the tree. "They all look like they're sleepwalking or something."

"It's this place, these woods ... this house. Evil! Pure evil. If I was you-"

Brian expelled a cough of a laugh and put a hand on the man's shoulder. "I'm sorry. I'm not laughing at you, really. It's just that ... just that I've heard all these stories all my life. It's just a house, that's all. And now-" He swept his hand in front of him. "-Now it's a beautifully restored house."

The mason agreed – sort of. "Yes, sir. It sure is a beautiful house. Sometimes."

"And what, exactly, do you mean by that?"

"Look, I'm tellin' ya. Cut your losses while you can and walk away from this place." He looked at the house, his eyes wandering up to the roof and then back down. "Walk away while you can."

"Have you got any idea how much money my wife and I have sunk into fixing this place up? And you want us to just chuck it because of children's ghost stories? You must be out of your mind."

The mason looked at the ground. "Ayup, ton a-money. And I know I ain't gonna convince ya t' give it up. No, I can see that for sure. But don't say you wasn't warned."

He side-stepped Brian and started back toward the front of the house. At the corner he stopped and turned back. "House don't wanna be changed. It ain't gonna let ya do that; it's only gonna let ya think ya done it. Don't move int'it. Paper and a match, that's my recommendation."

Brian watched him disappear around the corner. *It's a good thing he's a good mason*, he thought, *'cause he's certainly certifiable.*

"The house don't wanna be changed," he mimicked. "The *House*? The *HOUSE* doesn't want to be changed?" He laughed, and a chill ran through him like a sudden cold breeze that blows up in the middle of summer out of nowhere and is gone as fast as it came. He shook it off and walked back around the front. The mason was kneeling down again, working on the pointing, as if he'd never stopped. He cocked his head in Brian's direction, shook it once and went back to finishing up.

Brian took a last admiring look at the house and climbed into the truck. Everything was going well, the crazy mason notwithstanding, and he and Annabel should be able to move in by the end of the week. He turned the key and dropped the shifter into DRIVE. The tires crunched down on the gravel as the F-150 wound around the circle. When he turned onto the main drive he gave the house one more glance in the rearview mirror and slammed on the brakes. The truck skidded to a stop. He twisted around to look out the back window. Looking at it straight on, everything looked fine. But in the mirror he had seen the house standing there as it had been seven months ago, untouched and falling apart.

"Looks like the loony got to ya, Brian, old boy. Now you're seeing things." He twisted back around and looked up in the mirror. And it was there again. It almost seemed to be mocking him. He swiveled back again. Just as it should be. Without checking the mirror again, he stepped on the gas and sped down the drive toward the main road, keeping his eyes straight ahead and telling himself that houses don't remake themselves – telling himself that it was just an illusion dredged from his childhood by a crazy mason's ravings. That was all it was. No more real than confusing the sounds of a house settling for something clomping menacingly up the cellar steps to get you after you've finished watching a monster movie. It was all subliminal suggestion. Nothing more.

Thirty yards before the driveway reached the street, the truck stalled. Its engine clicked and coughed and sputtered as it rolled to a dead stop. Brian cursed, tried the key a few times and cursed again. He threw his door open so hard it bounced back, catching him on the shin as he stepped out. Another battery of curses echoed away into the woods.

"You com' t'see me, child. You com' now. You know where. Mot'er gon' be waitin, so don't you dawdle none." The voice (Jamaican or Haitian, he didn't know which) was feather light, but it wasn't carried on the air; it was in his head. "You com' t'Mot'er."

Brian leaned against the fender and shook his head, trying to clear it. He ran a hand through the thick, black tuft of hair that hung just below the crown of his left ear and exhaled. The last thing he wanted was to let himself start getting carried away with superstitious nonsense. He wanted to believe that maybe all he really *had* heard was just the wind whistling eerily through the tree branches. But that didn't really go down so well. If he were hearing things or, worse, making them up in his head, why in the hell would he add an accent to it? It just didn't figure.

"You're losin' it, kid. Let's keep it together, okay? Stop spooking yourself. You didn't hear anything and you know it. Just some more of the leftover mumbo-jumbo from that crazy mason." He opened the door and climbed in. What happened next didn't just nudge Brian into the strange; it grabbed him with both hands and shoved him into the world of the surreal. The key twisted itself to the right; the truck rumbled to life and the steering wheel turned itself all the way to the left.

"You know where t'com', child. Now stop makin' me wait. This is important."

## Chapter 7
## BLOOD and BEER

**1**

"*Belle*," Henry continued, settling back in his wheelchair and smoothing the afghan across his lap, "I know you're going to dismiss everything I have to say here as either the ramblings of an old, confused man, or just plain silly hogwash. Either way, that's your decision. I can't force you to believe what I'm telling you.

"Too many tales and stupid stories have circulated about that house up there for too long. I know you've heard them all. I know you don't believe in spirits and goblins or whatever you want to call them. Just remember this-" Henry paused, took a deep breath and fixed his eyes on Annabel. "-there's evil out there. Pure evil. You can see it in any daily headline or breaking news story. Evil. I know it'll be hard for you to accept that a house, or grounds or ... oh, I don't know what ... can be evil in itself. But it can. I know; I was there."

Henry leaned forward as far as he could and took Annabel's hand. "I know you believe in good. I know you know that there are a lot of good people out there in the world. So believe this too – there's no good without evil, just like there's no right without wrong or up without down. It's the Yin and Yang of the universe.

"Now, I don't want to go getting all metaphysical on you, so let me just finish my story." He sat back and held up his right hand. There was a sickle-shaped scar that ran halfway across his palm starting just below the little finger. "I got this when I pulled that door *open*."

**2**

"...*open*." Henry grinned. "I got the damned thing open. Come on."

Tommy gave Henry a clap on the back. "Way to go, my man. Great job!" He turned toward Matt. "Grab the cooler. Parrr-tyyy tiiiime!"

Henry stood there holding the door as the others passed through. Just as he was about to go in, a strong wind arose from nowhere and ripped the handle-ring out of his hand, slamming the door shut.

"AHHH!" screamed Henry, cradling his injured hand in the other. Blood oozed out of a deep gash that curved across his palm like the blade of a scimitar. It ran down his fingers and dripped onto the stone floor with an echoing *plop*! *plop*! *plop*! He could feel his stomach starting to knot up and willed himself not to be sick.

"Hey," he yelled. "Open up you guys; I cut my hand ... bad."

When the door didn't open and no one answered, Henry thumped on it a few times with the edge of his fist. "Come on, I need some ice or something. Open up!"

"It's stuck again." The voice was muffled, distant; Henry could barely make out the words.

"Well push harder," he yelled. "I'll try to pull from out here with my good hand."

Henry wrapped his fingers through the ring, closed his eyes and yanked. He had no way of knowing whether or not his efforts were being augmented on the other side. While he tugged with his left hand, he kept his right pressed up tight against his thigh, hoping that would help stop the bleeding.

Remembering how he had opened it before, he placed his foot up against the wall, took a firm grip on the ring and...

*Wham!* The door flew open before he could pull on it, sending him flying backward. He landed hard on his rump and slid sideways down the ramp, coming to rest up against a wall just before he reached the bottom. Another three feet and he would have gone into the pool and been completely soaked.

*Guess I have some good luck*, he thought. *At least I'm not drenched.* By the time he worked himself to a standing position, Tommy was there next to him.

"You okay?"

Henry held up his hand. "I'll live, but I gotta stop the bleeding."

Tommy yanked a paisley bandana from the hip pocket of his jeans and wrapped it around Henry's hand, tying a tight knot. "There. That oughta hold ya. Come on, we got us some beer to drink and some fun t'have." He clapped Henry on the shoulder and the two of them trudged back up the tunnel to the door.

Henry gave the oaken sentry a bad look, thought about kicking it but decided against it, and stepped through. Tommy followed. As soon as they were in, the door slammed over again. The sound of it was as loud as a gunshot. Lucy screamed, Amy jumped, and Tina and Janet both slapped their hands across their hearts.

Tommy and Henry both jumped too, whirling around at the sound. Matt let out a little shriek, which he hoped had been drowned out by Lucy's scream.

Tommy started laughing. "Man ... that door's really fucked up."

"What are you laughing about?" asked Matt, his heart still beating against his rib cage. "What if we can't get it open again? Huh? What if we're all trapped in here?"

Tommy turned and leveled his eyes on Matt's. "What if; what if; what if? Jesus on a fuckin' go-cart. So what if it won't open? We're not goin out that way anyway, are we? I mean, Christ, we're here to explore this place. We'll leave by the front door when we're ready."

"Oh yeah, sure we will. Then what?" snapped Matt. "Forget about the damned fence? You know, the reason we climbed down that stupid well in the first place?"

Tommy let out a phony laugh. He *had* forgotten about it, but there was no way he was going to let the others know that. "Don't worry about it. We'll get out. One way or the other." He turned to Lucy. "Get me a beer; I'm thirsty ... and get one for Henry here, too. The man who got us inside."

### 3

Henry had expected it to be pitch black inside. It wasn't. The room was small, the walls made of the same rough and uneven stone the tunnel had been cut through, but there were candles on large sconces all around that Tommy had set to burning. A steady *plop ... plop*

...*plop* marked time as condensation rolled off the stone and dropped onto the floor. At the far end was another door. This one looked like the one they had just come through, but larger. It also had a doorknob and flip-latch.

"What's in there?" asked Henry, taking the beer that Lucy handed him. He nodded his thanks as he worked at pulling the tab without dislodging his makeshift bandage.

"Don't know," said Tommy. "Haven't got that far yet. Remember? You were stuck outside and we had to get you in?"

Tommy chugged half his beer, belched and nodded at Matt. "Go see what's behind that door. And grab yourself a beer for Christ's sake; what're ya waitin for?"

When Matt bent over to pluck a can from the cooler, Tommy gave him a gentle push on the butt with his foot.

"Hey man, what was that for?"

Tommy winked. "For screamin' like a little girl. Think I didn't hear ya, queer-o?" He walked over and put an arm around Matt's shoulder. "But it's okay. We all still like you, anyway."

Matt shoved the arm away. "Yeah, whatever ... jerk-wad."

The two boys smiled at each other. Matt shook his head and then popped his beer open on the way over to see what was behind the other door. "Hope it's a way out and not just a stupid closet or something."

## Chapter 8
## MOTHER CASSANDRA

It took more than a few attempts for Brian to actually get his hands on the steering wheel. He'd reach out, draw back and reach out again, each time not quite letting his fingers touch the molded, foam-injected plastic. Half of him railed at the idea of believing what he'd just seen. Engines don't start themselves and steering wheels don't decide where you should go. The other half of him knocked insistently against his skull with the facts: there's nothing wrong with your eyes; you saw what you saw. Your hands touched neither the key nor the wheel, yet the engine is running and the wheel is turned. Give it up! It happened!

He slowly rested his hands on the ten and two positions of the wheel and let his fingers curl around. He waited, wondering if the truck would suddenly start off on its own. It didn't. It sat there idling, a soft vibration running through his fingertips. Laying his foot on the gas pedal, he pressed down lightly and swung the truck back up toward the house. The "crazy" mason gave him only a quick glance from over his shoulder as the truck lumbered to a stop in almost the same spot from which it had just departed.

"Com' to de back," the voice in his head instructed. "Follow de old path dat lead into de woods. You do dat an' you'll com' t'Mot'er soon."

Brian rubbed at his eyes and climbed out. His legs felt a bit wobbly and his brain a bit fuzzy, kind of like he was making his way through a hangover morning. He nodded at the mason and walked around to the back of the house.

He lifted branches here, peered through brambles there and worked himself around until he found the beginnings of the path he was supposed to take. The woods that surrounded the back of the house had been clear-cut for a distance of fifteen yards to make a nice backyard. Where they did begin to ring the property, the shrubs were thick and overgrown, their arching branches and brambles overlapping and entangling one another. Any hint of an old path had been well concealed by Mother Nature. Nevertheless, Brian finally found it, just to the right of the property, winding into the depths of the woods from beneath a thicket of blackberry bushes.

He fought his way through, every now and then giving out with an "ouch" or "shit" as the thorns fought back. Once through, though, it was pretty much a clear shot. The path, thin and covered with all manner of detritus, wound its way through the pines, oaks, sycamores and birches. It would almost have been a pleasant afternoon walk, if not for the voice in his head (still beckoning him forward) and the weak and worn-out feeling that seemed to deepen with every step. And just when he thought he couldn't go any farther, the mouth of an old well loomed up in front of him.

On legs that were now more rubber than muscle, he staggered over and sat on the rim of the well. His head was aching, he couldn't seem to catch his breath and there was a horrid, high-pitched ringing in his ears. He leaned as far forward as he could, afraid that if he passed out he might fall backwards and plummet into the darkness of the well.

"Don' you worry, chil'. You gon' feel better soon."

Brian straightened up so fast he lost his balance, rocked forward, and fell face first into the dirt. The voice had not been in his head this time. This time it came clear and strong from the bottom of the well.

"You got t'git hold-a yourself now, child. Mot'er gon' com' t'talk wit' you. Don' be frightened. Mot'er would never hurt you. Mot'er need you, an' dat's de trut'."

Brian pushed himself up onto his hands and knees and his heart froze. A thin ribbon of gray smoke rose from the well, drifted over his head and coalesced into a wispy, smoke-like figure of an old woman. She held her arms out, the palms of her hands turned up. A broad smile stretched across her face and her eyes seemed to shine with a light of their own, a kind of hazy blue glow that reminded Brian of those nasty halogen headlights he hated.

"You work yourself upright, child, an' don' be afraid. Everyt'ing gon' be irey. Mot'er promise. We jus' gon' talk a spell." She slowly drew her right arm upwards, and as she did, Brian rose to his feet. "Dare. Dat be much better. An' you feel better now, too. Don' you? Of course you do. Mot'er can see it in your eyes."

"H-h-who-"

"Already tol' you, chil'. I'm Mot'er. Mot'er Cassandra be my true name. Now you sit yourself on de edge-a dat well an' we gon' talk. Don' be t'inkin' 'bout whys an' wherefores and hows an' such. Dey don' matter. You see me; I'm here; we gon' talk. You a'cept dat for now an' den everyt'ing gon' be irey." The old woman winked.

Brian sat there, half of him wondering if he was losing his mind and the other half wondering if something supernatural really *was* happening. Everything seemed disjointed. He was scared. And somehow, at the same time felt relaxed, almost comfortable. It felt as if he were about to be taken into the confidence of a kindly grandmother.

Mother Cassandra drew closer, held out her left hand and closed her eyes. A small eddy of wind, a miniature cyclone, appeared above it and then formed into a crystal ball that settled itself down onto her palm.

"Don' be confused, chil'. Mot'er knows all about your doubts. You jus' set dem aside a moment or two, den you c'n let your mind be open to de trut'. Den ... when you be relaxed good an' proper, you gon' see what need t'be seen ... you gon' see what *you* need t'see."

"Are you really going to look in this ball and try to convince me you see my future? Cause if you are, I gotta tell you right now-"

"Ain't gonna do no such t'ing. De ball ain't fer me t'look in. De ball don' tell nuttin. It what's inside a body dat does de tellin." She half laughed. "De ball is just cut glass. Ain't even real crystal. Only t'ing dat's real is what com's from wit'in a body."

The blue light in the woman's eyes seemed to grow more brilliant. A trick of the light or stirred imagination, Brian didn't know which, but he found it impossible to pull his own eyes away from them. They drew him in, pulled him out of himself. He began to feel light headed again and everything was hazy and indistinct.

The voice was faint and distant. It came in a soft cadence that was felt more than heard.

"Now you can look at de ball, child. Now you will see what de world we don' see – what de world dat goes on around us and knows infinity, sees. Look at de ball and see inside and outside of y'self, child."

Brian's eyes drifted down. Inside the ball, a great lighting storm raged. Gray-black clouds clotted the dome. Beneath the storm, a house rose from a muddy swamp. A finger of blue lightning stabbed into its roof and a column of billowing smoke rose upward. It merged with the storm clouds and filled the interior of the ball with black. Slowly, the cloud smoke settled to the bottom, shrank and reformed. A young woman's face grew from a dot in the center and rose to the surface. Her features were soft, but they soon deformed as the face followed the contours of the glass ball. The eyes were haunted, wide and non-blinking in a terrified stare. Her lips quivered, speaking words that Brian could not hear. The face swirled around and around the inner surface until it shank back to the dot from which it was formed. The dot spat out hot blue sparks, settled and then erupted into another face, this of a man. A high collar, white, but yellowed with age, covered a thick neck that looked too short. Bushy gray eyebrows overhung eyes that were set too deep. And the eyes themselves glared out at him with an all but palpable impatience, arrogance and hatred.

Brian took an unconscious step backward, and the face drifted forward to the inner edge of the glass. Unlike the young woman's, this face did not distort; it held its shape. Its lips drew back in an awful sneer, revealing teeth pockmarked with rot. And somehow,

somehow, the stench of its breath forced its way out of the crystal.

"No more," cried Brian, burying his nose in the crook of his arm. "Stop this! Stop it .... NOW!"

The old woman covered the ball with her hand, and it shrank to nothingness and vanished as she brought her palms together. She wagged her head slowly from side to side, the way one might do while watching the antics of a child. "Mot'er t'ink dat's enough seein' fo'right now."

"Whu-why-"

Mother snapped her fingers and thumb together, as if she were making a sock puppet talk. "You jus' stay quiet for a few ticks; Mot'er do de talkin'." She raised her hand palm out and slowly lowered it at the wrist. Brian sank to the ground in a sitting position.

"Dare now, dat be better. Mot'er don' have a lot of time. Mot'er ain't strong 'nough yet, but will be when de time's right. You gon' help Mot'er; you gon' help Mot'er an' you gon' help Abigail. In return..." The ghostly image bent over at its wavering, smoky waist and glared right into Brian's eyes. "In return, Mot'er gon' help you and your pretty wife."

Brian followed her with his eyes as she straightened up. His eyes seemed to be the only things that were still under his command. He sat there cross-legged on the ground, numb – wanting to get up, wanting to run back to his truck and back to home and forget all about whatever it was that was happening to him, whatever it was that he was seeing, or imagining he was seeing. Yes. That's what he wanted to do. Trouble was: his muscles wouldn't cooperate. So there he sat, numb, staring into the eyes of some spectral woman.

"Mot'er c'n see de fear an' confusion swirlin' aroun' inside you, child. Dat's natural. What you be seein' now, child, ain't what de world sees. Your mind knows dat. But it ain't me you got t'be afraid of ... an' it ain't me dat you got t'com' to an understandin' wit." The look on the woman's face hardened, turned almost wolfish. "De face o'dat man you saw in de glass ... dat's what you have to com' t'understand. Dat's what you have to fear."

A thin smile cracked the line of her lips as she bent toward him again. "But none o'dat's for now. For now, you gon' get up an' go on into your house. Dat's where you c'n get your mind right. You gon' go on in and forget about ol' Mot'er Cassandra ... leastways for a little while. But I'll still be der, hidin' in de back of your mind. But firs' you got t'rest a bit an let de mem'ry o'me fade away."

The old woman straightened up and winked. She drew her hand down over Brian's eyes and they closed. "You just rest a bit, child."

And then she was gone.

Chapter 9
## THE DOOR

**1**

At about quarter to four, Emma leaned into the study, one hand on the doorjamb.

"You gonna stay for dinner, Annabel? Pork chops, green beans from our own garden, and mashed potatoes."

*Not while gran'pop keeps trying to feed me nonsense* hung on her lips, but she just smiled and said, "I'd love to, Mom, but I promised Brian I wouldn't be too late." And that was the truth for a change. Lately she'd been making up excuse after excuse to avoid what she was sitting through now. Most of them had been thinner than onionskin paper and she knew her mother knew it. And each had been as sharp as a double-edged razor, slicing a bit off both their hearts. To her mother's credit, the most she would ever say was: *Maybe next time, then.* But that didn't stop Annabel from hearing the emptiness in the words.

"Well maybe you could call him. I could throw on a couple extra chops. Not that much trouble."

"Not tonight, Mom. Sorry. We really have

(*to get rid of that damned razor*)

too much left to do. We're supposed to move in in a couple of days and we're not even halfway through the packing." Her eyes fell to her lap, her fingers trying to make knots out of themselves.

"Well, that's okay,

(*Here it comes*)

"maybe next time." She started to leave and then stopped. "How about if you and Brian come to dinner on Sunday? We can do it early, and I have a lovely roast that's just been sitting in the freezer waiting for a special occasion. We can celebrate your moving in."

"Uh ... sure. That sounds great, Mom. Sunday. Roast."

"Okay then. You talk to Brain and let me know what time's best." She slipped out of the doorway the way a snake slips into the brush and was gone.

Henry sighed, a long, whistling sigh. "Well now, now that that's done, do you mind if I continue with what I'm telling you?"

Annabel raised her arms and shrugged. "Geeze, gran'pop, mom was just trying to be nice. You don't have to be so impatient."

"If I'm impatient, it's with you, not her. The sooner I get done tellin' ya what I have to tell ya, the sooner you can get back t'treatin' her like your mother." He cocked his head and arched one eyebrow. "You think I don't know you've been givin' her the runaround about visitin' cause o'me? Sooner we get this over with, the sooner it'll be that you c'n stop lyin' to 'er."

Henry shifted in his chair and the pops and crackles of his spine sounded like firecrackers in the intervening silence.

"Now ... where was I? Oh yeah. "Tommy had just sent Matt to see what was behind the door on the other side of the room. I was getting myself *another beer*.

## 2

"...*another beer*." Henry pulled another beer out of the cooler. He watched Matt cross the room.

Tommy pinched another cigarette out of the pack, lit it and leaned back against the oak door they'd just struggled with. There was a squeal as the door slid open and Tommy tumbled out, flat on his back with a cracking thump! The air whooshed out of his lungs in a long grunt. After a few seconds, he propped himself up on his elbow, slowly regaining his breath and looking a bit sheepish.

Lucy and Henry stood side by side in the doorway. Tina, Janet and Amy were crowded around behind them. Matt had stopped and turned just as he'd reached the far door. All of them (except Matt who couldn't see from where he was) were standing with their mouths hanging open.

"It wasn't *that* bad," said Tommy. "You all look like my head just fell off or something."

Lucy's mouth moved but nothing came out. She was pointing over Tommy's shoulder.

"What the hell is with you guys?" asked Tommy. He twisted at the waist to look behind him. "What the fuck?"

Instead of the tunnel through which they had come, they were now looking at a long, thin room. There was a single candle burning at the opposite end – a flickering speck of light.

"What the fuck?" repeated Tommy, getting to his feet. He looked at the others and then turned and headed across the room, his eyes focusing on the only thing there was to see: the candle.

"How the hell is this possible?" Tommy grumbled. "This has to be some kind of a joke. We just came in through here not five minutes ago. This ain't right."

Lucy pushed past Henry and started to trot toward Tommy.

Tommy turned. "Don't come in here empty handed, you silly bitch. Go get me a flashlight."

"Fuck you, Tommy," shot Lucy, but she went back for the light all the same. Stepping through the doorway, the door suddenly slammed over, cutting her almost right down the middle, as if it had waited for that precise moment. It had her pinned. Her right arm and leg stuck out on Tommy's side and the rest of her on the other. Blood trickled from her mouth and nose, her head turned to the side facing Tommy. She was trying to say something, or maybe just cry out in pain, but her lips were contorted to one side and smashed up against the stone jamb.

Tommy raced back and grabbed the latch ring and tugged with all he had. The harder he pulled, the more the door resisted, squealing on its hinges as it pressed Lucy into a soufflé.

Lucy whimpered.

Tommy cursed, grabbed the ring with both hands and shoved his foot against the wall. He pushed with his leg and pulled with his arms and the door swung halfway open and then wrenched itself out of Tommy's hands and slammed over with a stomach-turning cracking and squishing sound. Tommy stood there horrorstruck as Lucy came apart. Her skull cracked open like a melon hit with a hammer. On the other side of the door, the horrified screams and stunned gasps rattled through the emptiness.

Tommy's eyes went wide behind splayed fingers. The palms of his hands were covering the gaping O his mouth had dropped into. Somewhere inside him a cerebral breaker tripped. All he could do was stand there and stare. Blood had pooled around the body and pseudopod-like trails of it rolled toward Tommy's sneakers; the air was thick with its metallic *smell*.

### 3

"...*smell. That horrid smell.*"

Henry sat back and fumbled with the afghan on his lap. He drew his sleeve across his eyes in a half corkscrew so that the heel of his hand drew the last dabs of moisture from them. The color had run out of his cheeks making him look even older than he was. For a long time he just sat there staring down at his hands, watching his bony fingers try to remember coordinated movement.

"Gran'pop-" began Annabel.

Henry held up a shaking hand. "Just-just ... I just need a minute, Belle. The memory came more vividly than I had thought it would. That girl; that poor Lucy Darrow." He wiped at his eyes again. "She died right there in front of us. I can still hear the sound of it; I can still smell that awful metallic smell ... and the horrible smell of ... of..."

Annabel leaned over and took one of Henry's hands in hers. "It's okay, Gran'pop. You don't have to do this. There's no need to force yourself-"

"You gonna walk away from that house?" Henry's face hardened and his eyes blazed with an intensity that Annabel had never seen before. "Are ya? 'Cause if you haven't changed your mind about livin' there, then there's plenty of reason for me to force myself to go on. It's hard ... real hard; I ain't denying that. But I have to. For your sake and for Brian's."

"Gran'pop, what you just told me was a horrible, horrible thing. And-" She hesitated, trying to choose the right words, the right sentence. "And, well, if it did happen and you're not just mixing up stories from TV ... you know you do that sometimes ... well then it was just a horrible accident."

Henry snorted and turned his head away. "If. 'If', she says. If you're not mixing it up." He turned back. "Now you listen to me, Annabel. If your grandmother were still with us, she'd tell you. She never forgot it, either. I'm not lying, not confusing the real world with shit television episodes and I'm not-" He looked over at the door and lowered his voice. "I'm not senile. So you just sit there and listen like you promised. And then I'll never bother you with it again like I promised."

How many times had Henry played this scene out in his head? A hundred, a thousand or more? How many different ways had he thought of telling the tale so that the unbelievable became solidly undeniable? But it always ended pretty much the same way. Annabel would smile and indulge him, not really listening – maybe thinking about a grocery list, or wondering what new flowers to plant in the garden come spring – thinking about anything but what was being said. And when it was all said and done, she'd smile sympathetically, but knowingly, and leave with a promise to think about what she was told. But all she'd really think about was how her grandfather was losing it. That's how it always turned out, and Henry wondered what he could do or say to make the girl pay attention.

Chapter 10
THE HOLLOW

**1**

Wickersham Hollow had been carved out of a three and a quarter square mile area in the heart of Lancaster County, purchased from the Pennsylvania Dutch in 1693. It was settled by Torrance Wickersham, who used his influence as a former judge and ordained minister to bully the Amish and Mennonites aside when he moved down from Ipswich Massachusetts. Two years later he pushed them farther, acquiring some of the most arable farmlands the area had to offer. He established a church and began to grow his own town. Most of the early settlers came from Ipswich, personally invited by Wickersham. A few had filtered in from Peabody, Salem and what is now Marblehead. They all brought their hopes, dreams and fears with them, along with an unswerving devotion to Wickersham and his Puritan church (demanded before rights to move in were granted); and they would all plant the seed that would lie dormant for more than three hundred years.

The town grew, supported by the farming community. It buried itself in obscurity during the Revolutionary War, remaining neutral. It grudgingly supplied its government with wheat, corn and beef throughout the duration of the Civil War and stood upon its founder's religious principles to avoid conscription.

By 1900 the dirt roads had been paved and what used to be called Dutcher Road was officially christened MAIN STREET when the town incorporated in 1902.

Main Street ran straight up the center. At the northern end it crossed Weaver Hill Road, which was offset on either side. The two roads made a kind of misshapen cross, with one arm higher than the other.

The Hollow survived the great depression, both World Wars and Vietnam. By then their religious attitudes had softened, primarily from an influx of outsiders and their beliefs, and the advent of technology. The price of their softening was carved into the base of the Veterans' Memorial, erected on a tiny park-like plot of land just beside the municipal building. It was fronted by a defunct US 33mm M3 Anti-Tank Cannon painted the standard OD green.

Geographically, the Hollow was nearly horseshoe-shaped, and by 1981 boasted a population of just shy of a thousand. Most of the older residents joked that it was a good thing that the open end of the horseshoe was pointed northwest. That way, only some of the town's luck would spill out. The oldest living resident, at the ripe old age of 91, was Joachim Walcott. He was purported to be a descendent of Torrance Wickersham himself (in some capacity or other), but nobody was quite sure how. And he would never say. Amazingly, most of his faculties were still intact. He had only one arm, the right (another mystery he refused to explain), and sometimes, in just the right light, the reflection he caught in his mirror looked back at him with the face of a much younger man. Despite his age, he still managed to oversee the running of his farm, mostly from the kitchen table, writing out the day's list of things to get done for his foreman, Ralph Strunk. If anyone in town remembered its history and secrets, it was Joachim

Walcott – but he was just as mum on those subjects as he was on his lineage.

## 2

At quarter to five, Ralph Strunk shuffled up the worn and creaky back steps, stopped long enough to dust off the clinging bits of chaff, rapped twice and stepped into Walcott's kitchen. He paused a moment to wipe his shoes and then walked over and plucked a mug out of one of the cabinets and filled it with what was left of a pot of burnt coffee.

Walcott was sitting at the table squinting at the evening paper that was spread out in front of him. A week's worth of stubble made a raspy, ticking sound as he rubbed at it with the backs of his fingers.

"Goddamned taxes are gonna go up again, Ralph," he said, picking up the paper. "Did you hear about that? It makes me sick to m'stomach. Let's just keep breakin' the backs of the middle class ... they'll pay for everything. That's the damned government's philosophy." He let the paper slip from his hand and flutter down onto the table.

"Lower field's all rolled up," said Ralph, working his portly frame into a chair across from Walcott. He dabbed at his forehead with an already sweat-crusted red and white bandana he'd pulled from his back pocket. At only forty-eight, his hair was more salt than pepper and clung to his temples and forehead in saw-toothed strands. "Also got quite a few bales of hay loaded to take down to Farley's for Halloween. He's been cryin' for them since the second week in October."

Walcott never bothered to look up from his paper. "Been cryin' for it, has he? Well ... goodie for him. I sell it to him; he marks the price up and makes a bigger profit than I do ... and how? ... off'n kids that just wanna use it for dec'rations." He shook his head. "It's a waste. That's why I always wait. Gotta see what the other farmers need for feed and such first. Plus, bein' next to the last day ... I can charge him more and he'll pay it. Cut down on the old bitch's profit margin." A broad smile etched its way across his face. Amos Farley is a doofus, and I can't stand that nosey bitch of an aunt of his that really runs the show.

Ralph took a swallow of coffee, grimaced at the burnt taste and acrid aroma and promptly set the mug down. He'd been Walcott's foreman for almost twelve years now, long enough to know better than to trust that the coffee had been made fresh in the afternoon. When Walcott turned seventy-eight, he'd had his first stroke and had finally had to admit to himself that the farm was just a bit too much for him. When his wife of fifty-eight years passed ten days after his stroke, he had no alternative but to get help. And Ralph fit the bill perfectly. He'd already been working on the farm on and off for more than five years, working summers while he tried to get his associate's degree at the local community college. As it turned out, schoolbooks and Ralph Strunk never made a good partnership. So when Walcott asked him to be his eyes and ears out in the field, he took the job and ditched the books. Now, twelve years later, he did everything but keep the books. That was old man Walcott's bailiwick. Of course, there was always *The List*. Each morning he'd sit at the table and drink his coffee, while Walcott wrote out his list of things he felt *needed* to be accomplished that day. Most of them Ralph agreed with and had already planned on doing. At the end of each day they'd meet in the kitchen and go over the list, item by item, with Ralph explaining which hands worked on which tasks and how long it had taken them. The routine never varied.

Ralph dug the list out of his pocket and laid it on the table, smoothing it out as best he could.

"Never mind the list today," said Walcott. "Pretty sure ya done what you always do and things is up t'snuff." He wiggled the coke-bottle glasses off his face with a shaky hand and dropped them on the list. "Got something else I need t'talk to you about, Ralph."

Ralph leaned forward and interlaced his sausage fingers around the mug of abandoned sludge. Walcott had never before dismissed the list so offhandedly, and its dismissal today made Ralph feel a bit uneasy, nervous. Nothing had ever been more important (except maybe the balance sheet) than *The List*.

"I'd like to ask you to go into my study and get the big wooden box that's sittin on my desk and bring it out here. If ya don't mind?"

"Not a problem, Mr. Walcott. Not a problem at all." He started to get up and Walcott grabbed his forearm. "Wait a minute. I ain't done yet. First off ... I think it's high time ya stopped calling me mister Walcott. Walcott will do just fine. Don't care much for my first name, so we won't be using that." He shook his head. "Where in the world my parents ever came up with Joachim I'll never know ... but I wish they hadn't. Secondly ... what I want to tell you ... what I want to show you ... it stays between us, no matter what. If I can't get your solemn promise on that ... well then ... let's just call it a day and I'll see you at six A.M. tomorrow as usual."

Ralph had no idea what to make of this sudden secrecy and sudden breach of etiquette. Never before had Walcott allowed anyone, with the possible exception of his wife, to address him as anything but Sir or Mister Walcott. There was the look on the old man's face, too. He'd always been what Ralph thought of as an *overly* serious man. Smiles on Walcott's face came few and far between. The look on the old man's face now was more that serious; it was grave.

"Um ... well sure, Mist ... um ... Walcott. I can keep a secret as well as the next person, if that's what you want."

"Don't want. Need. And ya better keep it better than the next person ... or you'll be out of a job and I'll be..." He exhaled and flapped his hand. "Don't matter what I'll be. If ya give me your promise of secrecy, I'll take ya at your word."

Ralph sat back. "You can always count on me, Walcott. Been your foreman for a lot of years now, and I ain't never broke your trust once. Ain't about to start now."

"Fine then. Go get the dadblamed box and quit yackin'." A hint of a smile crossed Walcott's face and disappeared.

### 3

For a long time the two of them sat, just staring at the box that Ralph had placed on the table between them.

It was an old box, but well cared for. The wood was rich and oiled and the lid was engraved with what looked to Ralph to be grapevines. A black metal key poked out of the lock in the front, almost begging Ralph to reach out and twist it until it clicked over and revealed all the secrets it kept safe inside. He rubbed his hands together, sat on them, interlaced his fingers on his lap, moved them to the table and then back underneath his thighs. It felt as if the box were tempting him – begging him to reach out and open it.

At last, Walcott reached out and pushed the box toward Ralph. "Ya c'n hardly wait to open it and see what's inside, right? I know what you're feeling. It's like it's calling to ya, right? Ya can feel the power of it in your brain, like an itch ya can't quite get to t'scratch." He laid his hand on the top of the box and slid it closer to Ralph.

"Go ahead. Turn the key ... but don't lift the lid just yet."

Ralph extended his arms, pulled them back, extended them again and then let them fall to his lap.

"Ya want to ... but it don't feel right, does it? Kind of hard to explain, huh? Like needin' t'see what's inside someone's diary and knowin' it's wrong to do it." Walcott took his hand off the top of the box and then tapped it with his index finger. "Once you open this ... there ain't no going back. Just like learning somebody's deepest, darkest secret ... ya can't make yourself unknow it, and ya wonder why ya ever felt ya had to know it in the first place. But ya did ... and now it's done and ya can't take it back. This box ... and what's inside ... well, it's just like that."

"I'm ... I'm not really sure-"

"Yeah. I know. But here's the thing, Ralph. If ya wanna be sure ya can keep working here, ya got to open it. It's that simple ... and that difficult."

"Are you say-saying ... are you saying that you'll fire me if I don't open the box?"

Walcott laughed: a deep and honest laugh. "No, Ralph. I ain't gonna fire ya. That'd be stupid. You're the best worker I got and the only one I know that I'd trust to be m'foreman. No. No firing. The thing is ... well ... there's a chance I could lose the farm, and if that happens then you'll have to take over. And to do that-" Walcott bit his lip, fidgeted in his seat and then exhaled. "-To do that ... ya have to know everything."

"Why would you lose the farm? Except for the old Wickersham place, yours is the biggest parcel of land in the county and your mortgage has been paid off for years."

"Why don't matter. But we'll get to that." Walcott sat back and grinned.

"Wha-what's that look for?" asked Ralph, feeling more nervous now than when this whole thing started.

Walcott nodded toward the box, and with a kind of feeling of creeping horror, Ralph noticed that his hand had somehow crept to the key, his fingers almost massaging it.

"Go ahead, Ralph. It'll be okay. Open the box and let's get on with it."

Ralph's fingers tightened on the metal hasp and twisted it to the right. A set of double clicks, sounding as loud as gunfire to Ralph, told him that things he wasn't so sure he really wanted to know were now only a lid-lift away. He let out the breath he'd been unconsciously holding and sat back.

## Chapter 11
## WHISPERS

It was dusk by the time Brian opened his eyes. He felt groggy and disoriented. He struggled to get to his feet. He felt as if he were standing outside himself. Everything around him seemed to be melting, dripping away into unformed pools on the forest floor. He felt as if he'd had one too many vodka martinis. Everything was swimming in mixed circles, some things moving in one direction while others moved backward around them. He felt hot and feverish and chilled at the same time.

On legs more Styrofoam than muscle, he wobbled back to the front of the house. All the workers had already packed up and left. When he approached the steps, the porch lights snapped on and his heart jumped into his throat. A motion sensor, Brian. Relax. He shuffled up the steps, crossed the veranda and laid his hand on the chrome door lever. At its touch, the well and everything that had happened there slipped from his mind. A broad smile washed across his face at the feel of the cool handle. It was almost too much to imagine that this beautifully restored old place was really his ... theirs. The night he'd talked to Annabel about buying it and fixing it up they'd argued over how much money it would cost and whether or not it would be worth it. He *knew* it would; she wasn't so sure.

Brian pushed down on the handle and the four inch thick, arched walnut door swung open without a sound, its half-moon window gleaming in the glow of the antique porch sconces. Standing there, he took in the ten-foot wide vestibule, bounded on either side by rich, cherry wood panel walls. He stepped in and strolled toward the double pocket doors that opened into a spacious sunken-living room as richly appointed as the vestibule. A large bay window opened onto a view of the front of the property. The flooring was Brazilian Oak with matching molding. A double-sided stone fireplace occupied the wall to his left, stopping just short of the Roman columns that flanked an archway leading to an equally impressive library, set in the base of the turret that rose like a blister on the right side of the house.

He lifted his right leg, but before he stepped down into the living room, he stopped and took off his shoes, afraid to even take a chance of marring the floor. He set them down in front of the pocket doors. The floor felt slippery under his socks. He was the first one to feel the newness of it all soak in. He took a few more hesitant steps and then crossed briskly to the fireplace.

A wild idea struck him and he just couldn't resist it. He turned, started at a trot, got up a little speed and slid through the archway into the library. The floor was so highly buffed out that he almost made it all the way to the bookshelves on the other side, some twenty-five feet. When he came to a stop, he giggled a little and thought about doing it again in the opposite direction.

"Okay, folks, here comes the world renowned floor surfer, Brian Michaels, about to attempt the difficult fete of-"

"*Brrrrriiiiii-annnn*" The voice was so soft it could have been a whisper in his head. He stood bolt upright and cocked his ear toward the living room where it seemed to have originated.

"*Brrriiiiiii-aannnnn ... Briiiii-aaaannnnnnnnnn.*"

He crossed the library and stopped at the archway to peer around the corner. The room was empty. He listened.

Nothing.

He tried to tell himself that it was probably just a draft from the fireplace flu, the sound of air whistling through a freshly installed chimney liner. *He* was the one that had turned it into a word – had turned it into his name. It was probably all that nonsense with the crazy mason. It was just his imagination playing-

"*Brrrrriiiiii-aaaannnnnnn.*" This time the hushed voice came from behind him, seemingly out of the bookcases. He turned back into the library.

"Okay, it's not funny anymore. Who's he-"

*WHAM!*

The pocket doors slammed shut. He crossed the living room climbed the three steps up to the hall and threw the pockets open, convinced that maybe the crazy mason had stayed behind to try and frighten him away. He stepped into the hall and watched in awe as the front door slowly closed over, latching with a loud click. He gazed at the chrome knob of the deadbolt as it slid over and seated itself in its hasp.

"*Brrrriiiiii-aaaaannnnnnnn*" – from the library.

"*Brrrriiiiii-aaaannnnnn*" – from the fireplace.

"*Brrrriiiiiii-aaaaaannnnnnnn,*" from above him.

"*Brrrriiiii-aaaannnnn      Brrrriiiiiii-aaaannnnn Brrrriiiiii-aaaaaaannnnn*" – from everywhere at once and softer than a dying breath.

## Chapter 12
## BE IT EVER SO HUMBLE

**1**

Annabel leaned forward, still awestruck. She clasped her hands together and rested her forearms on her knees, a spray of red hair falling down over her left eye. "So this girl was crushed in the door? How horrible. Did you go to the police?"

Henry wheeled his chair over to his desk and rooted through the thin middle drawer a few minutes. He came back with a yellowed newspaper clipping clutched in his right hand.

"Course we went to the police. But that was much later." He waved the flap of paper in the air. "This here's all that was said or done about it, but we'll get to that in due time. Lots more to tell first."

Annabel turned her wrist ever so slightly and surreptitiously glanced at her watch. Four minutes to six. Brian would be home by now and wondering where she was. She thought about calling him on the cell but knew that would only annoy her grandfather. What she really wanted to do was just find a way to bug out and go home. How she was going to manage that she had no idea. She took another peek at her watch.

"Somewhere you have to be?" asked Henry with one eyebrow raised.

"Well, gran'pop, actually-"

"Yeah, yeah. I know it's getting late and you want to get home. But you have to realize that I'm trying ... I'm trying... Oh damn! This is going to sound so melodramatic, but it's true. I'm trying to save your life, here. I'm trying to convince you to save your own life and stay away from that damned house."

Annabel sighed. "That's quite a statement, gran'pop. It is a little over the top, don't you think? It's a house, that's all. Stone, wood, plaster, nails, screws, pipes, elec-"

"I know what a damned house is made out of. But that house ... *that house* ... is a whole lot more. *That* house doesn't care about plaster or nails or mortar or any of the rest of it. *That* house moves and breathes to its own rhythm and its own desires."

"Okay," said Annabel, rising. "I was willing to listen to your story; I really was. I admit that I didn't want to, but I was willing to give it a try. Now you're ... you're... Ah, gran'pop, I don't know what to call it. Maybe you just need a long rest; I don't know. But houses that ... what did you say ... breathe and move on their own. I think you're getting yourself all worked up over ... over ... I don't know... bad dreams maybe. But I have to go. Brian's probably already home and wondering where I am. I think you should probably eat something and then get a good night's rest."

"So you *do* think I'm senile, huh? Well I'm not." He wiggled a finger in Annabel's direction, his face so tight it almost seemed to smooth out the age lines. "You do what you want; I knew you would anyway. But hear me good; you two are putting yourselves into serious danger. I know. I've been in there and was lucky to escape with my life."

"I love you gran'pop. I really do. But I can't listen to any more of this; I can't. I'm going home and have dinner with Brian. I'll swing by tomorrow and see if you're feeling any more rational, how would that be?"

"Come or don't come. That's your choice. Either way, what I have to tell you, what I told you, what I want to tell you ... it won't change. It can't change because it's the truth, and if you don't take the time to listen to me ... really listen to me and hear what I'm telling you, you're not only a clod-pated, thickhead who thinks she knows all about how the world works, but you're reckless. You're reckless, and that's what's going to do you in. And...

I

(*THUMP!*) Henry's fist slammed down on the wheelchair's armrest.

don't
(*THUMP!*)
want
(*THUMP!*)
to see
(*THUMP!*)
that
(*THUMP!*)
happen!
(*THUMP!*)

Annabel just shook her head. "I have to go, gran'pop. I'll call you tomorrow. Tell mom I said goodbye." She turned and left before Henry could say anything else.

## 2

Emma watched from the front window as Annabel pulled away. When the taillights vanished, she let the drapes fall back into place with a soft rustle. She had heard the animated thumping as Henry had punctuated his words and knew that he was now in his study fuming and trying to get his temper back under control. Taking a deep breath and absently slipping a hand through her hair, she walked to the study and stood in the doorway. Henry had wheeled himself back over to his writing desk and was sitting there tapping the end of a gnawed pencil on the smudged and coffee-stained blotter.

"She'll come back, you know," she said softly, "probably sometime tomorrow after she's thought about it a bit. That's how she handles things, dad. She has to think about them a while."

Henry waved a hand in the air and blew out a long, low sigh. "I know; I know." He wheeled his chair around to face her. "Hell ... I don't know what I was really expecting, anyway. If somebody tried to tell me that ... that ... that that ... *place* ... wasn't right, and for the reasons I was giving her ... well, I wouldn't believe them either."

Emma walked over behind Henry and began to massage his shoulders. "You know, Dad, I overheard what you said to Belle about almost losing mom there. How come you never told me that before?"

Henry patted the back of her hand. "That place ... what went on there ... it's not something you sit down and tell a child."

"I'm not a child anymore, dad. Why don't I get us each a nice glass of brandy and you tell me what you wanted to tell Belle? All of it. If it concerns my daughter and her husband, then I think I have a right to know." The tone of her voice left no room for discussion. The only part of it that was a suggestion was the brandy.

Henry nodded and pretended to be smoothing out his afghan again (usually an unconscious habit, but this was deliberate). He watched her leave over the top of his glasses. Some things about parents were never meant to be known by, let alone discussed *with*, their children. That house and what went on in there with Emma's mother – with all of them – was certainly one of those things. At least as far as Henry was concerned. But he was trapped now and he knew it. Emma always knew when he was lying to her (which generally only entailed skipping a dose of medication or sneaking a few extra shots of scotch), or when he was blatantly omitting information.

When Emma returned with the drinks she found Henry in the living room, hunched over and staring into the fire with his hands outstretched before it. A pang of emotion tugged at her heart. Her father had grown old and she had somehow never noticed it happening. For the first time that she could remember (even through these last years of taking care of him) he looked broken and worn out to her. Swallowing the feeling, she walked over and handed him his glass.

"This'll warm you up, dad."

He took his glass in two hands and looked at her. There was a fire in his eyes. It was as if all the strength he'd ever possessed had climbed into his mind and was reflected out through his eyes. His gaze, and what was behind it, made her draw a breath and take a step back.

Henry smiled. "I don't bite, dear. Come on, pull up a chair. I wasn't at all sure I wanted to tell you what you want to know. But I've been thinking about it and I think that, with some exceptions, you should probably hear everything." He smiled again, but this one was more of a surrender smile. "Besides, I have a feeling you'd short-sheet my bed or spit in my food or something if I refused. You're as stubborn and pigheaded as I am."

"And I wonder just where I get it," said Emma, easing into a chair she had dragged up alongside of Henry's. "And don't even try to blame mom for that. Yes, she was strong all right, but you're the one who's always had the porcine will. And ... what makes you think that I don't already spit in your food?"

Henry chuckled and held up a free hand. " Okay ... you win. I'm guilty as charged, your honor. Of course, you do know that every stubborn decision I've ever made was for the good of the family. You do know that, don't you?"

"Yes, of course I do. I also know that you're trying to divert me into an entirely different subject. Tell me about the house." She swirled the brandy around the bottom of the glass, watched it spin and then took a healthy sip. "Tell me about what happened there and why you think Annabel and Brian should give it up after they've put so much money and work into it."

## 3

Annabel rolled the Jeep to a stop in her designated spot at the Willow Arms, right in front of one of the lighting stanchions (they paid extra for this each month, but Brian had insisted that Annabel always park in a well-lighted area). The first thing she noticed was that the spot next to hers (Brian's) was empty. The next thing she noticed was that kids had apparently taken to chalking both of their spots. A large white circle filled the center of them. The top three-quarters had been completely chalked in and had large spikes extending outward from the circumference. What remained in the lower right hand corner looked like a fingernail-moon. Annabel scraped at it with the edge of her shoe, smudging its outline.

"Kids!" She shook her head and hurried across the lot, through the doors and over to the elevator, making a mental note to call the Super to have it cleaned up. When the doors slid open, a short black woman with gray-streaked black hair that looked like an oversized Brillo-pad stepped out. She gave Annabel a wink of a smile and sidled past her. The long yellow skirt she wore was printed with various kinds of flowers in all colors. As she passed, she grabbed the sides of the skirt and gave it a little shake. Annabel flashed a quick smile back and stepped into the elevator. When the doors slid shut, the air grew sickeningly and overpoweringly sweet – glass-walled greenhouse on a hot summer day sweet. She fell into a corner, the crook of her arm over her mouth and nose.

There was a slight jolt as the elevator began its ascent, and the air cleared. She dropped her arm and took a hesitant breath. All she could smell was a hint of the oily solvent used to keep the stainless steel shiny. *Way too much perfume.*

Annabel watched the digits over the door light up and then go out. Their apartment was on the sixteenth floor, not quite a penthouse, but close enough. When the number 10 lit up, the car stopped, dropped a foot or two, and the lights winked off and then back on. Annabel's stomach climbed into her throat, hung there for a minute before deciding everything was okay, and retreated.

"Shit!" She slammed down on the red EMERGENCY button but nothing happened. No bells rang, no sirens whooped – only silence. She hit it again with the same result. She couldn't help but think that this was just the perfect ending to a perfect day. Grandfather trying to scare her into giving up a house that they had redesigned from basement to roof, and now this – stuck in an elevator between floors. She pulled her cell phone out and flipped it open. Before she could even hit a single button, a mechanical voice said: "The party you are trying to reach is unavailable. If you'd like to try again..." This was followed by a giddy kind of surreal laughter and then the phone shut itself off.

Annabel's first instinct was to throw the phone against the wall as hard as she could and delight in the starburst of its plastic casing and electronic guts. Instead, she flipped it closed, opened it again and pressed the ON button. A musical tinkling accompanied a white flash across the screen. Both disappeared as rapidly as they had come, leaving only a blank, gray screen and silence.

"Well ain't that just fuckin' spiffy." She dropped the phone into her back pocket and pounded on the elevator doors. "Hello? Anyone? Help! I'm stuck in here. I'm stuck between floors ten-"

The car vibrated. When it stopped, a voice, soft and ethereal swirled around Annabel's head.

"You don' want to be *here*, child. You want to be wit' your man. You got t'get on to de house where he is. Dat's where you need to be." The voice evaporated; and with it, the memory of it. But the seed was planted.

A sudden jolt knocked her off balance. She stumbled sideways, banging her left shoulder against the wall, as the car began to rise again. "NEVER MIND!" she yelled, and then mumbled: "not that anyone did."

Like a wave pounding onto a beach, the floor rolled under her feet and she was knocked sideways again. When her shoulder hit the wall for the second time, a flash of light enveloped her, one so bright she had to shield her eyes with her arm. The car shuddered and resumed its ascent to the sixteenth floor. When the bell rang and the doors opened, Annabel wasted no time getting out.

**4**

Meanwhile, at the house, Brian edged toward the front door. His heartbeat rose until he could feel it knocking against his breastbone. A hollow feeling spread down into his belly and he had to struggle to keep his legs moving forward without shaking; his hands were already doing that. As he moved across the room, the corduroys he was wearing rubbed together making a rustling sound that echoed eerily throughout the empty house.

He reached out his hand but stopped before letting it touch the chrome bolt that had slid over on its own. His fingers danced shakily in the air a mere inches from the metal knob, as if he were waiting for it to slide open on its own. Then, gently, the pad of his index finger traced its curved surface. Slowly closing his thumb over it, he rotated it back. There was a slight *click*! as the bolt was drawn out of its hasp, and the house reverberated with a high-pitched, almost childlike, laughter.

Brian quickly turned the knob over and threw open the door. He was about to step out onto the veranda when he remembered his shoes. As he turned back to get them, the door slammed over again and locked itself. This time, however, there was no high-pitched laughter. This time the laughter was deep, menacing and minatory. And somewhere beneath it, barely audible, was the sound of a baby crying.

## Chapter 13
## A SHADOW AWAY FROM DISSOLVING

**1**

"Want me to put another log on the fire, dad?" asked Emma. The fire had dwindled to a bed of glowing red embers. A flurry of sparks rose up and fell back whenever a pocket of sap exploded.

Henry held out his glass. "That would be nice, and I could use another one of these if you don't mind."

Emma shrugged. "I guess so, considering what you've been telling me. I can't say that I couldn't use another myself."

They'd talked for almost forty-five minutes, Henry telling her everything he'd told Annabel about the house and what had happened there when he'd gone in with his friends ... and Emma's mother ...seventy years ago. The telling had been slow. Henry had had to stop a number of times to clear his throat, or wipe a piece of "pesky fireplace ash" out of his eye, or clear his sinuses, or rub at the cataracts that made his eyes water. And each time, Emma would stare into the fire and pretend not to notice his tears.

Emma handed Henry his brandy, slipped another split on the fire, stirred the ashes with the poker and replaced the screen. She stood there and watched, waiting for it to catch: tiny white peaks with blue bases that skipped across the log in an un-choreographed dance of light. Flickering lines of shadow played over the side of her face, and Henry thought (not for the first time in his life) how much she looked like her mother.

Emma sat down and swallowed hard, swirling the brandy around the bottom of her glass.

"So ... Lucy ... Lucy..."

Henry nodded. "Yes. There wasn't a thing we could do for her. We were ... we were stunned ... no ... more. We were scared shitless *and* stunned and ... and whatever else you could be when something like that happens right in front of you. Nobody knew what to do. At first we kept trying to get the door open ... but after that second time ... after that damned door... Well, nobody wanted to go anywhere near it." He took a deep breath and followed that with a long, slow sip of brandy. "The problem was ... well ... we were on one side of the door and Tommy was on the other. We had to get the door open, but if we did that..."

Emma laid a hand on Henry's. "Why in God's name have you kept this to yourself all these years, dad? You should have told someone; you should have-"

"Should have what? Seen a shrink? Shared this nightmare with my children?" He grunted, "Ahhh! Your mother ... your mother and I spoke about it many times. Spoke about it without saying a word. It would seem to come up out of nowhere and I'd look at her and she'd look at me and we'd both know we were thinking the same thing. Didn't need to tell anyone anything. At least, not until Annabel and Brian went and bought that house."

"I'll be honest, dad," said Emma leaning slightly closer to the fire. "I'm not sure I really want to know the rest. Not after that. But I have to ... and you and I both know I have to. So let's both take a nice sized sip of this damned brandy ... and get on with it."

Henry let out a little laugh. "I realize now that it's more than you just lookin' like your mother, Emma; it's that you have her ways in some things, too. Never mind the falderal. Pleasant or not, if something's got to be done ... just do it. That's the way she was." He turned to look at her. "And that's the way you are. It's why Annabel came out the way she did. Smart as a whip and more stubborn than a mule."

"As I've already said, dad, I think you're responsible for some of that too. Runs in the blood, apparently."

"Un-hunh. I have no doubt. Stubborn. That's what your mother was way back then. It was her ... er ... she – she hated when I interchanged her and she incorrectly – anyway ... it was she that finally got us all *moving.*

## 2

"...*moving.* Come on guys; we can't leave it like this. We can't leave Lucy like that and we can't leave Tommy on the other side, alone." Amy closed her eyes, gritted her teeth and found a place on the door where she could put her hands that wasn't covered in any part of Lucy. Grunting, she started shoving against it as hard as she could.

It took a few minutes, but Matt and Henry finally stepped in and started pushing too. Janet was in a corner throwing up – Tina behind her holding her hair out of the way. Amy was close to doing the same but held it in. Standing this close, her hands just below what was left of the left side of Lucy's face, an avulsed eyeball dangling from its socket, was anything but stomach settling.

On the other side of the door, Tommy Vorland stood staring at what, five minutes ago, had been his date. His hands were still plastered in front of his face and he could feel his lips moving against the palms, his mouth trying to form words that wouldn't come out. Somewhere in the back basement of his brain a voice was calling to him, taunting him. *Big bad Tommy ain't so big and bad. Big bad Tommy just dropped a big bad ten pound load in his pants. Big bad Tommy is all steam with no pressure. You're a joke. You've always been a joke; you've just been very good at hiding that joke underneath a thin, onionskin-width veneer of self-importance, self-aggrandizement and false bravado. Tommy the leader is really Tommy the Timid ... Tomm-*

"...ommy! Tommy! What the hell are you doing over there? Pull for Christ's sake." Amy's voice shoved Tommy's basement voice back down into its sub-cerebral hole. "Help us, Tommy."

Tommy dropped his hands from his face, set his teeth together and growled – partly from determination, but mostly from anger. He had let the doubting little boy who couldn't get his hat back from the bullies find its way out of the basement. Thank God Amy had shoved it back ... and goddammit ... back is where it was going to stay.

"Uh ... okay. Hold on a minute," he yelled. He looked at the disemboweled remains of his date and flipped the basement door open long enough to push the disgust he was feeling down into the hole to keep his self-doubt company. Rubbing his hands along the sides of his jeans to clear the sweat, he stepped up to the door and grabbed hold of the iron ring. He braced one leg against the stone wall and took a deep breath.

"Okay," he yelled. "On three. You push; I'll pull. Ready?"

There was a full stop of silence and then Amy yelled: "Okay. On three. Count it off, Tommy."

"This is gonna be really nasty when it comes open," Matt whispered in Henry's ear. "I don't think I'm ready for it."

"Just close your eyes and push. That's all you have to do," Henry whispered back.

### 3

A soft clicking sound, the sound of a thousand rats skittering along a stone wall, began to rise. Anguished cries and pitiful wailing ran underneath it in a hushed and breathy voice, the pleading words unintelligible. Then the heavy, slapping, clunking sounds began – a wet and solid sound – a sound so familiar, yet vague and beyond total recognition. Then the laughter. But it was not the laughter of fun or enjoyment; it was the laughter of bullies in a school yard, the laughter of people at a party watching a drunk humiliate himself, the laughter that came at someone else's expense and despair. The sounds then faded away as quickly as they had arisen.

Tommy had gotten as far as *Two* when it started. Startled, he let go of the ring so fast, forgetting that he was also pushing against the wall with his foot, that he fell back on his ass for the second time.

"What the hell was that?" he mumbled. Then, louder: "Did you guys hear that?" He waited, but no one answered.  "Hey!  I asked if you guys over there heard that weird laughing."

He got to his feet and turned around to look behind him.  The tunnel that had turned into a room was now the tunnel again, and he could hear someone slogging through the deep water.

"Hey you guys ... I think ther-"  He turned back to the door and froze.  It was completely closed over and there was no sign of Lucy at all.  No body squished between the door and jamb; no body parts decorating the door and wall and no blood pool on the floor.

The slogging sounds behind him changed to the slap of wet feet working their way up the stone ramp toward him.  He stood there in total darkness listening to that sound slowly getting closer.  And it wasn't just the darkness or the sound of the feet that was making his heart race; it was the quality of the sound of the wet feet.  They weren't walking, moving steadily forward; they were scuffing, as if whoever it was could hardly lift them to take a step.

Keeping one eye on the blackness of the tunnel in front of him, he cocked his head over his shoulder.  "Come on, you guys.  Quit fuckin' with me and answer me.  What are you doing over there?"

He could hear the panic climbing into his voice.  He could hear the self-doubting Tommy banging at the basement door, demanding to be let out.

"Come ON, guys."  And then softer, almost a whisper: "please answer me ... please say something."

The dragging, slapping footsteps were closer now, almost to the top of the incline.  Soon, whoever ... whatever ... it was would come shambling out of the blackness right at him. He backed up, took a quick look at the door to be sure he wouldn't be leaning against Lucy's remains and placed his back firmly against it. There was nothing else he could do but wait. Nothing but wait and pray that whatever was coming for him was not one of the many images he had playing though his mind – zombies thirsting for flesh, red-eyed monsters with piranha teeth, something that looked like a clown but was much nastier underneath – scenes from every horror movie or book he'd ever seen or read.

"For Christ's sake," he yelled, now in a full panic. "One of you fucking bastards over there on the other side of that door better fuckin' answer me. I swear to God ... if you're playing some fuckin' sick-ass joke on me, I'm gonna loosen somebody's fuckin-"

A shape wavered ahead of him, still couched in shadow. The slap-brush of its feet slowed, as if it weren't quite ready to step forward and be seen.

On the other side of the door, Amy, Matt and Henry looked at each other.

"What's wrong, Tommy?" Amy hollered. "Why'd you stop counting? Come on, we have to get this door open."

Henry pressed his ear against the door and listened. "I don't hear anything."

Amy pounded on the old wood of the door. "TOMMY! What the hell are you doing over there? *Tommy?*"

# 4

"...*Tommy*." She kept calling his name ... *we* kept calling his name, but he wouldn't answer." Henry took another sip of brandy. "Of course, we had no idea about what was going on over there ... over on the other side of that curs-ed door. *We* didn't hear the noises he was hearing, or the laughter or the slapping wet feet. We didn't find out about all that until later. We did hear him fall, but had no idea what happened or caused it. We thought, especially since he wasn't answering us, that he must have just passed out."

"That's horrible, dad." The look on Emma's face conveyed more than the words had. "And mom was-"

Henry nodded. "Yep. Your mom was right there, right in the thick of it. In fact, at this point, she'd unofficially taken charge. She was pushing on that door with everything she had. I'm almost embarrassed ... no ... I *am* embarrassed to tell you that I was just kind of standing there with my hands on the door until she yelled at me to either help or get out of the way. And I'll tell ya, that damned door had no intention of opening."

"But you finally managed, right?"

Henry turned his gaze toward the fire, lifted his glass to his lips but didn't take a sip and rested it back on his knee. This part of the telling wasn't going to be easy. Not that explaining that a young girl had been squashed like a bug by a door that had a mind of its own had been easy. But this part was the part where, in the movies, everyone sympathetically claps the teller on the shoulder and pretends to believe what they're saying, while behind his back they're making little circles at their temples with their forefingers.

The fire crackled and popped, and so did the thoughts running through his brain. This tale ... all of it ... was never meant to be shared with his children. Amy and he had agreed on that not long after she first got pregnant. It had been an unspoken vow of silence between them, and although he understood why he had to break it now, that understanding didn't comfort him. He felt very much like he was breaking Amy's trust. And that was something he'd never ever done in his life.

Emma's hand on the back of his made him jump. "Where'd you go, dad?"

He patted the back of her hand. "I guess I just got lost in the thought of your mother, honey. That woman-" He wiped at another pesky splash of invisible dust in his eye. "-That woman was everything to me. Still is, kinda. Of course, that goes for you, too ... but-"

"I know, dad. I do."

Henry sighed. "I don't think I have it in me to finish this story tonight. I'm tired, very tired ... maybe even more than that. I'm worn out. Not just on the outside, but on the inside, too." He leaned over toward her and brushed the backs of his fingers along her cheek. "I love you so much, kitten. I truly do. And I promised to tell you the story ... the whole story ... but the rest will have to wait until tomorrow."

Emma caught Henry's hand in hers, drew it to her lips and kissed it. All her life, his hands had been so strong, so lovingly gentle and so protective. Now, they could hardly steady a glass, or hold a pen tight enough and long enough to write a few lines. They were exactly what he'd just said: old and worn out, but she could still feel the love that ran through them.

"Come on, dad. Let me get you to bed. We'll talk about all this tomorrow after breakfast."

Henry smiled, and then suddenly caught her by the wrist and pulled her in close. "In my office ... in the bottom left hand drawer of my desk is a fireproof box. I keep the key taped to the inside of the middle pullout drawer on the right side. If ... if for any reason we never get to finish this conversation ... you go to that box. You have to promise me that you'll do that. And you have to promise me that you'll sit down and show all of it to Annabel ... that you'll *make* her look at it ... really look at it."

"What are you talking about?" Henry's sudden change in demeanor sent a ripple of ice up Emma's spine. "Why wouldn't we get to finish it? Tomorrow...tomorrow morning, first thing."

"I know...but just in case-"

"In case what? Don't talk like that; you're scaring me."

Henry kissed the back of her hand and then patted it lightly. "It's okay, kitten. Just the ramblings of an old and tired man. Sure we'll finish it tomorrow. Right after breakfast. Just like we said."

Emma pasted a false smile on her lips. "Well, let me tell you, old, tired man, you better not be planning on dying or anything stupid like that. I won't have it. And if you do ... I swear ... I'll revive you somehow just so I can kill you for doing that to me."

Henry waved a hand in the air. "Ahhh! Don't worry. I ain't goin' nowhere. Now come on and help an old man t'bed. I'm bushed."

Emma wheeled Henry to his room, pulled down the covers and went over and looked out the window while she waited for him to finish in the bathroom. The porch light cast an oval yellow circle about thirty feet into the surrounding darkness until it was swallowed up. A light braying drifted over the field from the cow pasture, sounding like a gentle moan of contentment.

*Contentment.*

That's what this farm had always felt like to her. It was a place where nothing bad ... nothing really bad was allowed to happen. It was ten acres of safety and security. And somehow, Emma had the sudden feeling that that safety and security and contentment were only a shadow away from dissolving.

## Chapter 14
## THE BOX

### 1

Ralph sat there with his hands on the edge of the lid. His touch was tentative, light – almost no pressure at all, as if his fingers knew that lifting the lid would be a horrible mistake.

"Well?" The word was snorted more than spoken. "You gonna open it or not? I ain't getting any damned younger, you know?"

The look on Ralph's face was blank. His mind had skipped back to when he had opened the box that his father kept hidden on the top shelf of the closet, underneath his old army uniform. Opening that box had gotten him a good hide tanning and a week of house arrest. He wondered if opening this box would lead to the same kind of thing, only on a grander scale. The box on his father's shelf had contained a .45 caliber Colt. And as is the case with most young boys, finding a gun meant having to take it out to show his friends, if only for the bragging rights of having the coolest thing in your pocket on that particular day. The possible consequences associated with taking that *coolest* thing are no more than a blink of a thought when the weight of that *coolest thing* is in your hands.

Walcott cleared his throat for the third time. "Ralph? Hello? Are you in there, man?"

"Um ... yes. Sorry Mis ... um ... Walcott." He shook his head. "I think it's going to take me some time to get used to dropping the mister. Sorry."

"Forget the mister, or dropping it, or whatever for now. Just let me know if you intend to open that box or not. Time's a'wastin'."

Ralph nodded, pulled his hands away from the box, flexed his fingers, rubbed his palms on the front of his overalls and then reached toward the lid. This time, without hesitation, he grasped the corners and lifted the lid. He had one eye completely closed and the other narrowed to a slit, as if he expected something repulsive to jump out. Nothing did. He ran the back of his arm across his forehead in relief. Walcott laughed.

"Think I had a bomb or somethin' hidin' in there? Or maybe..." He let an evil grin spread across his face. "-Or maybe body parts ... you know, like maybe a piece of the last foreman who hesitated when I asked him to do somethin'?" Walcott shook his head and grinned again. "Better an' easier ways t'get rid of employees other than blowin' 'em up ... or tryin' t'scare 'em t'death."

Ralph grinned back, his face still a knot of nervousness. "Not really sure what I expected. But I guess it wasn't this." He peered into the box, relief slowly softening his features.

Walcott leaned back in his chair. "Well go ahead, heft all that outta there. Lots t'get done and we can't get nothin' done just starin' at it."

Ralph reached in and scooped out everything he could get his fingers around, mostly piles of folded, crumpled and discolored papers. Underneath them, at the very bottom, were two keys held together with a twist of wire, one of which looked as if it had been fashioned from a small piece of ivory. The other was a large, iron skeleton key. Beside them, lying on its side, was a small, golden chalice, no bigger than a baby's rattle.

One at a time, Ralph carefully removed each item and laid it on the table, watching the expression on Walcott's face as each was laid down, watching the man's lone arm twitch with ... what? ... nervousness? ... anticipation? ... fear? ... maybe all of them. That expression only changed once, when Ralph removed the chalice. For whatever reason, this item wrinkled his face into a sneer and made him shift his gaze away.

Ralph leaned over the box. "That's it, Walcott. That's all there is." A hint of a smile played across his lips; he didn't use mister, and it *almost* felt natural.

Walcott laid his hand on the stack of papers that had come out first. "This here is what we're going to deal with first. Everything in this box has a story ... a secret ... a secret darkness that should have never come t'be ... and a secret that should never be uttered aloud... but has to be. Leastwise, it has to be passed on t'someone just because o'what it is and what's coming." He leveled a shaking and bony finger at Ralph's nose. "And looks like you're gonna hafta be that someone. And I'm sorry for that. But for now, let's just start with the papers. Start with that one there with the blue backing."

## 2

As much as he liked anyone (and those people were few and far between), Walcott liked Ralph. He was a good foreman; he was honest and diligent and, above all, fair. He had a way of seeing everyone's side. It was what most people called "having a big heart." Yet he was capable and able to get those working under him to give him more by asking less. That was something Walcott did more than like; that was something Walcott respected.

He watched as Ralph slowly made his way through the document. From the look on his face there was no doubt that most of the language was beyond Ralph's comprehension. In the best of situations with the most educated, lawyer-speak is nearly unintelligible. For someone like Ralph, who had a great deal of common sense but very little formal education, it was like trying to decipher hieroglyphics without a Rosetta stone. But Walcott admired the fact that Ralph flipped through every page and went through every paragraph (sometimes twice) until he figured he'd at least gotten the gist of it.

Ralph refolded the document and set it in front of him. The disbelief he was feeling was so clearly written on his face it could have been stenciled there.

"Well?" said Walcott at last. "What do you think, Ralph?"

"I-I don't know what to think, Mister Walcott." The use of mister this time was intentional. "Am I understanding this right? You're going to sign the farm over to me?"

Walcott smiled. "No, Ralph. I'm not going to sign it over to you. I'm going to sell it to you, if you'll agree ... for the tidy sum of one dollar."

"But why? I mean ... but why?" It was all Ralph could think to ask.

"Because you're the only man I trust to run it right. Because there ain't no other family I could give it to.

And even if there was ... I wouldn't. Because I don't want it to go to no goddamn government estate auction when I kick." He drew in a deep breath and looked away. "And because there's a hitch."

"What kind of hitch?"

Walcott reached out and scooped up the other papers that had come out of the box. They were old and yellow and made of parchment. It was obvious that they'd been tucked away in there untouched for a very long time. Some of the folds had split open along the crease and they crackled under the light, shaky pressure of Walcott's fingers.

"These here are the hitch, Ralph, the proverbial bump-in-the-road. But these ain't no bump. These here are tiny mountains. These here are the reason you don't have no pen in your hand yet. 'Cause before I let you sign that there quitclaim deed, you have to understand ... really understand what you're getting into. And you have to agree to it all on your own. No persuadin' from me. I'm just gonna lay it all out. Then..." He looked up at the clock over the stove. "Well, actually, considerin' what time it is, maybe we'll talk about this in the morning.

Ralph looked at the papers in Walcott's hand. He looked at the rest of the things that were spread across the table and wondered what part they all played in the mystery that Walcott was spinning. Having the farm would be a good thing, he knew that. He also knew that Walcott was not one to be overly dramatic or rattle easily. Whatever it was that was in those papers truly unsettled the man. And that made Ralph both nervous ... and curious.

"Okay," said Ralph, "we'll talk about them tomorrow."

## Chapter 15
## USURPER

**1**

"What the fuck is going on here?" bellowed Brian, his hand yanking furiously at the immovable deadbolt. His rising fear was temporarily swallowed by his even faster rising anger. His mind chose to blot out the echoed laughter and cries, concerning itself only with why a brand new door (perfectly fitted to a perfectly installed new jamb) should keep closing arbitrarily, and why a brand new deadbolt stuck in its latch like a rusted old piece of junk.

Out of breath and frustrated beyond belief, he slapped his palms against the sides of his trousers. "SHIT! Shit, shit, shit and more shit!"

Outside, dusk had passed into twilight, which was giving up the last of its glow to night. Brian flicked on the light and padded back down the hall and skip-stepped down the three steps that emptied him into the living room. Still grumbling to himself, he crossed the room, opened the flue to the double-sided fireplace that fed both the living room and library, opened the gas jets and ignited them. A warm glow of oranges and reds sprang to life, bathing the room in dancing auras of color and shadow.

Brian found himself staring trance-like into the flames for quite some time. It was like everything inside him just shut down. The recalcitrant lock, the obstinate door, some disjointed memory of an old woman, and the minatory laughter and haunting cries of a baby he'd heard all faded away, smothered by the hypnotic light of the flames that reflected off the highly polished floor and curled into odd-angled shadows that wavered like distorted silhouettes along the mahogany walls. What never occurred to him (but should have) was that Annabel might be home and worried about where he was.

For a few more moments he stared absently into the flames, not thinking, just watching them flicker. He then shoved his hands in his pockets and sauntered around through the archway into the library. He stood in the doorway taking in the three full floors of shelves that wrapped around the inner wall of the turret. Craning his neck, his eyes traced the railed catwalks that jutted out from the casements where the second and third floors would have been. His eyes swept from one side to the other, following the contour of the shelves until they ended on the far side of the room at the top of a spiral staircase built of polished walnut. Behind the staircase, on the first level, was a small door that led into a roomy pantry that abutted the kitchen on the other side of it.

Brian studied the bookshelves, wondering how many years it might take to fill them all. Oh, he had plenty of books already – on all kinds of subjects. But there was no doubt that all of his books combined with all of Annabel's wouldn't even fill a quarter of the space they had.

He laid a finger on the edge of a shelf to his right and drew it along as he followed the curve around to the staircase. It was smooth and warm and somehow made him feel powerful. All this space ... his to command, to fill and use as he saw fit. Yes, there was power in a bookcase this grandiose. He turned around and walked back the other way, this time his left index finger tracing the outline as he went.

A soft gurgling sound mewed in his belly, followed by a rolling growl. He placed a hand over his stomach and shifted his gaze back over to the pantry door. Of course, it was empty; he knew that, but *what the hell*? It's worth a look, right? Like checking out the fridge late at night and finding nothing you want, then checking it out five minutes later, as if you had missed some tasty hidden morsel the first time around, or some miraculous fairy had come along and restocked it – just so you could have a snack.

Brian trundled his growling belly toward the pantry door. He swung himself around the bottom of the staircase with one hand on the slick rail, the way a monkey might arc from one branch to another. With a quick twist of the knob and a slight push, the pantry door wafted silently open on its hinges. He felt for the light switch on one wall and then the other, and then remembered that the light was in the center of the ceiling, powered by a dangling string. He gave it a tug and seventy-five watts of bare bulb blazed to life.

He had to blink twice, and then rub at his eyes with the heels of his hands. The pantry was little more than a spacious alleyway between the library and the kitchen. The walls on either side fronted with shelves. What made him blink and try to clear his eyes was the fact that the damned shelves (all of them) were fully stocked. From floor to ceiling, from library door to kitchen door, not an open space remained on any shelf. It was a bonanza, but one from another century. Huge sacks of flour and sugar, mason jar after mason jar of preserves of all types, burlap sacks tied with hemp at the necks marked COFFEE BEANS, square, wooden, hand-crank coffee grinders and pepper mills, and at the library end, on his left, bottles of various colored liquids, which Brian took to be booze.

*This ... this isn't right. We didn't stock this place; we ... we haven't even...* He let the thought trail off as he walked toward the kitchen door, his fingers bumping along over the odd array of items. Just before he reached the door, the light flickered, went out, buzzed a little and then came back on. Brian drew in a sharp breath and held it. The shelves were empty, devoid of everything. Not even a single mote of dust existed to mar the pristine wooden surfaces.

A deep laughter rang out from behind the shelves – seeped out of them, like sap from a resin-loaded pine tree. Brian backed toward the kitchen door, his hand feeling behind him for the knob. His fingers just touched its rounded edge when the door flew open and then slammed shut again. And the laughter grew louder and more intense. The shelves began jumping up and down on their supports, and the noise of it forced Brian's hands over his ears. That was enough; that was more than enough. He twisted around, fumbled the kitchen door open and slammed it shut behind him, his back falling against it to ensure that whatever was going on behind it would stay behind it.

The noise behind the door stopped as suddenly as it had begun. The shelves stopped jumping. There was a moment's pause, a breath of an interlude and then...

*BANG! BANG! BANGBANGBANGBANG!* The door waffled against his back, threating to topple him forward, threating to blow itself right off its hinges and send him flying across the kitchen like wastepaper in a whirlwind. The force of it was jarring. He lowered his center of gravity and dug his heels in, but the freshly laid tile floor was slicker than ice, especially since all he had on was his socks. He slid to the floor, panting, and wrestled his socks off as quickly as he could. Bare feet would give him a little better traction, or so he hoped.

## 2

As Brian was struggling with the immovable door latch, Annabel stood in the shower letting the hot water cascade down over her bruised shoulder. By six-thirty she'd given up waiting for him and figured she might as well soak her elevator-battered self into feeling a little better. Where Brian had gotten to was still a question. It was supposed to have been a quick trip to the house for him, a meeting with her grandfather for her, and a meet up back here at the apartment. She supposed that maybe he had stopped off at the office and gotten himself entrenched in some new design or other. It certainly wouldn't be the first time that had happened. Still, she found it a bit odd that he hadn't even tried to call.

She turned the water off, climbed out and toweled off. The only reasonable thing to do now would be to give him a call. But after what happened in the elevator with her phone, she decided to take the course of least resistance. She'd make herself a drink and try to figure out what they would have for dinner. Spaghetti and meatballs (the frozen, pre-made kind you could heat in the microwave) seemed the easiest course.

With the towel wrapped around her and knotted under her arm the way only women seem to be able to do without having it drop off two seconds later, she ambled into the bedroom to dress. After making sure the blinds were closed, she flipped on the light on her nightstand. Her heart jumped into her throat and a little scream escaped her lips. A young woman was sitting in her desk chair on the other side of the room. Annabel could see the lamp, the desk drawer and blotter right through her. The woman gave a faint smile, started to rise and then disappeared.

*You need t'find your man, child. He needs you. You know where you have t'go.* The voice was definitely that of a woman far older than the apparition Annabel had just seen. And her words hung in the air like the final notes of an echoed symphony, and with them, the overpoweringly sweet smell of flowers in summer.

Annabel wasted no time rummaging for fresh clothes. She threw on the same things she'd peeled off to take her shower, a pair of faded blue jeans and a gray Old Navy V-neck top. Out in the hall she eyed the elevator, shook her head and opted for the stairs. Thirty-two cut back sets of steps was a lot, but better than getting stuck again. At least it was *down*.

She burst through the exit door into the lobby, practically ran through it and out into the parking lot. As she pulled out into traffic, she kept repeating a single word in her head: Brian.

*Brian, Brian, Brian, Brain, Brian.* It was her shield, something to concentrate on so she didn't have to see the young woman sitting at her desk – a young woman she could see right through. *Brian, Brian, Brian, Brian, Brian.*

She wheeled the jeep out on to Rt. 23 and pushed the speed up to sixty-five. At that rate, she could be at the house in less than ten minutes.

*If you don't get pulled over, that is.* Somehow, that thought managed to squeeze itself in between the Brians, and that made her smile. She eased off the gas and let the Jeep drop to a nice cruising speed of thirty-five. No sense taking chances.

A moment later, a flash of reds and blues lit up her mirror. For the second time her heart jumped into her throat. But this one was a false alarm. She angled the jeep to the side of the road and let out a very thankful sigh as the cruiser sped on past. When it finally disappeared around a bend ahead, she eased back onto the road and brought the Jeep up to 40mph.

Eleven and a half minutes later she rolled to a stop behind Brian's truck. Halfway to the porch steps she stopped. Something wasn't right, didn't *feel* right. The hairs on the back of her neck prickled to attention. She had the strangest sensation that she was being watched, not by some hidden interloper, but by the house itself. A light flickered on in one of the upstairs bedrooms and then went out again. It was almost as if the house had winked at her. A sly wink of understanding – a deliberate confirmation of her irrational suspicion.

"*That's just plain ludicrous, Abigail,*" she thought, and started up the steps again. "*Gran'pop must have really gotten to you.*" Halfway across the porch she came to a dead stop. *Abigail? Why did I... who is Abig-*

A loud click startled her out of her thoughts and the front door swung slowly open.

"Br ... Brian? Are you there?" She eased forward, her head craned to peer around the door that now stood ajar, and then stepped hesitantly into the vestibule. The first thing she noticed was how quiet it was. The only sound she could hear were a series of crackling and popping sounds, somehow familiar, though she couldn't quite place them. When she turned to close the door, it slammed over on its own and latched itself. The scream she let out rippled through the house like an echo through an empty cave.

Not thinking, not even wanting to think, she flew down the hall and turned into the living room. She expected – no, hoped – to find Brian sitting there with a supercilious grin on his face, overly pleased with himself at having scared the b'jeebies out of her with his door trick. In her haste she forgot about the sunken living room, lost her footing on the steps and went sprawling across the hardwood floor, face-down. Her arms flew out in front of her to protect her, but she still managed to bang her chin hard enough to rattle her teeth and peel a layer of skin off the inside of her right cheek. A thin trickle of blood dribbled from the corner of her mouth.

"Shit," she mumbled. The word came out sounding like thit, while she probed the extent of her injury with her index finger. Satisfied it wasn't too bad, she worked herself up to a sitting position and then onto her feet. She gave the steps a reproachful glance and repeated herself. "Shit!"

A loud *POP!* drew her attention to the fireplace. She watched the flames flicker and dance across the logs in orange and red spikes – the source of the crackles and pops she'd heard back in the vestibule. It took her a few minutes before she noticed what was wrong with the scene. The logs were real. Thin ribbons of gray smoke and burning embers rose upward and disappeared into the flue, and the room was rich with the aroma of burning wood. But that shouldn't be. Their fireplace was gas. She edged closer, walking softly, her mind still thinking about the winking window and the door that closed itself.

"Brian?" she whispered. Everything was tightening inside. She felt like a little kid who suddenly discovered she was alone and lost in the maze of the Fun House mirrors. As she scanned the room in a slow circle, she began to realize that the Fun House simile might not be too far off the mark. The entrance, or what *had* been the entrance, to the library (Brian's pride and joy), was now just a solid block wall, the pointing of which was dry and crumbling. The passage that led to the dining room, remodeled with cherry wood molding, was nothing more than a small archway of peeling plaster. Beneath her feet, too, the floor boards had reverted to the worn and chipped oak they had had removed. Her breath caught in her throat. No matter how hard she tried, the scream inside her stayed lodged there. She could feel the world trying to swim away from her.

"NO!" she finally shouted, the word coming out with such force that it even startled her. She had the silliest thought that it must have startled the house, too, because when the cloud of panic that had seized her broke apart, everything looked exactly as it should, including the gas fire playing across the fake logs.

## 3

*BANG! BANGBANGBANG!* Brian pushed against the pantry door with his back, constantly readjusting his stance as his feet tried to slip out from under him. The door kept slapping against his shoulders, trying to knock him off balance, trying to open. A stentorian growl, like an angry feral dog, rumbled counterpoint to the banging. Brian's strength was ebbing. His knees were sore and his thighs burned something fierce. He had no doubt that, at any moment now, he was going to lose his footing completely and lose the battle along with it. Whatever wanted out was going to burst out, and, most likely, tear him to shreds. He could see it in his mind's eye: some amorphous lumbering beast, its breath feted, its large needle-shaped teeth dripping with thick saliva, its eyes glowing red within their deep dark sockets, and its clawed hands pawing the air as it bore down on him.

*WHAM! CRAAAKKKK!* A fissure split along the upper panel of the door. Time was running out. He looked across the kitchen at the back door, wondering if he could make it. When they'd had the house restored, a large and spacious kitchen was one of the first things he and Annabel had agreed upon. Now it seemed it might be his undoing.

Another loud bang, and a second crack peeled off the first, forming a pattern that reminded Brian of the symbol for lambda: $\lambda$. This was it: fight or flight. The door was going to give. He took a deep breath and pushed away from it at a dead run, his feet slipping on the tiles. He angled for the back door and (he hoped) the freedom and safety of the outside. Behind him, the pantry door exploded off its hinges, sending shards of split molding tumbling through the air. He didn't stop to look back. He slid into the back door, his chest banging up against the mullions and cracking one of the glass panes. Almost frantic now, he grabbed the knob and turned and twisted and pulled and yanked. It wouldn't budge.

*The locks, idiot, the locks.* He had to fight with himself to keep focused. His fingers fumbled with the knobs as he tried to keep himself from looking over his shoulder at the beast he was sure was closing on him. The room was filled with a ghastly, feted smell: long dead fish rotting in a summer sun. When the puff of a hot breath struck his neck, he turned, whimpering, sure he was done for.

"*NO!*"

The word reverberated through the house, its origin unknown. It was harsh and commanding. It was a voice Brian knew well; it was a tone he knew well. It was Annabel's voice, and it was a tone he had come to recognize as the one she used when she'd had enough of everything.

At the sound of the word, at its *command*, the thing behind him – no more than an immense cloud of gray with burning points of light where eyes might have been (had it been a physical being) – evaporated. Along with it, the pantry door repaired itself, splintered molding reassembled itself and reaffixed itself to the jamb. The feted smell of rotting fish became the sweet smell of honeysuckle.

"Belle?" he called, slumping to the floor with his back against the door. "BELLE? Is that really you?" He wanted to believe that Annabel had come, had found him, had somehow chased away his nightmare. He wanted to. But the house ... the house could play tricks on you. Maybe the mason had been right. Maybe the house didn't want to be fixed. Maybe there was something to the ghost stories Annabel's grandfather so earnestly espoused.

He took a deep breath, held it as long as he could to try and settle his mind, and then exhaled. "That's just plain ridiculous," he said, getting to his feet. "Ghosts. Houses that don't want to be fixed ... silly ... just plain silly." He looked around the kitchen, forcing himself to focus on the beauty and design. He took in everything. All except the pantry door. That, he found himself unable to look at. Each time his eyes moved in that direction, he unconsciously shifted them to another spot.

"BRIAN! Brian, where are you? I know you're here; your truck's outside. Please, for God's sake, answer me."

The call was coming from somewhere behind the pantry doors. It was damped, muffled. *Maybe she's in the library*, Brian thought. *Or maybe it's another house trick ... a bait-and-switch. Can you trust it? Do you want to trust it?*

"I have to," he mumbled, heading for the pantry door on wobbly legs. His hands were shaking so badly by the time he reached it, he needed both to get hold of the knob. Part of him (most, actually, though he refused to admit it) didn't want to open that door.

## 4

Annabel stared quizzically at the archway leading to the library, an archway that only a moment before had disappeared and reappeared like some nightclub magician's grand finale. Feeling a little separated from herself, disconnected, like a person watching herself in a dream, she entered the library turret. She watched herself pause to imagine the room full of furniture: Brian's desk, expensive but not ornate, sitting near the center of the room where golden shafts of light from the upper windows fell, and the flickering from the fireplace enhanced its ambiance. A plush sectional couch in front of the bookshelves facing him, fronted by a modest coffee table and flanked on one side by a coffee station and a minibar on the other.

"*STOP DAYDREAMING,*" screamed the observing Annabel. "*Find Brian. Find Brian before it's too late.*"

Annabel cocked her head to the side and looked around the room. Had she heard something? Had someone said something? She suddenly realized she was standing motionless in the center of the library, but had no idea how she'd gotten there, or for that matter, where the library itself had come from. A moment ago it was a block wall. When the past few minutes finally flooded back (the change in the room, the door slamming shut), her heart beat accelerated, whacking against her breastbone.

*Brian. I have to find Brian.* She made a slow circle of the room, found the door behind the spiral staircase that led to the pantry and headed for it. She grabbed the knob, turned it and stepped in. Her fingers fumbled on both sides of the door in search of the light switch before she remembered that it was a pull-cord in the center of the room. She tugged it and the light flared to life with a soft click. At the same time, the door opened at the other end.

"Jesus Christ!" gasped a startled Brian. Annabel exhaled a soft scream. They clung to each other for a long time in the glare of the naked 75w bulb. When the light flickered, Brian grabbed Annabel by the hand and practically dragged her out of the pantry and into the library. He slammed the door shut behind them and wished that he had had the forethought to put a lock on it. Of course, who could have anticipated that a simple pantry would require locking?

"We ... we should probably get out of here for now, go ... go home," stammered Brian. "Maybe everything ... maybe will be better tomorrow..."

Annabel put a gentle hand on his shoulder. "It'll be irey, Brian. Somehow it'll all be all irey." She couldn't imagine where the words that were coming out of her mouth had come from. She felt very far from feeling things were going to be all right. And *irey*? What the hell was that? Yet they kept coming. It was as if someone else, another Annabel, were speaking. She had the brief sensation that she was once again outside herself, a cold observer to the pantomime that was playing out. "Come on, Brian, let's go into the living room and sit by the fire. That'll cheer you up; that'll cheer us both up ... make us feel normal again. Come on."

She took his hand and led him around the spiral staircase, across the empty library and into the living room. Inside her head she railed: *No, no, no! This isn't right. Brian, this isn't me. Please take me home. Please make me leave with you.* Dazed and helpless, Annabel watched from some mental place outside herself as she led Brian over to the fire, eased him down into a sitting position and worked herself in between his legs with her back against his chest.

"Hold me, Brian. Just hold me tight and watch the fire. We'll both get lost in the flickering dance of flames. We'll relax ... and everything will be irey." Brian obediently enfolded her in his arms, rocking her gently from side to side. His chin rested on her right shoulder and his eyes were fixed on the fire.

"Kiss me, Brian. Kiss my neck; kiss my shoulder. Squeeze me tight."

*Stop it! Stop it, stopitstopitstopit*! cried the observing Annabel. *He's mine, not yours.* That thought, that mental proclamation acted like a cold slap in the face. Annabel suddenly realized that she really *was* no more than an observer, an onlooker to this horror. Whoever or whatever was sitting with Brian was not she. It was something else, someone else – an intruder, an interloper. And yet ... somehow... it *was* her. She could feel the pressure of Brian's arms around her. She could feel the cool wet of his kisses on her shoulders and neck.

"Mmm ... that's nice," said the Annabel in Brian's arms. "But wait a minute. We can make it better." She stood up, pulled off her shirt and bra and dropped them on the floor. Then she slid off her jeans and straddled Brian so she was facing him. "Love me, Brian. Right here; right now in front of the fire. Make love to me, Brian."

Annabel the observer recoiled. *Don't, Brian. Please, for God's sake, don't. It's not really me. It's not me. It's...* A sudden flood of sensation overwhelmed her as Brian's hand closed on her counterpart's breast and his tongue licked lightly across her lips. She could feel her hands undoing Brian's pants, feel them guiding him into her as she rocked up onto it. She could feel the strength in his arms as he grabbed her hips and thrust himself into her, matching her rhythm.

Forty minutes later, Annabel on her back and Brian on top of her, they climaxed. Their bodies were covered in a fine sheen of sweat. Brian rolled off her and lay on his back bedside her, panting. Annabel the usurper lay still, a mocking smile curving her lips as she focused her mind on observer Annabel. She reached over and took Brain's hand. At the touch of their fingers locking together, observer Annabel plummeted into a pool of blackness, and then swam back up to find herself lying beside Brian, sweating and exhausted. She wanted to scream. She wanted to get Brian up. She wanted them to leave. But there was nothing left, no strength, no real will. Brian had had her ... or her intruder ... in every way imaginable ... in ways they had never done it before. Her body was totally worn out.

"Br ... Brian, we ... we have to ... we have to get out..." Before she could finish, she faded into a fast, hard and dreamless sleep. Beside her, Brian rolled over onto his side and began snoring.

## Chapter 16
## HENRY STICKS HIS TONGUE OUT

***October 31***
***11:20 a.m. – 3:26 p.m.***

**1**

Henry wheeled himself into the kitchen. Emma folded the morning paper over, looked at the clock and then over at Henry and smiled.

"Eleven-twenty. Aren't you just a big old slug-a-bug this morning?"

"Don't start with me, Emma," grumbled Henry good naturedly. "It was a hell of a night."

"Didn't sleep well, dad?" She got up to get him some coffee and a glass of water.

"No, not really, if you want to know the truth. I guess digging up the past with Annabel ... and you ... wasn't such a great idea." He shrugged. "Even though I know I had to. Gave me bad dreams. Guess I should've expected something like that, huh?"

Emma set the coffee and water in front of him, slid his soufflé cup of pills over and sat back down. "Wanna share?"

Henry waved a hand and took a sip of coffee. "No, not really. Dreams are dreams, that's all. Besides, we still have a lot more to talk about, and I'm sure that'll be enough for the both of us without adding bad dreams into the stupid mix." He up ended the soufflé cup, took a swallow of water, took a second swallow to get the third, recalcitrant pill washed down and crumpled the cup into a ball and tossed it on the table. "And I'm sick of taking all these goddamned pills. I swear, the only reason that jackass of a doctor prescribes them for me is so that he and his jackass counterpart pharmacist can get rich. I don't feel any better or worse whether I take 'em or not."

Emma laughed. "That's right, dad. To hell with those stupid pills. Your blood pressure and cholesterol levels ... they'll just straighten themselves out. Who cares about strokes and heart attacks and all that silly nonsense?"

"Sometimes, girl, you're a real pain in my ass." Henry smiled.

"That's my job, dad. That's every daughter's job. I think it's genetic. All those little chromosomes and stuff ... they just fire themselves up and say ...'Hey, it's a girl we're in. We gotta make her a real pain in the ass to her old man, especially when it comes to something so mundane and inconsequential as his health'."

"Smart ass."

"I think that's in that code, too. What do you want for brunch? It's a little late for breakfast."

Henry held up his coffee cup. "I'm drinkin' it."

"Un-unh. Not enough. How about some scrambled eggs and bacon?"

Henry wrinkled his face into a sneer. "What? Those stupid eggs without the yolk and that tasteless, low-sodium turkey bacon you're always shoving at me? No thanks, I'll pass."

"Then at least have some toast. And don't give me a hard time about the margarine, either."

"Ha! More tasteless – no, not tasteless – *plastic* crap. But I suppose if I refuse that, you'll find something even more insipid to offer me, so, okay. I'll have a piece of toast."

"You'll have two pieces of toast. But I'll cut you a deal."

"Yeah, what kind of deal? Smile while I'm eating my tasteless toast and you won't take my coffee away?"

Emma laughed. "No. If you promise to be a good boy today, I'll let you have some real, unsalted, butter on your toast."

Henry clapped his hands like a five year old at a birthday party. "Oh boy, oh boy, if I'm really, really good … maybe I'll get a beanie with a propeller on it, too."

They both laughed.

"Now who's being a pain in the ass?"

Henry stuck his tongue out.

## 2

After they'd eaten, Emma busied herself with the chores, while Henry went out to the back porch and watched the birds flitting around the feeders. It was the dryer buzzer that snapped Emma out of her thoughts. She'd been standing at the sink, steam ribboning up, thinking about what Henry had told her yesterday. She just couldn't imagine what it must have been like to be standing there looking at that poor girl. When she looked down, the sink was nearly full, and the hot water was cold. She shut off the faucet, pulled the drainer, shook the water from her now pruned hands and grabbed a dishtowel to dry them.

Emma looked at the time. She was late. Henry's meds were due at one o'clock, and she'd been daydreaming. It was now going on for twenty-after. She filled the soufflé cup, grabbed a glass of water and headed out. When she reached the back door, the dryer buzzed again.

*You'll just have to wait, so don't start wrinkling up on me.* She pulled the back door open and elbowed her way through the screen door and let it slam over behind her. Henry was at the far end of the porch facing toward the little stream that wound through the property.

"I know you're going to be happy to hear this," she said, her shoes making a hollow clatter on the floorboards as she walked to him, "but it's time for your medicine again."

Henry didn't reply; he just kept staring off across the field.

"What? No smart remark? No witty..." Emma dropped the soufflé cup and the pills scattered.

"Dad?" Her heart was in her throat. "Dad! Wake up!" Even as she was shaking him she knew he wouldn't wake up, couldn't wake up. For a brief moment, she lost herself. All the strength she'd ever had abandoned her, along with her ability to accept that her father was gone. And she went right on shaking him and telling him to wake up.

### 3

For a long time she just sat on the porch next to him, huddled up against the wheel of his chair, her knees pulled up to her chest and her arms wrapped around them. The tears just kept coming. No matter how many times she wiped at her eyes and told herself that she had to get up, that she had phone calls and arrangements to make, she just couldn't seem to force herself to do it. She sat there crying. The image of him that morning, sticking his tongue out at her would come and go. When it did, she would smile, and then she would cry more.

Finally, she forced herself to her feet and kissed him on the cheek, rubbing his hand between hers.

"I love you, dad. I love you so much."

She gently placed his hand back on his lap under the afghan and wheeled him back into the house. The tears still came, but Emma was in control again. She rolled him into his study, facing out the window toward the birdfeeder, kissed him on the head and then left to start making all the phone calls that needed to be made. At the door, she stopped and looked at him.

"I miss you already, dad. It's going to be so hard without you." She closed the door quietly, as if he were sleeping, and went into the kitchen to begin the process of saying goodbye to her father forever.

## Chapter 17
## LOST NIGHT

**11:00 a.m. – 6:00 p.m.**

### 1

It was Annabel who stirred first, fumbling herself up onto her elbows and then up to a sitting position. For a few minutes, she just sat there watching the fire and listening to Brian's soft breathing. Then she gathered up her clothes and dressed, turned off the gas jets to the fireplace and walked to the bow window and stared idly out into the morning sunshine. Most of last night was a blur – a kind of fragmented and already faded dream. Beneath it, buried in the fragments, something tugged at her consciousness, something dark and amorphous. It made her feel almost as fragmented as her memory. Fragmented. Yes, that was it. For a brief moment she felt as if she could almost grasp what had happened. Sex. They'd had sex. But it had been... Been what? Different. Different how? She closed her eyes and tried to think, to feel. They had been in front of the fire. Then... Then what? An image of herself straddling Brian bloomed behind her eyes. She'd stripped. He had made love – no, not made love, not like they always did – he had ... fucked ... her. It had been almost brutal, primal. She had watched them... A cold shudder ran through her. Watched *them*. Watched! The memory of having felt like an onlooker, like she had been outside herself watching someone else ... *fuck* ... her husband, hit her like a slap from a wet towel.

Behind her, Brian grunted, opened his eyes and rolled onto his side. As if by some strange, dark magic evoked by Brian's awakening, everything Annabel had just remembered about last night fell from her mind the way a lone, desiccated leaf falls from an autumn branch. It fluttered away into the nothing of forgetfulness.

"You're awake," she said, turning and walking to him. "Thought you were going to sleep right through lunch. It's going on for eleven, sleepyhead."

Brian grunted again and began gathering his clothes and dressing. "What ... what happened last night? I can't really remember much of anything."

Annabel thought for a moment and then finally shrugged. "I'm not sure. I kind of feel like ... like I had too much to drink last night ... kind of fuzzy and out of touch."

"Yeah, me too. But..." Brian scanned the room. "But I don't see any bottles, and I don't remember bringing anything with me yesterday. In fact, I don't even remember when you got here. I thought we were going to meet back at the apartment."

"Now that you mention it," said Annabel, a quizzical look on her face, "I don't remember how I got here, either. I was..." She thought for a long time, her face screwed into a knot of concentration. "I ... was at the apartment. I came out of the shower and then ... then I woke up here on the floor beside you."

Unconsciously following Annabel's pattern, Brian walked to the window, folded his arms across his chest and stared out into the morning. He let his eyes wander across the front lawn, which was now late autumn brown. Unlike Annabel, no flashes of the night before intruded on his thoughts. A hint of a smile curled the edges of his lips.

"This really is a beautiful place, Belle. I think we're going to be very happy here."

"I-I don't know." She walked up behind him and wrapped her arms around his waist. "It bothers me that I can't remember last night, or how I got here. Something's wrong about that. I feel it. Don't you?"

Brian took her hands and unfolded them from around him and turned to face her. "Oh come on, Belle. Please tell me you're not starting to buy into your grandfather's..." He paused, trying to find a word that was a bit more sensitive that *lunacy*, which was what he thought it really was. "Into your grandfather's irrational misgivings about this place. Are you?"

"No. No, of course not. But don't you find it odd that neither one of us can remember last night ... not even a little of it?"

All the color drained from her face when Brian suddenly grabbed her by the shoulders. His face hardened into a mask of fury, his eyes burning with a kind of craziness she'd never seen in him before. "Stop it!" he growled, his nose almost touching hers. "Your grandfather's lost it. Senile, not playing with a full deck, elevator doesn't go to the top, lights on but no one home. I'm not going to let him infect you with it. It's just a fucking house, for Christ's sake. And a beautiful one at that. We've spent a lot of time and money making it what we wanted, and I'm not going to let that old fool ruin it for us because his mind's gone. Do you hear me?"

Annabel shoved him back, breaking his grip. "Brian! What's wrong with you?" She rubbed cross-armed at her shoulders. "You hurt me. You've never hurt me before ... and calling gran'pop senile?"

Brian swiped a hand over his face, his eyes mirroring confusion. "I ... Geeze, Belle, I ... I don't know what came over me. It was like ... like I was outside of myself, just watching. I know; that's crazy, right? Geeze! Are you all right? God, I am so, so sorry."

The two of them stared at each other for a long time, not moving, not blinking – not even thinking. It was as if some unseen hand had hit the PAUSE button on their lives. Then Brian coughed once into a closed fist and the spell was broken.

"What were we talking about?" asked Brian. "I must have zoned-out for a minute."

"Um..." Annabel smiled sheepishly. "I guess I did, too."

They each fixed on the other's eyes in silence, and then broke out laughing.

"Geeze, Belle, I think we're losing it." He stepped forward and swept her into his arms, kissing her gently on the forehead. "What do you say we go buy some groceries, picnic lunch type stuff, and then come back here and gobble it up on the back porch? You know, take the day off, get away from it all for a while. It'll be fun. What do you think?"

As if the night before had never happened, Annabel grinned like a shy schoolgirl being asked out on her first date, winked and said, "I think ... I think we'll need a couple of bottles of good wine to go with the food, don't you?"

"That's a great idea. In fact, why don't we get enough stuff for dinner and tomorrow's breakfast, too? We'll pick up a couple of sleeping bags and spend the night. We can stretch out right here in front of the fireplace."

"Hmm... How 'bout ... you grab the groceries and stuff, and I'll swing by the apartment."

"What for?"

"Maybe something slinky and alluring." She propped a hand on one hip, turned sideways and stuck her chest out. "You know what Mae West said: 'When I'm good, I'm very good. And when I'm bad ... I'm better.' Or something like that. What do you think?"

"What do I think? I'm wondering why we're still standing here."

Brian took her hand and they headed for the door. Outside, he gave her a peck on the cheek. "You go your way and I'll go mine. We'll meet back her for a helluva great afternoon and evening. And ... by the way ... pick out something really hot for tonight."

"Groceries, big boy," she continued in her best Mae West voice from earlier. "That's your mission, should you decide to accept it. In fact, you'll be very sorry if you don't. And don't you dare forget the wine. No wine ... no me."

Brian saluted. "Orders received and mission as good as accomplished already."

## 2

The afternoon sun sent shimmering fingers of gold through the branches to land in sparkling dots on the lawn and porch. Birds called to each other in pleasant tones and the temperature was near perfect for the end of October, standing at sixty-four degrees.

By the time Annabel got back to the house it was almost two. Brian was already waiting for her on the back porch, a picnic basket beside him. When she came through the back door wearing her yellow Harley *Street Angel* tank top and no bra, he whistled and then threw his head back and howled.

"Ain't you one hot looking babe? Wanna share some wine with the big bad wolf?" He grabbed at her breast as she sat down and she slapped his hand away.

"Lunch first, lecher. Then we'll see where things go."

He cracked open the wine and filled their glasses. "Here's to us ... and to a great house. And ... I might add ... one that's haunted only by the demons in my lusting soul. Bwooohaaaaaaa." He grabbed her leg just above the knee and squeezed, making her jump.

"I hate that. Stop it! You'd better behave yourself, or you won't be getting any of this at all." She pulled up her shirt and yanked it back down again, flashing him the barest sight of her breasts."

Brian sipped at his wine, set it down and passed her a sandwich from the basket.

"Look at that," he said, pointing to the vastness of the back yard and the surrounding woods. Beautiful. Simply beautiful. There's nothing haunted here, I'll tell you. If anything, it's practically heaven. Haunted. Ridiculous!"

They laughed about Annabel's grandfather's story. At one point Annabel leaned over and grabbed Brian's crotch yelling: "Watch out mister, here I come, the succubus of Wickersham Hollow, and I'm going to suck your bus but good tonight." They roared. Everything somehow seemed funnier and lighter. Everything seemed to have an almost dreamlike quality to it and neither of them ever remembered feeling happier.

"How's your sandwich?" asked Brian, a strand of beef hanging from the corner of his mouth dripping horseradish sauce down his chin.

"It's *really* good. Lots of meat. And they didn't forget the capicola this time, either." She took the sandwich in one hand and wiped the oil that had dripped from the end along the seam of her jeans. When she bit into it again, a slather of meat dropped out onto her lap.

"God, I can't take you anywhere," laughed Brian. "Not even outside to a picnic."

Annabel plucked up the errant meat, blew on it and shoved it into her mouth, her tongue working to keep it from falling out again as she laughed.

"Looks like you lose," she said, still laughing.

"What do you mean? How do I lose?"

"You're playing second fiddle now to a piece of capicola. It just got the first blow job."

"Oh-ho! So that's the way you're going to play it, is it?" He shot his arm out over the basket and snatched her sandwich, holding it up and away from her. When she leaned over to try to get it back, he let his sandwich drop to his lap and reached out and grabbed her left breast, giving it a firm squeeze before letting go. "Ha! Now we're even. I just copped the first feel."

"Just gimme my sandwich back, pig."

Brian held her sandwich toward her, and as she took it from him, he leaned in and gave her a kiss. "God, but I love you, Belle."

"I love you, too. Very much, Brian."

It was then that Annabel's cell phone rang. She ignored it and let it go to voicemail. After the familiar jingle that told her she had a new message, it rang again. She fished it out of her pocket and looked at the caller ID.

"It's my mom." She looked at it for a minute, turned it off and slipped it back into her pocket, very uncharacteristically.

"Aren't you going to answer her?"

Annabel shook her head. "Uh-unh. She probably just wants me to come back and listen to gran'pop spout off about how evil our house is. I'll call her back, later."

Brian stood up, pulled Annabel to her feet and drew her in, his arms enfolding him. "Well then," he said, a devilish look in his eyes, "I want you. I want you right now, right here ... right on the porch of our new home."

Annabel feigned innocence, her voice lilting with a southern drawl. "Oh my and fiddle-dee-dee. I swear, sir, you are incorrigible. Out here? Out in the open for all the wildlife to see?" She slid her hand down to his crotch and squeezed. "I'm a lady, sir. If you want me ... then you'll have to catch me."

She shoved him down a step and jumped off the porch onto the lawn. "Nuttin's easy, honey. Ya gotta work for what you want in this world." She stuck her tongue out at him and dashed across the yard, headed for the woods. The rest of the lunch and Emma's call were instantly forgotten.

### 3

Brian caught up to her at the edge of the forest. He snagged the edge of her tank top strap in two fingers. For a minute he thought he had her, but she dropped her shoulder and wiggled free – at the expense of the strap. She almost made it into the woods this time but was suddenly yanked backwards by her hips. She screamed and laughed as she was wrestled to the ground, face down. Brian began tickling her. His fingers stroked and poked and wiggled along the lower edge of her hip, just where the legs meet the crotch. His full weight was on her back and she was helpless. No amount of squirming could shake him free.

After a few minutes, when she was out of breath and panting, he slid his hands up and started to undo her jeans. He just managed to get the button undone when she gave a powerful kick with her legs and rolled over. Now she was on top, her back pressed against his chest. She grabbed his wrists and pulled his hands away, rolled off him and struggled to get to her feet. She didn't make it. Brian latched onto the bottom of her shirt and pulled her back down onto him, this time, chest to chest.

They kissed. They kissed again. They kissed hard and long, and each began to undress the other. They made love in the field behind the house, their clothes strewn across the lawn where they'd been flung. The first time was passionate, almost primal, and they lay there in the grass afterward panting and cooing. The second time, they fell in rhythm with each other and moved slower and more tenderly. They made love in the cool October afternoon air and then lay naked and sweating, watching the sun slowly dip toward the tree line.

Thirty-five yards behind, their new house loomed over them, casting a great shadow that stretched toward them. It watched them through its window eyes, and when their primal passion turned to tender love, it shuddered, the glass panes shaking in the frames.

Twelve feet away, in her jeans, Annabel's cell phone was ringing, unheard for the eighteenth time.

## Chapter 18
## NO CHOICE

**11:00 a.m. – 5:00 p.m.**

### 1

While Annabel and Brian were planning their day, Ralph sat across the table from Walcott, who had the yellowed papers clutched in his only hand. He had spent a restless night trying to prepare himself for whatever impending doom those papers might reveal. Even now, staring absently at them, he wasn't sure he really wanted to know what was in them.

Walcott smiled, almost cryptically. "I c'n see you're not quite ready for this yet," he said. "It's somethin' that has to be done, though. But ... I think you need a little more time to get yourself t'gether about it."

Ralph fidgeted, feeling a little self-conscious.

"Tell ya what," said Walcott, "why don't you check on the farm, and we'll talk about this a little later, maybe after lunch. It'll give ya a little time t'settle yourself. Sometimes, doin' somethin' normal and routine c'n quiet a body. You go walk the farm. But after ... we'll there's no puttin' it off again. Deal?"

Ralph pushed away from the table and nodded, wondering how in the hell he was ever going to be able to get himself ready for *this*.

## 2

Being outside in the sunshine and away from the house had actually helped. At ten minutes to two, he handed the reigns over to his second in command, Filipe Marquez, and walked back to the house. His hands were in his pockets as he plodded along, and a short piece of straw bobbed up and down from the corner of his mouth. The smells and sounds of the farm were some of the reasons he liked walking it. Hay bales, rolled and stacked, awaited pick-up and gave off a semi-sweet smell as they dried in the sun. The horses in the lower pasture could be heard neighing and snorting; pigs grunted in their pens as they wallowed and scavenged. The cows meandered around their pasture, lowing. It was almost enough to make him not want to go back inside and talk about what had to be talked about. But there was no getting around it. Walcott wanted him to take the farm. And the condition was that he understood everything he was getting into.

"Ya got t'understand it all," Ralph mimicked in a voice very close to Walcott's. It wasn't very often that Ralph found himself talking to himself, but he was sure doing it now. "Sometimes I think I ought to have my head examined. A person knows better than to think anything good comes without a price. On the surface of it, it doesn't seem like much of a price to understand what somebody wrote down a long time ago. But I got a feelin' in my gut that it's going to be a whopper of a price. Can't say how ... just feel it."

When he reached the front porch steps, he spit the straw out, pulled his hands from his pockets and shuffled up. Just before he reached the door, he turned and walked back to the edge of the porch. He let his head turn slowly from one side to the other, taking in the view. A sigh of contentment slipped out of him. It was almost a scene taken straight from *Of Mice and Men*. Rolling pastures, cut into rectangular swaths by the dirt access roads, stretched out to the horizon on the north side and ran up to the foot of the woodland on the east. In the distance, men (no more than moving specks of silhouettes) went about their duties. Just looking at it made Ralph feel that, maybe ... just maybe ... whatever the price was, owning this farm and being able to carry on Walcott's tradition of keeping it going would be worth it.

He pulled himself away, opened the screen door and went in, making sure to wipe his feet thoroughly. The grandfather's clock that stood sentinel next to the living room fireplace told him that it was almost twenty after two. He went into the kitchen, grabbed a glass of iced tea and then went out to the back porch. As he stepped out the back door he looked at the tea in his hand and wondered if he should have poured himself something stronger.

The temperature was a little brisker outback where the sun was blocked by the house and the porch overhang. It didn't bother Ralph that much, he liked the colder weather. Why Walcott insisted on coming and sitting out here every afternoon when he despised the cold was a mystery. But mystery or not, that's exactly what he did. Bundled in a thick jacket and two heavy blankets thrown over his lap, Walcott could always be found rocking in his chair (sometimes with a beer, more often with something stronger) enjoying what he called

The Golden Hour of the Afternoon. "*It was when the sun actually felt warmest,*" he would always say, "*even though it ain't back here.*"

### 3

Ralph pulled a fan-back wicker chair up alongside of Walcott and sat down. "Filipe's going to finish up with the barn clean-out and then drive eight bales of hay down to Farley's. I'm assuming that's okay with you."

"To hell with Farley, and fuck his bales of hay. You about ready to get down t'business?" asked Walcott without looking up.

"Yeah ... I suppose I am."

"Those papers tell about the past and about ... well, they tell about Torrance Wickersham. They don't come right out and say everything, but they sure as hell hint at a lot of it real strong, and it ain't nice. Most of it seems to be some kind of secret agreement, like a contract of some kind. And from what I could gather, it wasn't no ordinary contract, more like a pact with the devil or somthin'. Of course, I don't mean an actual pact with the devil for real. That's silly. But it sure reads like one of them weird tales on TV, you know, like some kind of curse. To be honest, I don't really know what it means, but it ain't good."

Ralph opened his mouth to speak and then closed it again. He wasn't sure what to say to that. He wasn't even sure what Walcott was trying to get at. In the back of his head he saw a black and white scene out of "The Twilight Zone." Two men sitting, having a calm discussion about hexes and curses as if such things really existed. If that's what old man Walcott was getting at in his roundabout way (which in itself was unusual for him), then he wanted no parts of it. The idea of curses being real and substantial things was not in Ralph's belief system, but the fact that Walcott might believe it ... actually and truly believe it ... scared him. No, it more than scared him; it gave him enough doubt to almost believe it himself.

"Walcott," said Ralph, "I have to ask if you're expecting me to think that your farm is cursed because of something Wickersham did ... what? ... some three hundred or more years ago? Is that what you're really asking me to believe?"

Walcott drew in a deep breath and exhaled slowly. "Yes, Ralph. I guess that's exactly what I'm asking you to believe. More 'an that, I'm asking you to accept it as fact. That's important. It's also the only way I'll let you sign that quitclaim deed on the farm."

"I don't know. It all sounds pretty..." Ralph didn't finish. He wasn't sure what word to use. The last thing he wanted to do was insult his longtime friend and employer.

"It all sounds pretty much like something a senile old lunatic might come up with. Right? Hell, Ralph, I know that. I know exactly how it sounds. Still in all, I believe it with all my heart."

"Okay." The tone of Ralph's voice was one of skepticism. "But even if what you're trying to tell me is true ... well ... why would it all start up now after all these years?"

Walcott waved his hand in the air, cursed and spat on the ground. "I think it started slowly about seventy years or so ago. I think it all got started when a bunch of stupid kids went in there and got whatever it is behind this all riled up and pissed off. They went into that goddamned house and got everything stirred up."

"You mean the old Wickersham place? The one that just got bought and renovated by somebody?"

"That's the one I mean, all right, Ralph. The one and only."

"I have another question, then," said Ralph, almost sheepishly.

"And that would be?"

"If old Torrance Wickersham is ... er ... was ... some relation to you, then you must have owned that house. I mean, it must have passed to you at some point. Why'd you sell it to them?"

Walcott wagged a finger in the air. "That's a story in itself, and one of the reasons that I know that things are coming." He shook his head. "I'm sorry, Ralph. I really am. The truth is, now I'm not sure if you have a choice or not. It could be that by me just lettin' you touch those old papers ... well ... I might have dragged you into it whether you want to be there or not. I hope I'm wrong 'bout that, but I can't say I am for sure."

Walcott's eyes reflected a look that Ralph couldn't quite pin down. Was it regret, sadness ... or perhaps something else, something mischievous ... or maybe even a tad sinister? Whatever it was, it made Ralph just a wee bit uncomfortable.

## Chapter 19
## WHAT CONSEQUENCES?

**3:26 p.m. – 4:50 p.m.**

### 1

At three twenty-six in the afternoon, Henry Travis left his house for the last time. The two men who had arrived from the Holloway Funeral Home in a plain gray station wagon had been very cordial, if somewhat businesslike. They came in black suits and black ties and Emma couldn't help but think that they looked more like they belonged in the secret service than hauling bodies around. With tears in her eyes and her heart heavier than she'd ever felt it, she kissed her father on ther forehead and said goodbye.

At three forty-three she dialed Annabel's cell phone number for the twenty-third time and got the same result she'd gotten from the previous twenty-two: instant voicemail. In an uncharacteristic flare of anger mixed with sadness, she hurled the phone across the room and watched it splatter into pieces against the wall. Then her knees gave way and she slumped to the floor, her elbow catching on the seat of the dining room chair.

By four-oh-two she'd cried herself dry. Her eyes were red and puffy – bags packed for Seattle as her mother used to say. She worked herself up and went into the bathroom to freshen up. There were still so many things to do. The men who had taken Henry away had requested she come down to the funeral home (as soon as she felt able) to finish up The Necessaries, as they had called them. The casket had to be chosen, the fees for the grave opening and embalming to be paid for, an announcement in the paper that would require her approval for all those to be listed as "surviving" members of the family to be written, the type of service he would want and on and on and on. And Emma was not a person to put things off.

When she finished in the bathroom, she changed into a modest dress, dug all the appropriate papers out of Henry's safe: last will and testament, insurance policies, deed to the grave, etc. Slipping all these into a small briefcase, she took one last look at her hair in the mirror, adjusted it slightly with the palm of her hand and went back downstairs to try Annabel one more time, using the landline. She also made a mental note that she needed a new cell phone.

She was just hanging up from another straight-to-voicemail when the doorbell rang. The unexpected sound took her by surprise and she jumped, clapping her hand over her heart and letting out a chirp of a yelp. Then she laughed at herself, and for some reason, the sound of her laughter made her feel better and worse all at the same time.

"Coming," she yelled, still half laughing to herself and trying to stifle it. Laughing when your father was just carried out the door on his journey to the great beyond could definitely be considered unusual behavior. Not that she really cared what other people thought, that had never been a worry of hers. Still, appearances – as they say.

When she opened the door she was surprised to see Tim Holloway and his grandfather, Matt Holloway, the owner of the Holloway funeral home, standing on her stoop.

"Mrs. Lansing," said the old man, "I'm very sorry to hear of your father's passing. But I'm afraid I have to speak to you on a very important matter. May we come in, please?"

Emma swung the door open and stepped aside. "By all means, Mr. Holloway."

"Please," he said, offering her his hand, "call me Matt." The smile on his face slid off. "Of course, by the time we're done speaking, I'm fairly sure you'll have other names you'd prefer to call me."

Emma closed the door behind them feeling confused. "I'm not sure I understand, Mister ... Matt. Please, let's go into the kitchen, I find it more comfortable to talk there. Would you like me to make some coffee?"

Old man Holloway waved his hand. "No, thank you. That won't be necessary." He turned and looked at Timothy. "You know my grandson, Timothy, don't you? He runs things down at the home nowadays. But ... well, I still have the final say. So at least you won't take what I'm going to say out on him, I hope."

A stern look crept over Emma's face. "What *are* you going to say, Mister Holloway, that you think will upset me so much?"

Old man Holloway cleared his throat with a nervous cough and the younger Holloway took a slight step backward.

"I think we should sit down, if that's all right with you?"

Emma stretched out her arm. "After you. The kitchen's just through the dining room." On her way past the dining room table, she eyed the briefcase she'd placed there with all of Henry's papers in it and wondered what in the world an eighty-two year old man who ran a funeral home, practically in name only, could have to say that would make her want to call him names.

"I think I'm going to make some coffee, anyway, Mister Holloway. Are your sure you're not interested?"

The younger Holloway looked at his grandfather. He had taken a place in the corner and stood there with his hands folded in front of him. The old man worked himself into a chair.

"No, thank you. My doctor would be very upset with me if I accepted, for whatever good he's doing me. But I will accept a glass of water, if you don't mind."

Emma scooped the coffee into the filter, poured the water into the maker and hit the on button. "Not at all, Mr. Holloway." She pulled a glass from the cupboard, filled it with water and placed it on the table in front of him.

"Now," she said, taking a seat opposite him. "What's this all about? The two of you look like you're going to try and explain how you backed over my puppy in the driveway."

"I wish it were that simple, as horrible as that sounds," said Holloway.

"If you're worried about my ability to pay the expenses-"

Old man Holloway laid a bony hand over the back of Emma's. "It's nothing like that. What I have to say does not concern money or any such thing. But it does concern the care and disposition of your father."

"Perhaps I should get his papers for you. They detail everything that he wanted in his will. It should help make things easier-"

"That won't be necessary, Misses Lansing. You see, well, the Holloway Funeral home will not be handling your father's arrangements and services. I've called Earl Davenport out in Lancaster and he's agreed to take your father and see that everything is done properly and according to his and your wishes."

"What? Why would you do that? I don't understand this at all, and I can't say I'm very happy with it."

"No, I didn't think you would be, as I alluded to when I met you at the door. Nevertheless, we ... will not be the funeral home of record for your father's passing. I'm very sorry."

"Sorry? You're very sorry? You're going to ship my father out like a piece of meat ordered online to some funeral home fifteen miles away and you're sorry? I'd really like to know the reason for this idiotic and discourteous service you're *not* providing."

"That, Misses Lansing, is exactly why I'm sitting here. I felt ... no ... I knew that you deserved a full explanation and not one over the phone. Believe me I do not go out much. Coming here was not an easy thing for me to do, in any sense."

Behind him, the coffee pot sputtered out the last of its dregs in a choking wheeze of steam. The younger

Holloway filled the cup that Emma had set beside the maker and set it in front of her without a word.

"Would you like Timothy to get you some cream and sugar?" asked Holloway

Emma looked at Timothy and then over to Holloway. "No, I could get my own cream and sugar if I took it, but I don't; I drink it black. But I would like him to take a seat. He looks like a vulture standing there in the corner."

Holloway chuckled and waved the younger into a seat. Timothy sat down as instructed, but the look on his face didn't change a bit. If ever Emma recognized pure annoyance in a person, she recognized it now in young Holloway's face. And she had a strong feeling that before this conversation was through she was going to give him a good reason for having that look.

## 2

Holloway cleared his throat again. "Now, as you may or may not know, I knew your father. It's true that we have not had any contact in many, many years. What you may not know is that I respected your father. I held more respect for him than of anyone else in this community. Nevertheless, we ... well ... I was going to say *drifted* apart, but that would not be entirely accurate. In reality, we *chose* to have no contact, and I'll get to the reason for that in due time."

He shifted in his seat, stole a quick look at his grandson and then placed his hands on the table and leaned in.

"I need you to understand, Misses Lansing, that it is not because I don't want to handle your father's funeral. To be totally candid with you, nothing would give me greater satisfaction. I would feel it an honor ... and, perhaps, a way of repaying what he'd done for me, what he'd done for us." He waggled a finger back and forth. "No. It's not because I don't want to handle Henry's passing; it's because I *can't* handle Henry's passing. It just isn't possible for me."

There was something in the way the old man had said that that struck a chord in Emma and spurred a memory.

"Matt Holloway," she said, her eyes turned sideways in recollection. "You were there, weren't you? You were the Matt in that house with my father all those years ago."

Matt nodded. "That is correct, Misses Lansing. I was indeed in that house with your father. And that is why I cannot handle his arrangements."

Young Holloway clasped his hands together on the table. "Forgive me if I speak out of turn here, but I have to say what I'm thinking, what I've already told my grandfather." His eyes darted over to the old man seeking permission to continue. The old man sat back and exhaled.

"Go on, say your piece if it'll make you feel better. But when you're through, go on back to the home. I'll call you when I need you. Misses Lansing and I have some very serious matters to discuss, and your input will not be required, Timothy."

Timothy pushed away from the table and stood up. "I believe that my grandfather is being a bit paranoid, shall we say. I have a stronger word in mind, but we'll leave it at that. Our funeral home is quite capable of providing the services you require, and were it not for my grandfather's fear and fascination with the past ... we would. But I've been overruled in the matter. And for that, I extend my personal apology. Quite frankly, I think his refusal to service your father is just plain stupid." He looked at his grandfather, looked at Emma and then threw his hands up in the air. "Stupid ... and insensitive to your needs, Misses Lansing. Now, having said that, I'll leave you to hear his ... his-"

"Ramblings, I believe is the word you're looking for, Timothy. But you've had your say so you may return to the home. I'll call when we're finished."

Timothy walked around the table and stopped at the entrance to the dining room and half turned. "I'm very sorry for your loss, Misses Lansing. And I'm very sorry I will not be allowed to help you."

"What can I say?" said Holloway after Timothy left. "He's adopted."

### 3

Holloway tapped his fingers restively on the table and grinned. "I guess the best way for me to begin is to ask you how much you know already of our little sojourn into the old Wickersham place all those years ago. Knowing what you already know will save time."

Emma's mind wandered back to last night's conversation with her father and immediately skipped to the part about a locked box in his desk and its key. "*If for some reason I don't get to finish my story,*" he'd said, "*you go to that box.*"

"I know a lot about what happened up there, but not all. At least not all, yet. I know about Lucy Darrow and the horrible thing that happened to her, but that's where the story ends for me. I do not know how you all got out of there or what happened afterwards. The last thing my father told me about it was that you and he and the others were on one side of the door and Tommy Vorland was on the other."

Holloway clenched his jaw and his lips meshed into a straight, taught line. "At the door. I see. Well, it seems there's a lot more I have to tell you." A sad smile crossed his face. "But at least you already know about poor Lucy. I'm glad I don't have to be the one to describe that to you."

"I don't see what any of this has to do with whether or not you'll bury my father ... your friend."

Holloway reached across the table and laid his hands on Emma's. "You're right; Henry was my friend, even though we hadn't spoken for years. And the reason we hadn't spoken for years is because we made a pact not to do so. We learned, not too long after getting out of that house, that whenever we were together, any of us who were in there, bad things would happen. That's a long story in itself. But for now, let's finish the story of that cursed house."

He drew his hands away from hers slowly and smiled. "If it would be all right with you, I'd like to take you up on that offer of coffee now. It won't make what I have to say any more pleasant, but maybe it will make it a little easier to get out." He smiled. "And it'll annoy the hell out of my doctor when I tell him."

Emma just nodded and got up. As she poured the steaming brew into the mug, she stared blankly out the window. A pair of cardinals were hopping up and down the perches of the bird feeder and her mind slid back to finding Henry on the porch. She had to blink three times to keep the tears from spilling over her lower lids.

It had been less than two hours since Henry was taken out and it felt to Emma as if it had been both five minutes ago and a hundred years ago. Sometimes the brain has its own unusual way of counting time. Like a watch that could only have been plucked from the pocket of Rod Serling, its second hand sweeps backwards as its minute hand creeps forward; the hour hand blurs to infinity and everything is jumbled together.

Emma set the coffee in front of Holloway.

"The last thing that my father told me about that house ... about that day ... was that you were all trying to get the door open for Tommy Vorland who had ended up on the other side. Maybe you should start there." She exhaled and shook her head. "That is, assuming that the story really has anything to do with why you're turning my father out like a bum behind on his rent."

Holloway flexed his wrist and tilted his hand back and forth. "No, no, Misses Lansing, it's absolutely nothing like that at all. I'm turning your father away because not to do so would be to invite..." He lowered his eyes to the table. "I'm sorry; I truly am. But I just can't handle your father's funeral. And yes, I think your suggestion makes sense. We'll start there, the three of us trying to get that door open and your mother urging us to *push harder.*

## 4

"*...push harder.* I think it moved." Amy leaned her shoulder into it and shoved with a long, low grunt.

"You-you ... you know she's gonna slide out of there like a squashed pumpkin once this door opens, don't you?" said Matt. "I don't think I'm ready for that. I don't think I'm ready for that at all."

Amy cocked her head around. "It doesn't matter what you're ready for or not. Now shut up and shove."

Henry put a hand on Amy's shoulder. "Wait a minute."

"No. We don't have time to wait. We have to get this open."

"I know that," said Henry. "I do, but I think we should talk about this. Just for a minute." He grabbed her by the shoulders and wrestled her away from the door. The look in her eyes when she turned to face him was one of unbridled anger, bordering on fury. He took a step back and held his hands up in a peace gesture. "I think this is important, so just hold your horses a minute."

"We almost had it. What the hell could be more-"

"Hear me out. Suppose all of a sudden it gives, pops open on its own, just like it slammed shut on Lucy. Suppose it pops open just wide enough and suddenly enough for one of us to fall halfway through and then it pulls its squashing trick again. I think we'd better find something we can slide between it and the jamb in case of emergency."

"That sounds like a really good idea to me," interjected Matt. He stepped away from the door and looked around the room, his eyes falling on the red metal Coleman cooler. "The cooler. I can get down at your feet, Amy, and as the door starts to move I can shove the cooler into the opening."

Amy looked at Matt, then at Henry and then at the cooler. "Do you think it's strong enough? I mean … look what happened to…"

Henry looked around. "I think it'll have to be. There's nothing else."

"Okay then. That's-"

"…God's sake, open the door." Tommy's voice came from the other side. It was muffled, as if he were speaking through layers of foam rubber. It was also unmistakably filled with terror.

### 5

Tommy had his back pressed into the corner, his palms flat on the wall by his thighs. The dragging, slapping footsteps that had crept up the tunnel were closer now, almost to the top of the incline. Soon, whoever … whatever … it was would come shambling out of the blackness right at him. There was nothing else he could do but wait. Nothing but wait and pray that whatever was coming for him was not one of the many images he had playing though his mind – zombies thirsting for flesh, red-eyed monsters with piranha teeth, something that looked like a clown but was much nastier underneath – scenes from every horror movie or book he'd ever seen or read.

"For Christ's sake," he yelled, now in a full panic. "One of you fucking bastards over there on the other side of that door better fuckin' answer me. I swear to God ... if you're playing some fuckin' sick-ass joke on me, I'm gonna loosen somebody's fuckin..."

His voice trailed off into muttered whispers. A shape wavered ahead of him, still couched in shadow. The slap-brush of its feet slowed, as if it weren't quite ready to step forward and be seen. His stomach was knotted and his heart pounded in his ears.

"Come to me." The voice was soft and gentle, no more than the flap of a butterfly's wings. "Come to me and be my lover. Rescue me from my dark prison of loneliness."

An arm slid out of the black, its palm turned up. A sheer white sleeve hung from the wrist in soft, curving folds. The fingers on the hand were bone thin and the color of spoiled meat. They slowly folded inward, beckoning him.

"Leave me alone. Please leave me alone and go away." Tommy's voice was broken, a hush of cracked breath beneath whimpered sobs.

"I know what you want," the voice from the darkness said. "I can teach you things ... things you've never imagined. Come to me and be my lover and I will fulfill all of your fantasies like no one else ever could."

Tommy covered his eyes with the heels of his hands. The words he was hearing were not coming through his ears; they were in his head. And behind them was the image of a beautiful woman dressed in a flowing white nightgown, her breasts fully revealed beneath its sheerness; her legs slightly open revealing the dark patch of her womanhood through the gown.

"Come and be mine, Tommy. I have been waiting so, so long for someone like you to come."

"You're not real," he screamed, his hands now cupped over his ears. "You're not real. Go away and leave me alone. Go away. Just go away."

It stepped forward into full view, its bare, wet feet slapping on the stone. Flesh hung in strands from the cheeks and forehead. The gown that had appeared white in Tommy's mind was gray and torn and splotched, and it clung to the naked and rotted corpse it covered. The hair dripped from her head in clumped and stringy patches, showing irregular discs of bone.

"You must come to me, Tommy. You must come-"

Suddenly, the oak door groaned on its hinges and was thrown open. The squishy sounding thud of Lucy's body falling to the ground and sliding off the cooler that had been shoved into the jamb echoed through the tunnel, and the shape in front of Tommy thinned and disappeared.

## 6

Holloway sat back and coughed into his hand. "I think I could use some more of that coffee, now, Misses Lansing." He coughed again.

"You can stop calling me Misses Lansing, and I'll stop calling you Mister Holloway." She got up and poured the coffees, handed him his mug and sat down.

"You must understand, of course, that we ... um ... Amy, Henry and I, had no idea what Tommy had seen or experienced at this point. We heard nothing. In fact, we thought that he had knocked himself out or something when he fell."

Holloway raised the cup to his lips, blew on it and took a sip. "Good coffee. Nice and rich and strong. I hate weak coffee, don't you?"

Emma was anxious to get on with the story, but she could see on Holloway's face that it would take him a few minutes to gather himself enough to do so. She sipped at her coffee, still wondering what all this had to do with Holloway's refusal to conduct her father's funeral. It was all too surreal and she had to wonder just how much of it had been born of runaway imaginations. Except that that didn't really feel right. The one thing she did know for sure was that her father was not given to a runaway imagination, and he believed what he had told her. And so far, Holloway's story was matching up.

"I don't mean to be rude or pushy, Matt, but it's getting late. Please go on with your story and get to the part about why you're not going-"

"You're right. I apologize. It's just ... just a bit difficult. When I start talking about it ... which I haven't done in years ... it's just all too vivid. But I'll try to move along as fast as I can."

Holloway cleared his throat, sipped at his coffee and then set the cup down. For a moment, his teeth were clenched so tightly that Emma could see the muscles ripple along his cheeks. But when he finally spoke, his words were clear and strong.

"As I said, we had no idea what Tommy had ... I guess *experienced* is the best word. We found him huddled in the corner behind the door, his eyes closed and his hands over his ears. It took your father almost five minutes to pry them away and get him to come out. And even then there was a blank look in his eyes, as if he were seeing past us.

"We tried to move him a little farther into the tunnel, away from the door and Lucy's body, but he just collapsed to the floor and refused to budge. Henry finally had the ball… um … had the courage to move Lucy's body away from the door and out of sight. I don't think any of the rest of us could have done that. In the meantime, Amy-"

"You mean my mother. Please call her that, Matt."

Matt nodded. "Yes, of course. I'm sorry. Your mother sat next to Tommy trying to get him calmed down enough for us to all get out of there. She finally managed to get him talking, which is when he told us what had happened and that there was no way he was going down into that tunnel, exit or no exit."

"What did you finally do?"

Holloway smiled. "Your father. It was your father who got him up and moving. And it was your father who led us all out of that tunnel, dragging Tommy along like a limp ragdoll." He let out a puff of a laugh. "Your mother and your father were certainly meant for each other, I'll say that much. While your father was dealing with Tommy, your mother went back inside for Janet Egan who was not in much better shape than Tommy. Tina Farley was in shock and as white as a ghost herself, but at least she was moving … following along. To be totally honest, I don't know what we would have done without your parents."

"Humph! And yet you still won't handle his funeral."

"I'm getting to that, Emma. I am, as quickly as possible, but I can't leave out any of the important details or it will only make less sense to you than it does now. And I'll add this; there was something in the way that Tommy told us what happened, and the look on his face as he did, that sent a cold shiver up my spine. And I had no doubt that everyone else felt the same way. It scared the hell out of us. We believed him."

They sat in silence for a while, each only half looking at the other, as if making eye contact would break the reality of what they were both feeling. Emma wondered if her father would have told her that it was he who had moved the body. Probably not. He would have delicately and deftly left that part out. Holloway sat wondering if Emma believed what he was telling her. He also wondered if coming here might have been a mistake. When he had decided that it was what he had to do, he knew there would be risk. Even as he stood on the front stoop before ringing the bell, he was sure he felt a twinge of something settle over him. They had all, long ago, decided never to meet again. And here he was, sitting at the kitchen table in Henry's house. And he wondered if this breach of their pact, necessary as he felt it was, would bring consequences that he didn't want to think about.

Emma stirred, lifting her eyes to Holloway. There was a puzzled look on her face and her head was dog-cocked to one side. She asked a simple question and Holloway jumped, knocking his coffee cup over. They both watched it roll lazily toward the edge of the table and drop off, shattering on the linoleum.

"Wha-what did you say?" He had heard her clearly but needed to hear it again to believe it because there was no way she should have asked that question.

"I asked you ... what consequences?"

## Chapter 20
## FIRE BIRDS

**5:00 p.m. – 5:45 p.m.**

### 1

Ralph sat staring blankly out across the back field. The afternoon sun edged toward the western treetops in a lazy arc, casting irregular shadows of the house across the field. An intermittent breeze added a slight bite to the air and carried the somewhat pungent but pleasant scent of freshly bailed hay along with it. Ralph inhaled deeply, let it out slowly, and then turned to Walcott.

"Guess we should start getting' down t'the specifics, huh," said Ralph, "though I can't say as I'm really looking forward to knowing any more than I already do. But if it's what has to be done, then I guess I'm as ready now as I'll ever be."

Walcott worked himself up. His legs wobbled for a moment. "Old age sucks! I ever told you that before?" He cocked his head in Ralph's direction. "It *really* sucks. I'm goin' in and make myself a drink; then we'll get started."

Ralph watched him all the way to the bend, waited, and sighed again when he heard the screen door slap shut. He closed his eyes and drew in another deep and calming scent of the farm. In the distance, the muted sound of a ringing bell told him that the Orthodox Church on Weaver Hill Road was calling it's ministers to vespers. Ralph was not a religious man but blessed himself nonetheless. It seemed to him a bit too capricious a timing for the church to be calling for prayer when he was about to go through the doings of Torrance Wickersham. With an involuntary shudder, he looked down at the papers and had the greatest urge to just burn them up and be done with it.

## 2

*Ya got to do this*, thought Ralph. *There's really no way around it and you know it. So just get it done as quick as ya can.* A circling hawk suddenly dove into view, its talons extended. In a well-practiced maneuver, it gripped its prey and sped skyward again. From his place on the porch, Ralph couldn't make out what had been taken, although he assumed it to be a rabbit from its size.

*It's like that, ain't it? It's just like that. One minute you're here, scurrying around doing all the things you think are so important to get done – and the next – POOF! You're carried off to whatever it is that comes next.* "When you're young-" He let out a snort of a laugh. "-Or even middle aged, death is only something that happens around you. When you're older-" He turned and looked toward the spot where Walcott had disappeared around the corner.

He tried to imagine how it must feel to go to bed at night and wonder if you'd just spent your last day. His mind could grasp the reality of it, but not the feeling of it. The unexpected screech of the hawk made him jump, and the papers slid off his lap. As he bent to pick it up, a raven flapped over and perched on the porch railing just to his left.

Ralph waved an arm in its direction. It jumped up and then settled back down, its head cocked to one side, one beady eye trained on Ralph.

"Go on. Scat!"

The bird spread its wings and erupted in a series of loud caws. One at a time, more ravens took their place beside it until the entire railing was full of black shapes, each bobbing their heads and vocalizing some unknown discontent.

Working a farm opens one to some odd sights and sounds associated with animal behavior, but Ralph had never seen the likes of this before. He was stunned – and a little scared. He felt the goosebumps crawl along his arms. A nervous chuckle escaped him, as his mind wondered if Hitchcock were now staging Poe. He laid the papers in his lap and leaned forward, resting his forearms on top of them. The birds stopped cawing and flapping.

"Okay, you
*(got me talking to birds)*
got my attention. Your move."  He kept his eye on the one he figured to be the leader, the one who had landed first. And it sat staring back at him. He spread his hands in a so what now gesture. He had the greatest urge to just leap out of the chair, flailing his arms and screaming at them at the top of his lungs. He resisted, figuring it would probably only set them to jabbering and flapping away again. But deeper inside, he thought: *or maybe worse.*

For the second time in less than ten minutes, he jumped. The *BANG*! made his heart skip a beat, and the ravens took flight.

"What in God's great creation is going on out here?" growled Walcott, shuffling around the corner.

Ralph just pointed up at the sky. When Walcott turned his head, he could hardly believe what he was seeing, and it took him a minute to figure out exactly what it was. A large, swirling mass of black undulated across the evening sky.

"Ravens," said Ralph.

"I can see that," barked Walcott. "What the hell are they doing?"

"If you think that's weird, you should have seen them a minute ago."

Walcott worked his way over to the railing and stood there gazing at the throng of swirling black shapes that hovered over his field.

### 3

Walcott and Ralph stared at the sky, watching the birds dip, dive and weave in and out among themselves. They rose and fell, moved left and then right, all in hectic unison. It was an avian ballet, but not one that either Ralph or Walcott felt comfortable watching. Suddenly, they all changed direction and swept upward, aggregating into a single black and menacing cloud.

"What in the hell-" began Walcott, but was stayed in mid-sentence by a burst of blue lightning that shot from the center of the bird mass. It struck the ground not five feet in front of him and its impact knocked him off his feet. He could feel the emanations of its electrical charge crawl across his skin like thousands of spiders.

Ralph, too, felt the charge, but managed to keep his feet. He started to help Walcott to his feet when the second burst of lightning fingered into a tree at the far end of the porch.

"Help me up and let's get outa here," yelled Walcott.

The lightning bursts started coming faster and faster. Ralph dragged Walcott to a standing position and started working him toward the door.

"No, no, no," said Walcott, his voice strong but calm. "The truck. We got to get to the truck. It's the only safe place."

Out in the field, bird carcasses fell like thick balls of black rain, each singed, some aflame.

Ralph didn't waste any more time wrestling with Walcott. He picked him up and ran off the porch, skirted the side of the house and made it to the truck just as a blue ribbon of electric fire slammed into the chair in which he'd just been sitting.

Safe inside the truck, Ralph let out the breath he hadn't even realized he'd been holding. And all of a sudden, he *knew* what it felt like for Walcott to go to bed wondering if he'd have another morning to awaken to.

## Chapter 21
## PIG-IN-A-POKE

**4:50 p.m. – 6:10 p.m.**

### 1

Matt Holloway cleared his throat, his mind spinning around Emma's question: "What consequences?" His postulation had only been an un-vocalized thought, yet she was addressing it as if he'd said it to her face. It unsettled him. It was not the first time this sort of thing had happened. In fact, along with more bizarre and less innocuous occurrences, it had been the reason that the "house group" had made the pact never to meet together.

"Ahem … well, I believe we should continue with our story. As you pointed out, it's getting late." He shifted in his seat and kept his eyes on the table.

"Matt, I asked you what consequences. You said that you wondered if there would be consequences from you just being here. I'd like to know what you meant."

Matt brought his eyes slowly up to hers. "Actually, Emma, I never said any such thing-"

"But you most certain-"

He held up a hand and shook his head. "No, I didn't. I *thought* it, Emma. And somehow you heard it; that startled me. But it does not surprise me. What just happened … your question … is the secondary part of this story, and the part that has made it necessary for me to refuse the honor I would normally have had in serving a great friend's passing."

"You didn't say there might be consequences? You didn't say that?"

"No. I didn't. I only thought it."

"But I heard-"

"It clearly," finished Matt. "Yes, of that I have no doubt." His eyes softened. "I'm more sorry than I can tell you that this-" He shrugged. "-whatever it is, has come home to roost, so to speak. I know that Henry ... your father ... never wanted any of this to touch his family."

Emily's mind turned. She was seven years old, splashing around in the blowup pool her father had just bought her. Her father was sitting on their back stoop with a glass of iced tea in one hand and a folded newspaper in the other. The sun glinted off the water as she laughed and giggled each time she jumped in.

## 2

"Watch me, daddy! Watch what I can do," she yelled, her legs pumping. The grass tickled the souls of her feet as she raced across the lawn, hefted herself in the air and landed in the middle of the pool, bottom first. She let out a squeal of delight as the water splashed up around her and swelled over the sides in splattering waves.

"Careful, honey," said Henry. "Pool's very shallow. Don't want you to hurt yourself."

"I won't, daddy," said Emma, her face aglow. "This is so much fun. You and mommy should come in and play, too." She flopped onto her belly, grabbed the edge of the pool with both hands and started kicking her feet.

*Pool's very shallow.* The words echoed in Henry's mind and then warped into: *I think we're all going to be up to our waists soon.* The voice was Tommy Vorland's, and Henry found himself back in the tunnel. He pinched his eyes shut and tried to chase the memory out of his head. When he opened them again, Emma was standing in front of him.

"Don't go there, daddy. I don't like it. It's dark and scary." Her face was knotted and her eyes wide with fear. "It's too dark. And that water scares me, daddy."

Henry took her by the shoulders and pulled her to him, enfolding her in his arms. "What's too dark, honey? Look, it's bright and sunny and warm and your pool is right there-" He floundered for more words, something soothing, but could find none. His heart was beating hard against his chest. He wanted to deny it but couldn't. His seven year old daughter had just seen into his head.

### 3

Matt reached across the table and laid a hand on Emma's. "Are you all right? Your face just all of a sudden went blank. For a minute there, I thought maybe you were-"

"Having a seizure?" Emma finished for him. "No. Just a very vivid memory. It seems that this isn't the first time I've ever ... um ... seen, I guess you'd say ... into someone's head. I didn't remember it until this very moment, but a long time ago-"

It was Matt's turn to finish the sentence. "You heard what your father was thinking."

Emma shook her head. "No! Not just heard it ... I saw it. I saw the dark, wet walls and the pool of water ahead of him ... ahead of all of you. For a brief, frightening moment, I was there."

"How long did the vision last?"

"I'm not sure. Not that long, I don't think. I think my mother came out and ... and... I don't know. She said something, but I can't recall what it was."

Matt sighed. "Well, I guess it doesn't matter all that much in the long run. I just don't understand what might have triggered it. Usually-" He waved his hand. "Doesn't matter. I think we should go back to the story. We'll cover this kind of thing-"

"Usually you had to be together." Emma cocked her head to one side. "Two or more of you from that house had to be together for something like the visions or telepathy or whatever you want to call it to happen, right? That's what you were going to say."

Matt nodded once.

"Then that was it. I remember now what my mother came out to say. She said that Janet Egan was in the living room and wanted to talk to dad."

A salacious smile spread across Matt's face, crinkling the corners of his closed eyes. He inhaled deeply, as if he'd just stepped into a florist's shop. "You know," he said, opening his eyes, "I can still somehow seem to smell the perfume she wore. We had quite a thing going back then. Janet was ... well, I guess she was my first love. Of course, now, looking back, I'd say more of an infatuation. It felt real at the time, I suppose." He closed his eyes again and the smile slid off his face. "But that damned house. That one, stupid, impulsive need to be in that house ruined it."

"You and Janet Egan?" Emma's face cracked a slight smile of its own. "Somehow, you don't seem the type to get involved with-"

Matt laughed out loud. "With a girl who turned Goth and opened a tattoo parlor? Honey, young men do not make choices based on status, reason, long term compatibility, or anything approaching the rational. In fact, they don't make choices at all. Their hormones do that for them. It's all inconsequential now ... mostly. And what *isn't* ... is part of the other side of the story, the side we'll return to *after* we finish what happened in that damned house."

"But if you could read each other's minds, you must have thought that was something special, something to be cherished and used."

"At first, yes. At first, we thought it was the greatest thing ever. But it turned out to be a pig-in-a-poke. And we soon learned the price of having it was more than any of us could afford." He glanced at the time: 6:02 P.M. "Please, I beg you, let me finish with the house, and then I'll tell you everything that happened *after* we got out of there."

## Chapter 22
## ON THE WING

**5:45 p.m. – 6:30 p.m.**

### 1

Ice-blue tendrils of lightning danced around the truck like the tentacles of an octopus groping for its prey. The radio switched on and off, sometimes squealing in high-pitched, ear-piercing tones, and sometimes in bursts of chaotic static. Ralph and Walcott watched the assault, Ralph a bit more nervous than his older companion.

"Sure glad we made it to the truck. Thank God for rubber tires."

Walcott snorted. "Ain't the tires that keep us safe, Ralph. It's the metal frame of the truck."

"What? How can that be? Metal conducts-"

"Yes it does. And that's exactly how it protects us. It has to do with the physics of electricity and all. What happens is that the metal of the truck acts like what they call a Faraday Cage. It directs the lightning over the surface of the metal and directly to ground, protecting everything inside."

Ralph looked astonished. "Where'd you learn that?"

Walcott laughed. "Watch a lot of nature and science shows on TV. Rest of the crap on that silly box ain't worth sittin' through. Worse than that, you can't even get it for free anymore. You got to pay to pick through the crap."

Ralph opened his mouth but a finger of lightning split the darkness and punched into the ground in front of them with a tremendous crack of thunder and power. The truck shook as if it had been kicked by a giant. A moment later, a flaming raven bounced off the hood and the storm was over. The evening stars, obscured by the electrical tumult began to wink into view.

Walcott looked toward the house. "Don't see no smoke rising. Maybe we got lucky and the place ain't gonna burn down."

Ralph looked skeptical. "I saw a bolt of lightning strike the porch. Hit the damned chair I was sitting in. How could it not have started a fire? Maybe it's a trick, a trap?"

Walcott studied the house and as much of the surrounding farm as he could see in the twilight. "I don't think so. I think it's over ... for now. Let's go see what the damage is."

Ralph grabbed his arm. "Are you really sure that's wise? That whole thing was ... was... Hell, I don't know what it was, but it wasn't normal; I can sure as hell tell you that."

Walcott jerked his arm free, opened the door and stepped out. "There's not too much that I think is going to be normal from this point on. The shit's in the air and on its way to the fan. There ain't no doubt about that in my mind. Come, we're safe for now; that much I can feel in my bones. Let's go see what's what."

Ralph hesitated, his hand on the door handle. When Walcott reached the side of the building, fighting to keep his balance, Ralph climbed out and ran over to help. At the back of the house, the damage was visible, incomprehensible but visible. The chair that Ralph had been sitting in was reduced to cinders. Aside from that, the only evidence that anything had happened were the scorched, charred or ashen corpses of hundreds of ravens scattered across the backyard, some still smoldering.

The two of them stood there looking between the pile of ashes that was the rocker and the avian carnage that decorated the lawn and porch roof..

"Come on, Ralph, let's get in."

## 2

"It's a goddamned shame is what it is," grumbled Walcott. He eased himself into his chair at the kitchen table. "Loss of a good rockin' chair, if ya ask me. Anyway, I guess it's time I try to explain what's goin' on … and why."

Ralph poured them both a generous tumbler of bourbon. Walcott drained half of his on the first swallow. Ralph sipped a little more judiciously. The burn coursed into his stomach, splashed down and seemed to chase itself back up again. He burped.

"Excuse me."

Walcott just waved his hand. "I don't believe I'm going to be able t'recount the whole thing verbatim, but I'll sure as hell hit all the salient points." He took another swallow and looked into the burnished liquid.

Ralph took a bigger gulp and laughed. "You might try starting with explaining what the hell just happened out there. That'd be a good page to start on in my book."

"Can't explain it. Don't think anybody *could*. Now … understanding it … that's a whole other thing. And that's what Wickersham's story ... and mine," he said in a lower tone, "will most likely do. Help you ... help us ... to understand." He raised his eyes to Ralph. "And not just about that craziness out there, neither. About what's coming. I got a feeling we just got a dribble off the ice cream cone. What's coming is sure as hell gonna try and shove the whole goddamned thing down our throats."

Ralph had no idea what to say to that. He downed what was left of his bourbon, fetched the bottle over to the table and refilled both their glasses. "Guess there's no sense in doin' this sober," he quipped. The smile on his face looked like it had been finger-painted there by a three year old. And it might as well have been.

"I'll try to give you the short version, in as much as is possible without losing nothing. From what I gathered from them papers," said Walcott, "Torrance Wickersham ran this whole place. Anything he wanted, he got. Took is probably a better description of it. He was the be-all and end-all of Wickersham Hollow: minister, mayor, chief constable ... oh he had some people appointed to a couple of these positions, but they were just puppets on the ends of his strings. He did what he liked and there was nobody to challenge him or stop him.

"The real trouble seems to have come, from what I gathered from them papers, when he wanted something that someone else finally wasn't willing to give him. He wanted..." Walcott paused, a look of disgust plastered on his face. "He wanted ... a ... a woman, a young woman to serve his perverse sexual needs. His problem was her mother had a whole other idea about that. The mother's problem was ... he had all the power."

"The mother went up against him." It was a half statement, half question. Ralph thought he knew where this story was going. "She went against his wishes and he did something that, somehow, started all this mess."

"Yes and no. The problem for us, Ralph, is that those papers don't come right out and say exactly what happened. But I'll tell you what I put together from all of it. Some of it's guesswork, some of it's just common sense deduction. The point is, we'll never exactly know what went on. But we'll know enough to see what might be coming from that mess."

## Chapter 23
## SOMETHING WICKED

**6:00 p.m. – 7:50 p.m.**

**1**

It was going on for six by the time Brian and Annabel collected themselves and headed back. They strolled to the house hand-in-hand, the picnic basket bopping lightly against Brian's thigh with each step. Behind them, the sun was nearly gone, no more than a flame of oranges and pinks streaked across the horizon. As they stepped into the kitchen, Annabel's phone rang again. When she pulled it out, she was momentarily startled by the number of missed calls it registered from her mother. She flipped it open and the kitchen door slammed shut behind them and bolted itself. Time stopped. They stood there, frozen. Around them, things began to change, slip backward. The house shuddered, shook off its new façade throughout, and reestablished its former countenance. Modern furniture melted as décor grew from the floors, walls and ceilings. A log fire sprang to life in the fireplace. The bookshelves in the turret library were absorbed back into the walls, leaving only the stone block facing of its former existence. An iron, spiral staircase wound around its walls between floors from basement to conical roof. When the transformation was complete, the cell phone in Annabel's hand vibrated and then shattered, bringing Brian and Annabel out of their temporal catatonia.

Startled by the scene before them, Annabel blurted out a staccato scream, and the picnic basket dropped from Brian's hand. He started to speak and was stopped in mid-sentence by an overwhelming wave of dizziness. Brian pitched forward onto his knees. He fought to regain himself, but the whole world was swimming in circles around him. His head was pounding with the intensity of a blacksmith's hammer, and a thin line of blood trickled from his nose. Strange and dark thoughts, cold and pitiless images of a time long gone, coursed randomly through his mind, as if he were some ghostly observer to a time long past.. And then the thoughts solidified. He was no longer just observing; he was experiencing as well. He suddenly felt as if he were two different people – as if someone had stepped into his body and taken control.

    He descended the familiar spiral steps that led to the belly of the house. The lantern he held in front of him swung gently to and fro, creating dancing shadows on the damp, curved walls. At the bottom of the steps, he opened a trap door and continued down until he came to a thick oaken door. He carefully selected a key from the large ring that hung from his belt and slipped it into the lock and twisted. When he pushed it open, a blast of musty air hit him in the face. He stopped and inhaled deeply. There was no doubt in his mind that the scent he really smelled was fear. And it sent a shiver of exhilaration through his body.

    He stepped in, passing through a short, narrow hallway that emptied into a twelve-by-ten room. Raising his arm a little higher, the lantern illuminated more of his surroundings. He crossed the room, purposely jingling the ring of keys in his hand as he passed the woman on his left, who was shackled to a four-poster metal bed. She whimpered through the gag. He smiled but did not acknowledge her. At the far end of the room, he set the lantern on a slab altar and lit the two five-candle candelabras on either end.

"I must tell you how beautiful you look, my dear," he said, turning, "that filmy white gown revealing all you charms. It won't be long now. Just a few more preparations to make and then..." He walked over to her and ran his index finger from her throat to her belly. "And then we will create the instrument of my immortality. I am so looking forward to having you. I must confess ... it is really straining my patience and self-control to have to wait. But all things at their proper time, eh? Still, perhaps just a little taste."

He leaned over and ran his tongue across her left breast, feeling the nipple stiffen against it beneath the gown. He did the same to the right, his hand gliding along the smooth skin of her left thigh between her splayed legs. "So delicious. Just so delicious. But now ... now we must commence the ritual. It is time."

Inside his head, Brian was screaming. The woman on the bed was, at least in appearance, Annabel. He wanted to make himself unlock her, set her free. But he was not the one in control. As he knew the woman on the bed was named Abigail, he also knew that he ... or at least the power that now held sway over his body ... was Torrance Wickersham. From inside the prison of his mind he watched and felt and railed against the ritual he was performing. His twenty-first century mind had no basis for accepting the things his seventeenth century usurper was doing. Yet he watched through the eyes and felt through the fingers every action Wickersham performed, helpless to change or stop any of it. Everything he was witnessing and doing had long ago passed into the abyss of unchangeable history.

## 2

While Brian unwillingly participated in the past, Annabel swam in her own pool of vertigo. When her head finally cleared, she found Brian lying on his back on the kitchen floor. His eyes were open and moving rapidly from side to side, and his hands and legs twitched erratically. Thinking he was having a seizure, she reached for her cell phone. When she couldn't find it, she searched his pockets for his. Nothing. She got up and headed for the landline hanging on the wall and, for the second time, though this time voluntarily, she came to a dead stop. Her eyes widened in shock and surprise at the change in the kitchen. Everything modern was gone. The grill top, double-oven gas range they had agreed to splurge on was now a large open hearth in the center of the back wall. A long oak table took up most of the free space in the center of the room.

"What the..." She turned in a slow circle, not believing what she was seeing. "This ... this can't..." She glanced over at Brian, and then down at herself. At least they hadn't changed; Brian was still wearing his faded jeans, and she still had on the yellow "Street Angel" Harley top with the torn shoulder strap. None of this made any sense. Yet, there seemed to be a familiar feeling to it. Her eyes moved to the large wooden cabinets that stood against the left wall. Without having to open them, she knew ... she *knew* ... what was in them: two twenty-pound sacks of flour in the bottom right hand cabinet, a half empty ten-pound sack of sugar and six containers of various spices in the left. The upper cabinets held the pewter plates and cups. The temptation to open them all was strong. Not so much to prove herself right, but in the hopes she was wrong. She almost gave in. Instead, she went back and knelt by Brian. As she felt for his pulse, his eyes blinked and he started to sit up. She quickly threw an arm behind his back to help support him.

"Damn!" He blinked a few more times. "Wh-what happened? I'm having a little trouble focusing. I-I was in the middle of the strangest... I want to say dream, but it really wasn't a dream ... it was something else. I just can't explain it."

For the briefest of moments, Annabel thought she saw a face behind his face. It was like a double exposure. It wore a minatory grin. And ...*Oh Lord ...* did it wink at her before it vanished? An unformulated terror began to well up in her. She withdrew her arm from around him and took a few steps back.

"Geezuz, Belle! What's wrong?" He shook his head, still trying to clear it. Things were still fuzzy, out of focus, but he could see the fear spread across her face. "Did ... did I do something to you while I was out? You look really spooked."

"Brian, you ... it's ... there was a..." Out of the corner of her eye, she noticed that the kitchen was just as it was supposed to be: no hearth, no long table, no plain wooden cabinets. She wondered if she had also had some nightmarish hallucination. Taking control of herself, she forced herself to stop voicing the absurd.

Brian managed to stand with some difficulty, took a shaky step forward and stopped to steady himself.

"It's okay," she said, wrapping him up in her arms. "I just guess I got a little woozy. Thought I was seeing things. Silly, huh?"

"I'm beginning to think it's more scary than silly. Again, I'm not subscribing to your grandfather's interpretation, but whatever just happened to us was definitely weird. Anyway, I think I'm feeling a little better now. How about you?"

Annabel swept her eyes around the kitchen, relieved to find things still the way they should be. Trying to push it all aside, she said: "I think I could use a drink. Where's the booze, big boy?"

Brian escorted her out of the kitchen, unconsciously choosing to avoid the pantry route. Rather, he led her the longer way around through the dining room. He wrapped his arm around her waist, occasionally allowing it to drop down so he could pinch her ass. At the entrance to the living room, a brief wave of dizziness struck them both again. When they recovered, they walked straight to the wet bar next to the fireplace – a wet bar that, like the furniture they maneuvered around, shouldn't have been there. Everything seemed and felt perfectly normal. And neither of them heard what echoed through the stillness of the house: the baby's cry and the sonorous, hollow laughter that followed it.

"Scotch, bourbon, rum or vodka?" asked Brian, swinging the drinks cabinet doors open.

Annabel suddenly shuddered. A cold chill brought goosebumps up across her chest. It felt almost like icy fingers had been dragged lightly over the bare skin of her breasts. She shuddered again and the feeling was gone. Neither she nor Brian saw the specter that had passed between them, stopping just long enough to touch the object of its desire.

"Two fingers of vodka," said Annabel, smiling. He held up his hand with the thumb and pinky splayed.

## Chapter 24
## THE HOUSE (3)

**6:34 p.m.**

Twilight gave up the last of its bluish hue to the ebony of night. Owls echoed their mournful cries through the surrounding woods and the house shuddered, rousing itself to the fullness of its nocturnal existence. Floorboards creaked, shadows passed down the walls of stairwells, cries of shame and pain and sorrow filled the upstairs hallway, mixing with the laughter of sadistic delight. Deeper, in its bowels, the shrieks of anguish and anger rippled through the foundation and the house shifted. Plaster peeled away revealing cold, stone block. Light fixtures shriveled and reformed into sconces fueled by oil. The walls expanded and contracted as the house breathed in the air of its former existence.

Seventy-five yards away, in a stand of trees that ringed it, the old well spat out plumes of blackened water and chunks of stone and mortar. Cracks spread through the circular stonework of the well's base, and the fingers of a hand, long devoid of flesh and missing a little finger, slipped through a fissure to feel the air again for the first time in three hundred years.

As the moon rose into the Halloween night sky and shed its pale light on the roof, the house settled back down, the stone walls of its old existence once again slipping silently behind the plaster of the new. It's time had come. *His* time had come. Soon ... very soon ... all things would be in play. The battle would begin and Torrance Wickersham had no doubt that, when it was over, he would be whole again. His consciousness, and the beast (an incubus) that shared his existence, reached out from their prison. Their minds touched on Brian and Annabel. Wickersham needed Brian's body. The incubus lusted after Annabel. Using the beast's powers, their essence coalesced into a spectral form that once again could roam the halls and corridors of house.

## Chapter 25
## THROUGH THE DOOR and BACK AGAIN

**6:00 – 7:04 p.m.**

### 1

As dusk faded to night, Emma went around turning on lights. When she returned to the kitchen, she made a fresh pot of coffee and made a couple of ham and cheese sandwiches. Matt declined more coffee, preferring a glass of milk instead. They ate in silence, Emma thinking about what she already knew and wondering what was to come, Matt wondering if she was going to believe anything he was about to tell her.

"Thank you," he said, pushing his plate to the side and patting his belly. "I must admit that I hadn't realized how hungry I was until you so graciously offered dinner."

"Just sandwiches," said Emma, clearing the plates away and stacking them in the sink. "I thought we might be here a while, so we might as well eat. And now that we're done…"

"Yes. We must get back to business, because I feel, somehow, that time is growing short."

Emma had the same feeling. She didn't wait for the coffee maker to finish its brew cycle. When there was enough for a full cup, she poured it and returned to the table. "So, my father and mother got everyone moving. Tommy had seen some kind of … ghost or something, I guess you'd call it."

Matt laughed, but there was not a drop of real humor in it. "Actually, despite everything that had happened at that point, we all kind of felt that he was just hallucinating. He wasn't a stranger to drugs, and it was much easier and safer to believe in hallucinations than ghosts. But that would change very shortly."

Emma sipped at her coffee. "So you're telling me that you believed it was actually a ghost?"

"As I said, at first, no. Later... What's important for you to know is ...and I hope it doesn't color your objectivity ... that I do now. What happened in that house and what came afterward just plain make it too hard for me to ignore."

"Then I suppose you should continue with the story."

Matt folded his hands in front of him and closed his eyes. "There's something about this whole thing that I never understood. And now, with Henry's passing, I doubt I ever will."

"And what would that be?"

"How your mother and father could have married and stayed together all those years when..."

"When any of you being together was somehow detrimental."

"Yes, exactly."

"I'm afraid I can't answer that, though that question crossed my mind too."

Matt patted her hand. "No, Emma, I didn't expect that you could."

"At any rate, Henry was helping Tommy to his feet and your mother had gone back in to get *Janet*.

## 2

"... *Janet*. Come on, we have to get out of here." Amy found her huddled in a corner, her knees drawn up to her chest and her arms wrapped tightly around them. She was rocking back and forth, occasionally banging her forehead against the wall. Amy grabbed her under the arms and hauled her to her feet.

"I know you're scared," Amy whispered in her ear, "we all are. But you have to pull yourself together so we can all get out of here. Tommy's a wreck and Tina's in shock. I *need* you."

Janet blinked, rubbed at her eyes and took a step back. "What? I'm sorry, what did you say?"

"I said ... I *need* you to get it together." Amy took Janet's hands in hers and looked her straight in the eyes. "You're stronger than this, Janet. We both know that. What happened to Lucy ... my God ... but we have to get past that and-"

Janet blinked again and squeezed Amy's hand. "I'm okay ... I'll be okay. Thanks. Sorry I lost it there for a minute."

Amy hugged her. "No apologies necessary."

"You've always been such a good friend, Amy." She hugged back. "Now let's see if we can't shake Tina out of it too, and get the hell outta here before things get worse." She looked over Amy's shoulder. "Where's Tommy?"

"He's in the tunnel with Henry and Matt. Tina's there too."

Janet started toward the door and Amy stepped in front of her. "Hold up a second. We can't trust that damned door. We have it blocked open, but I'm not sure it'll stay that way. We're going to have to be super careful when-"

*Cree-eeeeeeek*! The door swung all the way open.

"I don't think I like that at all," said Janet.

"I'm *sure* I don't," said Amy.

'Hey you guys," called Henry. "Stay where you are for a minute. I don't trust-"

"Neither do we," yelled Amy and Janet at almost the same time. They looked at each other and started to laugh. Janet punched Amy in the arm.

"I got it," yelled Matt. He walked over and leaned his back against the door, squatting down so that his knees were bent and his heels dug in out in front of him. "Even if it moves, I'll be able to get out the way fast enough like this. Just come through one-at-time when I tell you … and be quick about it."

Henry added, "Get a running start and jump as far through as you can, like you're trying to win the gold in the broad jump event." He turned to Tina. "Stand here with Tommy." He shook her by the shoulders until she focused on him. "Stand here with Tommy, okay?"

Tina nodded and sidestepped a little closer to Tommy, who was now on his feet but refusing to take his hands from in front of his eyes.

Henry walked over and planted himself off to the side of Matt and took hold of his shirt with one hand and his belt with the other. "Okay, if you even feel the slightest pressure, just nod, and I'll yank you out of the way."

"Wait!" yelled Tommy, suddenly dropping his hands. He looked down the tunnel. *You can do this; you can do this; you can do this*. He walked over to where it started to angle down, to where the she-thing had come out of the darkness for him. Repeating to himself, you can do this, he turned his back on the tunnel and faced the open door. "Okay ... when I say go ... run like hell and jump into my arms ... I'll catch you. Janet ... you first."

### 3

"So Tommy finally came around," said Emma

"Yes and no. He managed to pull himself together...but it was an on and off thing. It'll be clearer when I finish." Matt sat forward and placed his hands into the small of his back and stretched. "I need to stand for a little bit, maybe walk around a little. The back ain't what it used to be, as they say in the vernacular."

Emma stretched, too. "I know what you mean. Why don't we amble into my father's study? The chairs are a little more comfy in there. Or we could sit in front of the fireplace in the living room, whichever you'd prefer."

Matt smiled. "I'll defer to you, it's your home. I can be comfortable anywhere ... well, within the bounds of my age." He let out a puff of a laugh.

They both worked themselves out of their seats and Emma led the way to the living room. Matt stood in front of the fireplace with one hand on the mantle and the other still welded to the small of his back. When he was confident that he'd chased as much of the stiffness away as he could, he took a seat.

"Might I impose on you a little further, Emma?"

"What can I do for you?"

"Have anything to drink?"

Emma smiled. "Bourbon, gin, scotch or rum?"

"A nice rum and coke would go down well about now, if it isn't asking too much."

"Not at all. Actually, a few fingers of bourbon would suit me right about now, too. Ice?"

"Please."

"Do you think you should call your grandson and let him know you're still here and all right? It's been quite a while." Emma fixed the drinks and took a seat.

"And I think it will be quite a while longer, but I suspect Timothy is just as well pleased that I'm gone and out of his hair. Oh, he likes me well enough; I even suspect he loves me in some way that is possible for him. He just ... well, he just has a fairly strong infatuation with himself, if you know what I mean."

Emma laughed. "I do. I think all the younger people suffer that affliction today to one degree or another."

She took a sip of bourbon and dabbed at a single tear that threatened to spill from the corner of her eye. The room was cozy, too cozy and way too familiar. Last night her father had been sitting telling the same story.

"So," she said, clearing her throat and hoping her mind would follow, "what happened next?"

"Well," said Matt, unconsciously imitating his host by clearing his throat, "The only light we had was coming from a few sets of candles set into sconces on the wall in the room where Janet and your mother were. All we had outside that room was whatever light that managed to flicker through the doorway. And as it turned out, it was a good thing they were inside and not out. As to our situation, I was pressed against the door, trying to keep it plastered against the wall. Your father was next to me, waiting to pull me out of harm's way should the need arise. Tommy was standing there with his arms wide open calling for your mother and Janet to *jump*.

### 4

"*Jump*! Get a good running start and jump through, I'll catch you."

Janet and Amy hugged and then moved closer to the open doorway. Amy winked and nodded, and Janet was off. She took a few quick steps and leaped into the air, her arms folded across her chest. A second later she was in Tommy's arms. They both turned and looked at Matt and Henry.

Matt shook his head. "It didn't move an inch."

Tommy sent Janet over to stand with Tina, who was beginning to focus a little more, and faced the doorway again. "Whenever you're ready, Amy." He had his arms wide and his eyes drilled into Amy's.

"Get ready," said Amy. "Especially you, Matt." Her mind circled the games the house had been playing so far and decided to try a little trick of her own. "Make sure you're ready, Matt, do you hear me?"

"I'm ready, all ready. Come on, let's do this."

Amy backed up, drew in a deep breath and held it. Then she bolted forward. At the last minute, she jumped sideways instead of through the door. At the same moment, the door pushed Matt forward, his heels sliding along the stone.

Henry hated the idea of what he had to do but had no choice. He yanked Matt to the side, both of them tumbling to the floor. The door slammed over and opened again, its hinges squealing in apparent delight, thudding into the stone wall that supported it with a jarring crack. If Henry hadn't pulled Matt out of the way, he would have been crushed against the stone like a bug beneath a flyswatter.

"I thought so," said Amy. "Is everyone all right?"

"Good here," called Henry, climbing to his feet and helping Matt do the same. "You okay?"

"So far, so good."

Tommy threw his hands up. "Now what? Do we try again?"

The sound turned all their heads in the direction of the tunnel. Tommy twisted around. It began as a low gurgle and steadily rose in pitch. A few seconds later, water sloshed over Tommy's ankles, bubbling and swirling and frothing.

"Oh Christ," yelled Tommy. "Oh my fucking God. The water's rising. I mean *really* rising ... and fast."

By the time he'd finished the sentence the water was sloshing around his calves.

Matt moved first under Henry's prodding. "Go on, we don't have any time or any other choice. We're going to have to find another way out of here." He patted Matt on the shoulder and sent him on his way toward the open doorway.

Safe across the threshold, Matt yelled: "Henry's right! Come on, come on. You have to risk it ... all of you. And for God's sake, hurry up about it."

Tommy was the next one through, too scared of what was behind to worry about the door squashing him. Henry shoved Tina through into Matt's arms. He turned to Janet, who held up her hand and shook her head.

"I can do it," she said, and did.

The water was now up to all their knees and the force was getting stronger. Running or jumping was out of the question. Taking a big chance, Henry slogged his way over to the opening and then pushed off with his feet and dove into the water, disappearing beneath its surface. The strength of his push and the force of the flow carried him through, and slowed the closing door just enough. It whammed closed behind him, shaking the jamb and sending a spider web of cracks through the surrounding stone.

"Well, here we are again, back where we started; what fun ... we can swim home." Amy's sarcasm made Henry smile. Nobody else seemed to appreciate it. The water was now up to their waists or higher.

Outside, the water continued to rise, pounding against the door with the force of ocean waves against rock. The thin gap between the door and floor had slowed but not stopped its advance on the inside. The battering continued for another five minutes and then stopped.

"It's dropping," said Janet, "it's going down."

Ever so slowly, the level dropped until it reached the bottom of their calves.

"Oh my God! Do you smell that?" Tina pinched her nose closed. "Oh my God; it really smells bad."

Matt bent over and inhaled. "Christ, it's the water ... if that's what this is." He hesitantly dipped the tips of his fingers in and brought it up in front of him. His face contorted as if he'd just bitten into a lemon. "Ewww, this is gross."

The thick liquid dripped off the ends of his fingers in black threads and swirled away beneath the surface.

"Whatever it is now, it wasn't that way a minute ago," said Henry. "I was under it and it was just water."

"I think this house is trying to kill us," said Tina. "I know that sounds crazy, but…"

"I don't think it's so crazy. But it's not *just* the house; there's something else down here with us. She was after me, she came up out of the tunnel-" Tommy looked down at the liquid surrounding his legs. "-and she was dripping with this shit. And you know what else?"

Nobody said anything; they just waited.

"She wasn't alive, either. Maybe at one time, but sure as hell not when I saw her."

"A ghost? A ghost came after you?" Tina started toward Tommy and found that whatever it was they were standing in was thick, almost jelly-like. It took a great deal of effort to put one leg in front of the other. And it seemed that it got thicker with each step. She stopped.

"You guys, try walking in this. It almost feels as if it's grabbing at you, trying to hold you. I don't like this place. I want to get out of here and go home."

"We all want to go home, Tina," said Henry, "and we're going-"

"Oh shit!" shrieked Tina. Something just touched me. I felt it."

Tommy jumped, sending slow ripples across the surface of the liquid. "Me too. Christ, something touched me too. It felt like it was trying to... "

"Ahhhhhh/Yeeeeeeeeep!"

Tommy and Tina both screamed at the same time. What was left of Lucy came bobbing to the surface between them, her hair fanned out and one arm outstretched, the fingers cloying at Tommy's pants leg.

## Chapter 26
## THE HOUSE (4)

**7:04 p.m.**

The house kept watch over its property from every side, its window eyes blinking in the darkness. Its dark breath, invisible and silent, puffed from the chimney stack. Its voice of discontent cried out from the creaking floorboards. And within its walls, Wickersham and the incubus searched out their prey.

In the well outside the house, black water bubbled and frothed around the bony fingers that had breached their stony prison. Overhead, the white moon shone down, its half closed eye reflecting off the black surface of the churning water. And in the bubbling froth, it winked a knowing wink. On Halloween, the witches rise, the dead walk the earth unseen, and magic, for good or ill, is at its strongest.

*Tis de night for all t'ings t'be settled.* The words gurgled up. *Tis almos' m'time, an' I be getting' stronger. Soon ... I will com' into all and be free of dis prison for all time.* A hideous, squealing laughter rippled through the water and shook the well's foundation. *What was wrong will be put right ... an' a Mot'er's revenge will be final.*

## Chapter 27
## THE TRAP IS SPRUNG

### 7:04 p.m. – 8:48 p.m.

**1**

Matt Holloway stared into his glass. He watched his reflection waver in the amber liquid from the slight tremor in his hands. It was a visual reminder that he was no longer the boy (or even the man) he used to be. What used to be effortless now required concentration and determination: tying your shoes, buttoning your suit jacket, getting your fingers to work cooperatively to knot a tie. Even as short as twenty years ago (yes, when you hit your eighties, twenty years doesn't seem all that long ago – because, boy ...did they fly by) old age really seemed like something that was still out there on the horizon. And that horizon was just a point you kept edging toward, thinking you could never *really* get there. Then WHAM! You were not only there, but somehow – in some impossible way, the damned thing seemed to have slipped behind you. That's when reality not only slapped you in the face, it kicked you in the ass and the shins. That's when you realized that your horizon was now on the opposite side of your journey, and the only damned way to see it now was through the lens of memory.

He watched his face float and wrinkle and jig and wondered what he thought he was doing. He was eighty-five for Christ's sake, and here he was talking about battling ghosts and haunted houses. That was scary enough, but what was deeper in his mind was ridiculous and terrifying. Actually, it was ridiculously terrifying. As he described what had happened in that house all those years ago, he came to the unhappy recognition that the telling was just a prelude to what had to be done. Matthew Holloway, respected funeral director, one time president of the Wickersham Chamber of Commerce and annual Grand Marshall of the Hollow's Fourth of July Celebrations, eighty-five year old Matthew Holloway – would once again have to go into that house. Eighty-five year old Matthew Holloway would have to dig into his memory of youth to find the strength and the courage to do the unthinkable. He only hoped that the old saying was right – that at least he had wisdom. A smile crept across his face at that thought, for if he truly had wisdom, he'd never consider doing what he knew he had to do. The funny thing was, though, somehow in some strange and miraculous way – whether it was wishful thinking or not – he felt younger, stronger. Maybe even capable of pulling it off.

Emma touched him lightly on the shoulder. "Woolgathering?"

Matt swirled his face into oblivion and drained it off. He held the glass out and raised one eyebrow. Emma grinned, got up and refilled his glass, adding an additional splash when he followed the withdrawing bottle with his glass.

"I just had a thought," he said. "Actually, I had a few, but one in particular. And I think that it was your thought and not mine."

"What was that?"

"The box. Perhaps you should get the box that Henry ... I mean, your father ... told you about. If I we're a betting man, I'd bet there's more in it than just the tale I'm telling you. At least ... at least I hope so. Because what I'm going to suggest is going to take crazy to a whole other level."

Emma stared into his eyes for a moment and then got up. She stopped at the archway to the dining room and turned back. "You're going to suggest that we ... you and I ... go to that house, aren't you?"

Matt shifted his eyes to the clock on the mantelpiece and noted the time. "It's a little after seven. I'd like to finish up the story and-"

"And then go over to that house."

"Yes. But not right away."

Emma cocked her head to the side and studied Matt's face. More than that, she studied what was going on behind his eyes, eyes that seemed to have taken on a completely new vitality.

"You want to wait until the children are all off the streets, done Trick-or-Treating, don't you?"

Matt gave a somber nod. "Yes. And by the way, now that you mention that ... is it customary for you to have no Halloween visitors. Not a single child has been here."

"No, it's not customary. Usually we get tons. Dad always made such a fuss..." She wiped at her eyes, and then changed the subject. "I'll get the box."

When she returned, she set the box on the table between them and inserted the key. Matt reached out and stayed her hand.

"Not just yet. First, I need to tell more of the story."

Emma took a swallow of her bourbon and sat back. Matt leaned forward and clasped his hands together on his knees.

"Tommy and Tina screamed. And I don't mind admitting now that I almost did the same. There she was, our friend Lucy ... at least, what was left of her ... bobbing around in that foul water like a rotten apple in fetid cider, her lifeless fingers clutching at the cuffs of Tommy Vorland's pants. And him standing there yelling for someone to get her *off*.

## 2

"...*OFF*! Get her the fuck OFF OF ME! Get IT the fuck off of me! Somebody!"

Tommy kicked and jiggled and shook his leg to no effect. Lucy's fingernails remained firmly embedded in the cuffs. The churned up water from his efforts made the half of face she had left wobble up and down, as if she were trying to lift her head. Her one gray-clouded eye stared up at him, and he knew she was looking at him ... through him ... into his very soul, and accusing him.

With a final kick so hard that it sent him splashing into the mucky water, the fingers came free and the body floated to the bottom out of sight. A moment later, the water rushed out under the door the way it had come in. It went with a speed that rivaled any storm current. It was gone in seconds, leaving the saturated pieces of corpse splayed out on the stone, its arm still outstretched in Tommy's direction, its vacant staring eye still accusing.

The group searched each other's faces, wondering the same thing: should they try getting out through the door, or should they try to find another way? That's when it happened for the first time. Their heads bobbed up and down a couple of times until their chins came to rest on their chests. Eyes twitched behind closed lids; fingers played invisible pianos at their sides, and in their heads, a thousand colors sprang up and fell back like rainbow fountains. Those fountains were the thoughts of everyone in the room. Most of them variations on the same theme, individual iterations of the same fears and concerns: *how were they going to get out of here; what was happening; what were they going to do about Lucy.* Some were more frantic than others. Only Tommy's thoughts were different. His mind could not let go of the nightmare image of the woman oozing toward him from the wet abyss of darkness. He could still see the water dripping from her decaying, beckoning hand, could still hear the sickening sounds of her bare feet slapping against the wet stone as she came for him. But most of all he could still hear her siren voice enticing him to join with her. His fear dominated the rest of their thoughts, delivering them into the here and now of that moment. In that instant, they all stood at the top of the tunnel; they were all beckoned forward, and they all *knew* the horror of his reality.

The moment passed. Their fingers stopped playing, their eyes snapped open and their thoughts disentangled. But the memory and image of what they'd shared remained.

"Did you all..." Amy was the first to speak, or ... try to speak. She had to search for words, as if the pages of her mental dictionary had been somehow rearranged, pulled out of order.

Henry nodded, and Amy could see that he was having the same problem. His mouth was moving without sound, his face contorted into a knot of concentration until he was able to finally force something out.

"Thinking ... I ... thoughts ... no, wait ... I thoughts heard ... I..."

"Me ... um..." Matt slapped the heel of his hand against his forehead several times in rapid succession, as if he were trying to knock the words back into order - a child's game of *get the little silver balls to sit in their depressions.* Only his method was more brute force than gentle tilting and coaxing.

Finally, Tina formed the first coherent sentence and it catalyzed everyone else. It was the articulation of all their first thoughts.

"Christ, did we really just hear each other thinking?" The next thing she said was the second thing they all wanted to know. "Jesus, Tommy, who the hell was she? Where did she come from?"

Tommy had no answers. He could still see that woman reaching for him, and he could still feel Lucy's accusing eye staring at him as her dead hand clawed at his leg. He shrank back against the wall and folded his arms across his chest, his head in constant "NO" motion. It was then and there that his sanity decided it was almost High Noon and time to get out of Dodge.

"Henry, we really, really have to get out of here." Matt speared the oak door with an apprehensive gaze and then pointed toward the door at the far end of the room. "If I get a vote, I'd vote that way."

"Me too, said Tina. "I refuse to try to get through *that* door again. And I'm sure as hell not going down into that damned tunnel even if we could. No fucking way, Jose! And that's all I have to say on the subject."

Janet's eyes were riveted on the floor. "What … what are we going to do about Lucy? We can't just leave her here like this."

"I'm afraid we're going to have to," said Amy. "And I'm afraid there's not going to be getting around telling the cops what happened and bringing them back here."

"Yeah, that's if we get out," mumbled Tina. "And I'm not so sure this house is going to allow that. I can feel it. Can't you all? It's not going to be happy until we all end up like…" She looked at the remains that lay at her feet and quickly looked away.

*Click! Creeeeeaaaakkkkk*! The door at the far end of the room drifted open.

"An invitation?" asked Matt. "If so, I'm not sure I'm all that keen on accepting it."

"We don't have a choice," cried Tina, her voice shrill. "We have to! We have to because I'm not going the other way. I'm not; I'm not."

Henry looked around, found one of the flashlights sticking out from under Lucy's body and wormed it out. He didn't like what he was thinking and what he was going to suggest. Not one bit did he like it. But he also thought it was the only thing that made any sense.

He clicked it on and shined it around the room. Confident it was working properly, he said: "Everyone wait here. I'll go through and see where it might lead. I'll stay close, though, within earshot."

"Are you sure that's wise?" asked Matt.

"Probably not," said Amy. "But I agree. One of us has to check it out. We all can't just go rushing in there, and we certainly can't go back through that tunnel."

"That's exactly my point," said Matt. "If we can't go back ... then, for good or bad, that door down there is our only way out. That being the case, no need for exploration, we just all go. It's the only thing to do. And I for one don't think we should separate again."

After a little consideration, Amy agreed. Forward seemed much better than back, at least at this point it. "Okay. Together."

Janet cocked a thumb in Tommy's direction. "What about him? Look at him; he's completely lost it. We're going to have to drag him along like a lost dog. And that's not going to speed us up any."

"Tommy," said Henry in a voice as calm and reassuring as he could muster, "are you going to be okay? I need you to keep it together so we can get out of here."

Tommy's eyes blinked and he squeezed his arms in even tighter against his chest.

"He's gone," said Janet. "I don't think there's anybody home anymore."

Amy walked over and put her hands on Tommy's shoulders and drew him in. She whispered in his ear. "We can't stay here; you know that. You led us in here. If you can't lead us out, that's okay. But you can't just turn yourself off. You have to try and stay with it." She shook him back and forth, his head bobbing like a caricature doll on some dusty dashboard. Then she stepped back and slapped him twice across the face. The second one hard enough to make his teeth clack together.

His eyes blinked again and his head bobbed up and down. But this time it was a clear assent. He unfolded his arms and put his hand out.

Amy enfolded it in hers and gently pulled him forward. He came slowly but willingly, being extra careful not to step on or look at Lucy.

"Okay." Amy guided Tommy around the body and over to the other door. "Tina, you take Tommy's other hand. Henry ... you're out in front." She smiled. "No pressure or anything like that, Henry, but we're all counting on you now to get us the hell out of here."

Henry smiled back. "Pressure? What pressure? Just a walk in the park."

"You mean a walk in the dark, don't you?" quipped Matt.

"How can you people make jokes?" asked Tina, her eyes still filled with fear. "This place is trying to kill us, and now you're going to just lead us through some door that goes God knows where?"

"Can-it!" snapped Janet. "You don't want to go-" She turned and pointed to the door that ate Lucy. "-there's the other way out. Have fun. I, for one, am more willing to risk this way than that. So what are you going to do?"

"You don't have to be snotty," said Tina. "I'm scared, that's all."

"Don't worry, honey, you're definitely not alone in that department," said Amy. Her admission wasn't quite the slap in the face she'd delivered to Tommy, but it did have a galvanizing effect on Tina, helping her to settle down and feel a little calmer. She rubbed her hand down the sides of her jeans as if she were smoothing out a skirt.

"Okay," she said, her voice still a bit jittery but not as high-pitched. "I'm not happy about it, but I guess I'm as ready as I'll ever be to follow you all through the looking glass." She tried to smile, but it looked just as strained as it was.

"All right, then," said Henry. He snapped on the beam of the flashlight and carefully pushed the door further open, his heart racing in his chest and his legs ready to jump him out of the way if it moved on its own or gave the slightest resistance.

Tina and Janet moved closer together. Amy wrapped her arm through Tommy's, waited for him to nod that he was ready, and stepped forward. Henry held his breath and stepped through the door into a darkened hallway. Matt slid around to take up the rear.

"Hold on a sec," called Matt. He dashed over to one of the sconces and plucked a thick tallow from its base, protecting the flame with his cupped hand. "Okay, I think we're ready now."

### 3

Emma suddenly shivered and sat forward. Something had happened, something that scared her on a level she'd never felt before. When she looked over, she could see that Matt felt it too. The pictures in her mind, painted by his words as he told the story, had taken on a life, a reality. She could feel the dampness of the place soaking into her pores like a thin layer of skin cream. The dank smell of the stone walls filled her nostrils; the echo of their voices – the kids' voices – reverberating around the hollowness of the house assaulted her ears. She was no longer just listening to a boogeyman story, *"a tale told by an idiot, full of sound and fury, signifying nothing"* as Shakespeare put it. It was now real, and she was living it, breathing it, feeling it ... and she was doing it from inside Matt's mind.

Matt stopped talking. He didn't look at her; he didn't have to. Their thoughts were braided together: a Gordian Knot that no blade could undo. He took a gulp of his drink, set the glass down, closed his eyes and reclined. There was no more need for words. He drew his thoughts back to his tale, and there, in the darkness of that house seventy years ago, a ghostly figure of a woman wavered in the air beside him. She hovered there, no more solid than he was – two wispy figures of smoke hiding in the shadows and watching silently and helplessly as six teenagers struggled to awaken from their unified living nightmare.

**4**

The hallway they entered was long and narrow. Henry's flashlight spread an opaque white cone of light before them until it was overwhelmed by black. They moved along the hall huddled in a tight group. Amy had to keep coaxing Tommy along with a tug now and again. Janet and Tina also had their elbows interlocked, and Matt walked solemnly in the back, his candle held high. The sound of their footsteps fell on their ears like the beating of unseen drums, promising that they would all be some form of stew for heathen cannibals. Only they all knew that the cannibal in this case was the house itself. And they were already deep inside its belly.

The group walked in silence, Tina and Janet beginning to feel claustrophobic. The farther they went, the narrower the hall became. At last, they came to another door. Henry looked at the others and shrugged. With a gentle push of his hand, the door swung inward.

"Can we trust it?" asked Amy.

"I don't think we have much of a choice, as usual. Through or back." He shone his light into the room and stepped through the doorway. "It's empty. But there's some kind of passageway on the other side."

Matt stepped past Amy, pushed the door all the way open and put his back against it. "I'll hold it, just in case."

Amy just nodded and stepped in. Janet followed and Tina brought Tommy with her. By the time they were all in, Henry was on the other side looking through a stone archway. "Hate to tell you this, guys, but it looks like the only way from here is down. How far, I can't really tell; the steps wind around the wall. It must be that turret room you can see from the front of the house."

"Down?" questioned Matt. "How can it go down? I thought we were already as down as down gets. We came into the basement through a tunnel, for Christ's sake."

Henry shrugged. "I don't know. All I know is there's no other door and the steps go down."

"I don't like it," said Tina. "We need to find a way up. Up and out of this hellhole."

"Hey!" said Henry, with just a tinge of exasperation in his voice. "I didn't build the damned place."

Amy moved in beside Henry and looked down. "I don't like this either," she said, "but it doesn't look as if we have much choice."

The group moved down the steps in single file. The eighth step opened onto a small landing, where the group paused. Henry was about to start down again when his flashlight began to dim. What had been a bright cone of light was now just a yellow dribble in the dark.

"Oh, that's just great," said Tina, who was at the end of the line, just behind Tommy. "It isn't bad enough we're stuck in this loony funhouse, but now the batteries are gonna ... gonna give up the ghost." She waited for a response but no one laughed. "That was an intentional pun, guys. Come on, it was at least worth a feigned groan or laugh."

"Oh yeah," said Janet, "We all want to stop for comedy hour."

"Chill, guys," said Matt. "We still have the candle. Let's just keep going. There has to be a way out. There *has* to be."

"Wait a minute." Amy stopped and inhaled a few sharp breaths and coughed. "Oh God, do you smell that? It smells like-"

"Aww," cried Tina. "Shit. It smells like shit."

"Come on," said Henry, "try to ignore it. Breathe through your mouth. Let's just keep moving. No matter what, Matt's right. There has to be a way-"

*Waaaaa ... waaa-waaa ... ahhwaaa.*

The baby's cry rushed at their ears like a windstorm in a tunnel. It was near deafening in volume. It faded away, only to be replaced by a deep and hideously maniacal rumble of laughter. Everyone's heart froze at the sound of it. Tommy slumped down on the steps, his back against the wall, his hands thrown over his ears. Tina could feel her legs beginning to shake and fought to keep them steady. Janet huddled up against Matt. Henry looked at Amy and knew she was thinking the same thing he was. If they didn't get everyone moving right away, they might never.

"Get him up," Amy said to Tina, her voice firm, sure and commanding. "Get him on his feet and let's get the hell out of here."

"Do ... do you really think there's a baby in here somewhere?" asked Janet.

"I doubt it," answered Henry. "I think it's just another house trick. Come on, Amy, get them moving; I'm gonna scout ahead a bit."

Henry was starting to lose his patience. He began to wonder if there was going to be a big piece of cheese waiting for all of them at the end of this, because he certainly felt as if they were all just rats in an elaborate maze. Run this way; scurry that way. Climb up; climb down. Let's all go round and round on the hamster wheel, getting nowhere. It was all beyond frustrating.

Another burst of minatory laughter rang through the stairwell.

Tommy slapped his hands over his ears and pushed his way past everyone, almost knocking Henry down the steps. Amy made a grab for him as he bolted by but missed. He disappeared into the darkness below, leaving behind only the sound of his echoing footsteps.

"SHIT!" screamed Henry. "Come on, let's go get him."

With Henry in the lead, they all trundled down the stone steps, each entangled in his or her own thoughts, suppositions and fears of what might be awaiting them in the belly of the beast. When they reached the bottom, they found Tommy slumped against the wall, his hands still over his ears and his head between his knees.

"Stay here with him for a minute," said Henry, "while I check this out."

The stairs emptied into a circular corridor that bent around to the left. Henry's flashlight was all but dead. Only a small circle of yellow illuminated its end, just barely enough to keep away total darkness. He moved along the corridor with one hand gliding along the stone wall. In less than five minutes he found himself back where he started – at the steps and the group.

"It's solid," he said, shaking his head in disbelief and frustration. "There's no door, no nothing. It's a solid wall that just goes in a complete circle."

"Nothing?" said Amy. "That doesn't make much sense. Why would a stairway lead to nowhere?"

Henry just shrugged. "How's Tommy?" he whispered in Amy's ear.

"Not good, obviously. We got him to take his hands down, but he won't get up and won't look at us. Henry? What are we going to do? If there's no way out down here, and we can't go back..?"

Henry pinched his lower lip in thought and stared into the darkness at his feet. He could feel the frustration inside morphing into anger. Everyone was looking to him for answers, answers he didn't have. Tommy was supposed to be the one in charge. Now, everything had fallen on his shoulders and he had no real idea of what to do. He could almost feel everyone's eyes on him, all of them waiting for him to come up with some miraculous plan. He had no plan, miraculous or otherwise. And the frustration finally boiled over.

"FUCK!" he yelled, and hurled the flashlight against the wall. The base of it struck a small square stone just to the left of Tommy's head. A moment later a grating sound filled their ears. A moment after that, the wall behind Tommy swung inward and he fell backwards into the blackness. At the same time a foul gust of wind erupted from inside and blew out the candle in Matt's hand.

### 5

Matt coughed and the connection was broken. They found themselves back in Emma's living room.

"We better finish," said Matt, not wanting to waste any time on suppositions or explanations of why they'd suddenly lost their mental connection. "At least, as much of the rest as I know. Now let me see…

"Your father had just stepped into the room he'd opened by accident when he threw the flashlight against the wall. Tommy was inside, too, curled into a fetal position. The rest of us stood outside waiting. And I can tell you, we were all wondering the same thing. It was your mother who vocalized it. She stood just outside the doorway and asked your father: 'What if this damned stone door closes on you *like the wooden one that ate Lucy?*'"

# 6

"...*like the wooden one that ate Lucy*? Sometimes, I don't think you think at all."

"Hey!" snapped Henry, "I'm doing the best I can to get us out of here. Some damned chances have to be taken. Any of you have any better ideas?"

The uncharacteristic outburst of anger stunned Amy and she recoiled. It wasn't just the vehemence in his voice; it was the timbre – a deep rumbling growl, spat out. The others heard it, too. Matt took an unconscious step back and Janet moved a little closer to Tina.

"What the hell is wrong with you, Henry?" Amy's momentary shock abated and she suddenly found herself overwhelmed with anger. "We're *all* struggling here, you know. You're not the only one stuck in this Godforsaken nightmare. Get a grip and grow the hell up."

Matt stepped forward and put a hand on Amy's shoulder. She swiped it off and turned on him. "What the hell do *you* want?"

Matt raised both hands. "Hey, calm down. What's got into you two? I've never heard either of you talk like that, especially to each other. I think this house is trying to set us against one another."

Amy started to growl something back at him and caught herself. She took a deep breath, closed her eyes, fighting to regain control. At last she opened them and laid a hand on Matt's shoulder. "You're right. We shouldn't be acting like this. We're going to have to be very careful."

Although she couldn't see it in the dark, Matt smiled. He stepped around her and moved into the doorway, though not close enough to get hurt if it suddenly decided to make him a carbon copy of Lucy.

"Henry," he called. "Maybe you should come out of there." Inside, the room was blacker than black. He couldn't see Henry at all. He couldn't see anything. When Henry didn't answer, he tried again, a little louder. "Henry? Where are you? I think you should-"

Suddenly, one at a time like a series of Christmas lights, torches flared to life around the stone-walled, half-moon shaped room. Henry held the center. To his right was a long wooden table with a large rounded wheel at its head. Iron chains dangled from the rack's foot posts and turning wheel. At its foot, a small table held an upturned hourglass, its sand nearly drained from the upper bulb. Behind Henry, a large granite slab supported by two upright stone supports served as an altar. Beneath it, between the supports, rested a glass box with a shattered end pane. A baby lay on its back in the box, kicking and mewling. It had only one arm; the right side of its chest was a gaping hollow, through which the child's heart could be seen beating. Matt gasped and started to back away from the door. Amy stood there in shock, a hand covering her mouth.

"It's okay, guys. Come on in. I think I found a way out," said Henry, his hands on his hips and an odd grin on his face. "It's over here; we can finally get out of this stinking place. Come on."

Tommy, still lying in a fetal position in the doorway, uncurled and stood up. In a surprising burst of speed that caught everyone off guard. He shoved Matt aside and grabbed Amy by her shirt and whipped her into the room. Before the rest of them could react, the stone door swung shut and the wall was once again sealed.

## 7

Matt put a hand over his mouth and looked down at his shoes, too embarrassed to look at Emma. "I'm afraid that this is where my part of the story ends. We were all locked out. Whatever happened in that room ... well, neither your mother nor your father ever said. And Tommy, well, whatever happened to him took his mind. All I can tell you now is how we got out of the house."

Emma massaged her temples, hoping to avert the sickening headache she felt coming on. The rest of her felt like she'd just finished a double-header Iron Man contest. She was weak and sore and all but totally worn out. "I think it's time we see what dad left. He promised me the truth about what happened, and I'm betting... She picked up the box. "I'm hoping ... it's in here."

Matt laid a hand on the lid. "Emma, there's something else, something I didn't remember until right this very minute when you picked up the box. We were all locked out of that room, staring at each other, wondering what to do. And then ... then... It grew cold, very cold. I remember us all joining hands and we ... we started to chant something ... a name. It was as if... No, not *as if*, we *were*, all of us, in some kind of a trance. We just kept saying, 'Mother', over and over and over again. That's all I can remember until that stone door swung open again and they came out." He drew his hand away from the box and sat back. "How could I not have remembered that? Thinking back on it, I can still feel how cold and empty I felt, as if I was no more than a puppet. How in the world could that have-"

"Because it wasn't time for you to remember it, Matt. Maybe that's a good sign. Maybe it means that now really is the time that's right, the time for us to do what has to be done."

"Go ahead, Emma. Open the box. Let's see what there is to see and know what there is ... I hope ... to learn."

## Chapter 28
## TIME and TRUTH

**6:30 p.m. – 8:12 p.m.**

*Tick ... tick ... tick ... tick...* The eternal companion to everyone swept forward at its steady pace into the future. Time. It is not judgmental; it cares not for the joys or woes, comings and goings and doings of man, beast or nature. It just is, though some would claim it doesn't exist at all, a foible of man's consciousness, created solely for his convenience. Others believe it to be the quantification of the fourth dimension, space-time. A convenient tool, another dimension, an enigmatic companion – by whatever name or description, it moves from event to event in one *perceived* direction.

*Tick ... tick ... tick ... tick...* And so it moved forward in Walcott's kitchen. Ralph Strunk kept track of it by the number of scorched crows his mind kept recounting. To Joachim Walcott, the tracking of time was a waste of it. To him, it was neither a companion nor a dimension. It certainly was not a convenience by any stretch of the imagination. To Joachim Walcott, time was ... something else, entirely.

Tick ... tick ... tick ... tick...

When the grandfather's clock in the living room sounded a single chime marking the half hour, precisely 6:30 p.m., Walcott took a big swallow of his bourbon, poured another and leaned forward. He bore a troubled look on his face and his eyes seemed distant, almost vacant. It looked to Ralph as if the old man were looking at something far off in his memory, as if he were trying to gather disjointed thoughts and organize them.

"What I told ya a little while ago," began Walcott, "wasn't the truth. It skirted the truth, comin' close, but not quite hittin' the mark. I guess old habits, like tryin' to keep secrets ... and shameful things from the light of day ... I guess those habits are harder to break than folks realize. Anyways, secrets or shames, it's beyond high time the truth finally came out. I got to tell you what really happened to Wickersham, all he done and what it cost. And I got to tell you 'bout me ... what I done and what it still might cost, 'cause the final bill ain't been delivered yet. Pay attention, Ralph. It's gonna be more than a bit hard to swallow. It ain't gonna sound rational, 'cause it *ain't* rational. But it'll be the truth ... and that's somethin' I've been avoidin' for a very, very long time."

"Mr. Walcott, whatever it is, no matter what, you know you can trust-"

Walcott waved Ralph into silence. "Let me just think a bit about how I want to tell this. Then, once I get going, you just sit there an' listen till I'm done. Then ... *after* I finish ... then you can ask all the questions ya want. And believe me, there will be questions. Agreed?"

Ralph nodded, now, more than ever, dreading what was about to be revealed.

"I guess I'll start," said Wickersham, his eyes closed and his brow furrowed, "by tellin' ya straight out that what I said before about not believin' in the occult ... that was a boldfaced lie. Those papers, the all yellow and crinkly ones that I told you were some kind of a deal with the devil, well ... that's exactly what they were. It was a covenant. Ya know what that is? It's a contract that Wickersham bargained for so's he could live forever. More than that, I guess ... probably power, too. But livin' forever was the basic idea. The whole story's more twisted than you could imagine."

Walcott opened his eyes, fixed them on Ralph and leaned forward, resting his forearm on the table. He swallowed hard, forcing himself to go on, to accept the fact that now was the time for everything to come out.

"You know most of the history of this place, so I won't bore you with those details. But to understand what's going on now, you got to know what happened back then. Torrance Wickersham came here in sixteen ninety-three. That much you know. What you don't know, what nobody in this cursed community knows, is why he came here. It wasn't by choice, least ways, not the relocating part. Yes, he *chose* the Hollow as the place to settle, but that was only because he was forced out of Ipswich. Sixteen ninety-three was the year that the Salem Witch trials were put to an end. The concept of guilt by what they called spectral evidence was no longer accepted as evidence of witchcraft. Wickersham, however, continued the practice of hunting witches in Ipswich. Eventually, the colonial governor, William Phips, forced him out. So here he came, and he brought his loyal followers with him. He also brought as many of his prisoners as could be gathered and concealed, including a very beautiful young woman. She was the daughter of a Jamaican peasant he thought he'd killed during trial by water. A lot of that story is missing, and even I don't know what happened. But ... that's where our story and this mess we're in begins."

Walcott cleared his throat again, took a deep breath and went on. "The name of that peasant woman was..." He paused, sighed, and looked down at the table. "The woman's name was Cassandra Wanelus. Her daughter's name, the one Wickersham took away with him, was Abigail. She ... she was a beautiful girl, young and lithe and fair skinned for a black girl. But more important to this story, she ... she was my mother, Ralph. My name was changed to Walcott to protect me. But we'll get to that."

Ralph sat there stunned, not knowing quite what to think or what to say. Walcott raised his hand, preemptively. "Remember our deal, Ralph. Hold off your disbelief and let me finish. Then you can have your say and ask your questions.

"At precisely the stroke of midnight on October 31, 1697, the skies poured forth a torrent and flashed with angered lightning ... and in the midst of that cursed maelstrom my brother and I came forth. We were born inseparable, conjoined, two halves of an unholy union between man, demon and woman, forever bound to each other's fate."

"Mr. Walcott, you can't be seri-"

"More serious and earnest than you could possibly know, Ralph. Please, let me just get to finish. I know how it sounds, but you have to let me get it out. You see, that unholy birth, that abomination, was not the true beginning of this living nightmare in which we now find ourselves. No. The true horror began some days before. I have never been able to determine exactly how many, but it was no more than six and probably a great deal less. It began on the night that Torrance Wickersham learned that my grandmother, Cassandra, was on her way to save her daughter. How he learned this, I do not know. Probably from one of the many spies he had serving him. He knew she was coming for him. What he did not know was that my grandmother wielded a formidable power through that ancient art of voodoo. And when he found she was coming to stop him, he accelerated his plans, drawing on the same dark forces for which he had condemned others.

"Needing to have the object of his desire, my mother, Abigail, he had one of the prisoners he kept in a shack on the property brought to him. Shackled and collared, she was taken to the bowels of the house, to the dungeon room at the bottom of the turret. Abigail was already there, bound to a small cot. Now, you might be wondering why, if he already had her, he hadn't yet taken her. That was my grandmother's doing. Her power was strong, and she had used some kind of incantation that prevented him from touching her. Don't ask me the specifics, I don't know or understand them. All the same, he realized that if he were going to have what he wanted, he would need someone who could break the spell that prevented it. The woman, Jamaican by birth, who was summoned to do this was Tyanna Walcott. It was she who eventually saved and harbored me after the events of that unholy Halloween night."

Walcott paused, poured another round of bourbon for the two of them, wiped his lips with the back of his sleeve and went on.

"When my grandmother arrived, a terrible battle ensued. Tyanna, a powerful witch in her own right, was forced into battle against my grandmother. You see, Ralph, Wickersham had her son sequestered in a secret place. She would either fight or lose the boy; she had no choice. From what I understand of it, my grandmother and Tyanna were equally matched. The turning point came when Wickersham cajoled Tyanna into summoning a demon. And here is where things went blacker than black for everyone."

"Whoa," said Ralph, waving his hands in the air like a cop at a traffic stop. "A demon? You really believe that? You *really* believe some kind of witchcraft and demon spirit is causing what's happening..." He paused, thinking. "What *is* happening, anyway, Mr. Walcott? I'm not even sure I know that. And you being born, what, hundreds of years ago? No, I don't think I can believe that."

"No, Ralph, I guess hearin' someone tell he was over three hundred years old would be a lot to swallow. And I know you don't know what's happening. But you sure as hell saw them birds drop from the sky ... blasted out of the sky, I should say. Ya saw that with your own eyes, didn't ya? Ever seen that in your life before? Think that's an everyday, normal occurrence? Well, if'n ya do, you're wrong. It ain't. Not by a longshot.

"Look, Ralph," Walcott laid his hand on the back of Ralph's, "truth is, we're runnin' outta time here. I ain't got the time to dance around all this with you, so I'm gonna' show you somethin'. This is gonna be a shock, so don't jump outta your pants; it don't change nothin'. It's just so's we can get past all your questions real quick and move on to doin' somethin' about this horrible mess."

Walcott sat back in his chair and closed his eyes and slowly opened them again. Ralph watched with a mix of horror and fascination as the wrinkles on Walcott's skin smoothed, the gray stubble on his lips and chin and neck receded. He watched as the skin tightened and the musculature firmed. He watched Walcott's eyes clear and turn bright blue, and his hair grow back, thick and full. He flopped back in his chair, a hand thrown across his mouth in awe as the old man he'd been speaking to was replaced by someone who looked no older than thirty.

"Don't be scared, Ralph. I'm still the same person I always was. I'm just lettin' you see the real me for the first time. Nothin' else has changed. I ... I needed to do this to get you to believe ... to get you to let me finish as quick as I can so's we can start to figure out what we're gonna' do."

Ralph just sat there in silence, shaking his head no, his hand still plastered over his mouth.

*Tick ... tick ... tick ... tick...* Time swept forward at its steady pace, caring not for the comings and goings and doings of man, oblivious and indifferent to the truth that had just been revealed. Unwinding ... and running out.

## Chapter 29
## END of the BEGINNING

**8:48 p.m. – 10:14 p.m.**

### 1

Emma leaned forward, her eyes drawn to the box on her lap. The story of her father's visit to that house was chilling enough. Thoughts of what might be revealed inside the box frightened her. She suddenly felt older, more tired and worn down. It felt to her as if she'd lived a lifetime in a single afternoon.

*Brrrring-brrrring. Brrrring-brrrring. Brrrr-*

Matt and Emma exchanged a questioning glance. Emma's hand hovered over the receiver for a moment, and then she plucked it from its charger. "Hello?" No one spoke. "Hello?" The line suddenly filled with static, which was quickly replaced by a high pitched squeal. She snapped her thumb down on the OFF button and the phone went silent. Just before she settled it back in its cradle, a voice filled her head.

"Don't hang up. Don't hang up; we're still connected."

Emma raised the phone back to her ear. Silence, not even the sound of static.

"Can you hear me? Are you there, Emma?"

Emma suddenly realized the voice was not coming from the phone. The voice was in her head. She closed her eyes and thought: "*I can hear you, Janet. But you're-*"

*"Not really on the phone,"* finished Janet. *"I know, but don't hang it up or we might lose each other. I don't know how long we can hold our connection, so just listen. I'm on my way. I'm on my way back to you, and I have Tommy Vorland with me. Don't leave, don't go to the house until we get there. We-"*

Another loud burst of static crackled from the receiver and the line went dead again, this time, it took the connection between Janet and Emma with it.

Emma hung up the phone and turned to Matt. "Did you get any of that?"

He shook his head. "No, but I know who it was, and I know what you heard did not come from the phone. You were connected, weren't you?"

"Yes. She said she was on her way here with Tommy Vorland.

"Tommy Vorland? How could that be? He's ... he's ... as far as I know ... he's been locked up in some mental hospital down in Philadelphia. How could she possibly be bringing him? And ... well, even if she somehow could ... do you think he'd agree to going back in there? It doesn't make sense to me."

"All I know is that's what she said. She's on her way with Tommy and told me we're not to go to the house until they get here."

Matt let out a little chuckle. "I guess there's still some kind of link between all of us if she knows what we're planning. But it's still kind of funny if you think about it. A bunch of old people coming together to do what? Battle evil forces? Save the day? Hell, we don't even really know what the hell we're doing – what we're getting into – just some intangible feeling that we have to put an end to whatever that house is about. Do we have a plan? Nope. Hell, we don't even have youth on our side anymore. And even with all that..." Matt looked at Emma and smiled. "Even with all that, we're still going to try to do something. Who knows, maybe we'll get lucky. Maybe God really does protect fools."

"Do you really feel that way, Matt? Do you really think we're fools?"

"Perhaps, but at least we're brave fools. And even without a plan, even without our youth, we're the ones that have to do whatever it is that has to be done. I know it; you know it, and, apparently, so do Janet and Tommy. If ... if we can believe that ... it actually was Janet speaking to you?"

A puzzled look took over Emma's features. "What do you mean, *if* it was Janet? Who else could it have been? Who else but someone connected to us ... to you ... could have known what we're planning?"

Matt shrugged. "The house is evil. Or, if not evil in itself, there's some kind of evil in it. Whichever, I guess, doesn't matter. But I'd bet my bottom dollar that it isn't a weak evil, and I'd be willing to bet my life that ... if it somehow has an inkling that we're trying to stop it ... well, I don't think it's just going to throw up its hands or whatever and surrender. Perhaps ... just perhaps, Janet's call was its way of stopping us from coming, or at least delaying us. I don't know. But we should probably consider the possibility that it's strong enough to throw curves at us at the very least."

"So, what do you think we should do?" she asked, pulling her eyes away from the box and back to Matt's "Do we wait, or do we go?"

"I think we should do exactly what we're doing. Go ahead, open the box."

Emma drew in a deep breath, picked up the box and laid it on her lap. There was a soft click as she twisted the key, and the lid popped up a fraction of an inch. With her thumbs on the corners, she lifted it open, her eyes fixed on Matt's. When she looked down into the box, a hollowness grew within her chest, as if a great, unseen vacuum had sucked out her very being. Tears welled up in her lower lids. The last words her father had spoken to her were of the contents that now lay at her fingertips. They stabbed at her brain like an ice pick fashioned of a warning she had been too foolish to acknowledge: "*If ... if for any reason we never get to finish this conversation ... you go to that box.*" If we never get to finish. Did he know? Was she too dense to listen?

"Emma," Matt laid a gentle hand on top of hers, "are you all right? Are you sure you want do to his, now?"

An embarrassed and conciliatory laugh escaped her. "Sorry ... I was just ... just-"

"Thinking of Henry ... of your father." He squeezed her hand and then gave it a light pat. "I guess I'm supposed to say it'll be okay, and I'd really like to. But I'm not at all sure that will be the case. What I can say ... what I *will* tell you ... is that if we have any hope of getting through this, whatever your father left for us in that box is going to be needed. At least ... at least I hope so. I hope he left us something we can use, because I really have no clue as to what we're supposed to do. Your father ... and mother ... were the ones that got us through and out safe all those years ago. Let's hope that whatever magic and wisdom they'd had then has been handed down in some fashion."

Emma nodded and wiped at her eyes. Very carefully, she removed everything in the box, one item at a time and laid them on the table between them. When the box was empty, she closed the lid and set it on the floor at her feet. More than a little surprised, Matt and Emma stared at the small box with Tommy's name printed on it. Emma coughed and said: "Maybe, if Janet and Tommy are truly on their way, maybe we should wait for them to go through this stuff."

Matt thought for a moment, studying Emma from the corner of his eye. An almost imperceptible smile played across his lips. In this light, there was no denying that Amy and Emma were mother and daughter. He could see the battle raging in her between fear and strength, and he had no doubt which was going to win.

## 2

Emma got up and started pacing.

"Are you all right?" asked Matt.

"I'm sorry. I guess I'm just a little on edge. Aside from all this, I still haven't heard from Annabel or Brian."

Matt rubbed at his chin. "Why don't you try giving her a call again? I'll make us some coffee. Much as I'm enjoying the liquor, I think maybe we should have our heads on straight for the act of lunacy we're about to commit."

That made Emma give out with a little laugh, and Matt could see some of the tension wash away. Her shoulders, which had been hunched up around her ears, dropped down and the tightness in her features softened, as she dropped back into the chair.

"Do you like your coffee strong?" he asked, pushing up out of the chair.

"I can make it." She started to rise and Matt gently pushed her back down.

"I'll make the coffee. You try to reach Annabel or Brian."

"Strong is good."

"Ata girl. Can't stand weak coffee. You take it black, right?"

Emma nodded and reached for the phone.

"I'll be back in a jiff," said Matt.

Emma dialed Annabel's number. It rang three times, then a deep voice said, "They're here with me. We're having a hauntingly good Halloween. Why don't you and the old geezer join us for some fun?" And the line went dead.

As if she had just hung up from talking to an old friend, Emma set the phone back in its base. She smoothed out her dress and let her eyes wander to the stuff on the table. Her mind also wandered. She wasn't quite sure what she *should* be feeling: fear? ... concern? ... disbelief? She only knew that what she *did* feel was a sudden well of anger, bordering on rage. Someone or something was playing games with her daughter, and it took all her strength to stay sitting in the chair and not go charging off to that house. That would be a mistake, and she knew it. That simple understanding made her realize that what she'd just heard on the phone had been a taunt, a morsel of bait. She forced herself to remain seated, despite the desperate need she felt to do something. Sitting idle and waiting was the hardest thing she'd had to do all day, and this day had been filled with impossibly hard things.

"Here we go," said Matt, coming back with the coffee. "Piping hot, black and strong enough to pour itself." He grinned a sad grin as he handed her a cup. "Did you get ahold of Annabel or Brian?"

Emma shook her head. "No. I got the house, or whatever it is that thinks is running the show." She sat forward and clenched her fists in her lap.

Matt almost dropped his coffee. "Wh-what?"

"Whatever answered Belle's phone told me they ... or it ... had them, Brian and Annabel, and then invited us, me and you, to come and play."

"Christ! It's trying to scare us. And I can't say it isn't working." Matt's hands were shaking and he had to steady his cup with both of them.

"No. I don't think so." Emma's face was a mask of determination. "I think it's just the opposite. I think it wanted us to run over there willy-nilly and unprepared. It's hard to explain, but I got the distinct sense that whatever it is, *it's* the one that's afraid."

Matt set his coffee cup down and laughed, a long hearty laugh. When he stopped, he wiped at his eyes and looked into Emma's. "Well, in my book, there's no doubting that you're Amy's and Henry's daughter. By God, if you didn't just sound like your father. And the look on your face ... it was like looking back in time at your mother when she barked at me about helping with the door that squa ... you know ... Lucy."

This time it was Emma's turn to laugh, though not quite as boisterously. She knew exactly what look Matt was talking about. Quite a few of her childhood antics had garnered that look.

"Let's see if Henry's left us some wisdom," said Matt.

Emma drew a deep sigh and sat. She glanced at the box with Tommy's name on it, pushed it aside and picked up the bundle of papers. She unfolded them and smoothed them out on her lap. It was almost too much for her. Her father's words stared up at her in line after voiceless line. She let her fingers glide over the page, as if she could feel the essence of his touch, the essence of him, in the print. In doing so, an odd thought crossed her mind. Was this how Hamlet felt when he gazed upon his father's spirit on those cold Danish ramparts? She smiled, and started scanning through the papers. What she needed to find was the spot where Matt's story ended and her father's and mother's began.

"Here it is," she said, her finger stopping on a line partway down the third page. She began to read: "I am ashamed of what I must tell next. Though I was not myself, I cannot escape culpability for my weakness, for being unable to resist, for not having been stronger."

Emma wiped a tear from the corner of her eye, and Matt gently pulled the papers from her hand. "Here, let me," he said, and continued.

"After the wall sealed the rest of our group out, a greenish mist began to seep up out of the floor. Tendrils of it, like octopus tentacles, curled around my legs and crawled up my body. I was unable to move. It soaked into me, and I was no longer alone within my mind.

Worse, I was no longer in control. *He* was. I ... we ... walked over and looked at Amy, still in Tommy's grasp. What I didn't know, at least at this point ... though he did ... was that Tommy had been taken the moment he'd fallen into the room, taken by something truly evil and lecherous – an incubus. He stood there grinning at Amy and said to her: *'Welcome to the party, Amy.'*

### 3

"*... the party, Amy,*'" said Tommy. His eyes were as vacant as the look on his face. And the grin he wore was unnatural, a caricature of a human smile. "Torrance and I have been waiting for you. We thought you'd never get here."

Amy's heart jumped into her throat. Henry's face was in flux. One second it looked like Henry, the next like some old man whose flesh was slowly rotting off the bone.

"What shall we do first?" asked Tommy. He grabbed Amy by the throat and hair and wrestled her to the floor. Despite her best efforts, she couldn't break his grip. Her lips were beginning to blue. Tommy sniffed along the length of her body. When he finished, he loosened his grip enough to allow her to breathe. "She's perfect. The bitch is a virgin."

Henry grinned. "Then she's just what we need."

Tommy yanked Amy to her feet by her hair, ignoring her struggling and screams of pain. He forced her down onto her back on the cot and started to manacle her wrists.

"No! The altar," barked Henry in Wickersham's voice. "Chain her to the altar. That is where we must have her." His eyes wandered to the emptying hourglass. "The time is neigh. Before the midnight hour comes, our fusion must be complete and she must be inseminated."

Tommy yanked Amy off the cot. As he dragged her toward the altar, he began to change. Hair fell from his head in clumps. His chest and thighs expanded, growing more muscular. Bat-like wings sprouted from his shoulder blades and a scaled tail with a serpent's head at the end uncoiled behind him. What grew between his legs made Amy whimper with fright. By the time they reached the altar his metamorphosis was complete. With one clawed hand around her throat, he pinned her against the cold stone slab and tore the clothes from her body with the other. He lifted her as if she were a rag doll and slammed her onto the altar on her back. The air rushed from her lungs in a single whoosh! She gulped at the air, tiny points of light swimming around behind her eyes, while the beast shackled her, spread-eagle on the cold slab. Rivulets of green slime oozed from the corners of his mouth and plopped onto her face and breasts as he drooled over here body. The arched claws of his fingers raked her thighs as his serpent's tail lightly toyed with her womanhood.

"Prepare," said Henry/Wickersham. He moved to the altar and stood over her. The beast sprang up and straddled their helpless victim. He crouched over her, eager to take her. His hands gripped her shoulders, as he rocked his pulsing member back and forth against her belly. A thick greenish fluid oozed from the tip of it and glistened against the smooth whiteness of her skin.

Amy's strength and will to fight were ebbing away. The feel of the beast on her flesh made her insides turn over. She struggled to keep control, to maintain her sanity against the unthinkable horror to come.

Henry/Wickersham grinned down at her, glanced at the hourglass and raised his hands. No more than a fistful of sand remained. "It is time for the fusion." He began the incantation. Beneath the altar, the baby in the glass box screamed and thrashed around. Its skin shriveled and reformed, turning first yellow, then a sickening brown and finally gray. The apex of its heart pulsed wildly in and out of the gaping hole in the left side of its chest. The flames of the torches that studded the walls licked at the ceiling and then shrank away to thin ribbons of white. The room filled with shadow and Henry began to convulse, his jerking movements, as well as his flesh, mimicking those of the baby. The demon crouching over Amy arched its back, threw back it head and shoulders and bellowed out a piercing howl.

The air grew hot and sticky. The walls undulated like waves of heat off hot asphalt. Amy screamed as the thing astride her grew translucent, its pulsing member grown to its full length and thickness. Henry staggered backwards. Filaments of red fire sprang up around his legs and spiraled upward. As they reached the top of his head they shot across to the demon and spiraled around him, moving from top to bottom. When they reached its clawed feet, they disappeared and Henry slumped to the floor. Wickersham and beast were one.

"We are one," growled the beast in Wickersham's voice. "It is time for the mating." He grabbed Amy by the shoulders and angled his member toward its virginal target. "You will give us the child of our immortality."

The room suddenly filled with the scent of honeysuckle. The hourglass exploded. A bright blue ring of fire rose from the floor, the white-gowned figure of an old woman shimmering within it.

"Dis girl not gon' be yours. Der still 'nough magic left in Mot'er t'stop dis."

The Wickersham beast jumped off the altar, spread its wings to their full height and width and strode toward the encircled woman. "You do not have the power to end this. You are no match for us. Together we are stronger than whatever silly charms you think you have left. Three hundred years ago we defeated you by combining the evil of the man and power of the demon. Nothing has changed. You cannot kill us."

Mother laughed. "Dat part be true. But Mot'er strong 'nough for dis ... *an'* ... you don't have de witch dat help you last time wit' you now. Dis not be de fight of fights; dat gon' come. An' de girl ... she is and is not de one dat gon' finish all dis."

"More foolish riddles. Useless ... like before." The beast grabbed for Mother and its hand burst into flame at the touch of the blue rings surrounding her. He drew it back and howled in pain and anger. "Arrrgh! The girl will not survive. She will deliver unto us the child of immortality and our use and need for her will end upon its delivery."

Mother closed her eyes and raised her hands, palms out.

"Beast and man wit' wings of flight. Mot'er's power hol' you tight."

Sparkling filaments of blazing blue light wrapped around the demon incubus in the shape of a glowing net. The thing howled out its rage in multiple, overlapping voices: Tommy's, Wickersham's, the incubus's.

"T'de boy in de beast whose mind must dare hide,
"Mot'er command you to step from inside."

The glowing net surrounding the demon incubus began to pulse faster and faster. The room filled with a vibrating hum. The beast wailed in agony. Its body rippled and bulged. Gaping fissures spread across its chest and up its arms. As it sank to its knees, the ghostly shape of Tommy Vorland stepped out of it, solidified and dropped to the floor.

Mother's hands dropped to her side. She staggered backwards and just barely managed to keep her feet. She was tired, worn out. The net surrounding the beast began to thin and pale. Her time was running out, but she was not done yet. Steeling herself, she drew on what remained of her strength and concentrated.

"Love is de t'ing dat free de soul.
"An' power be given to de one dat is bold
"Shake off your slumber, de dark of de night,
"An' reclaim de one wit' whom you'll unite."

Henry groaned, rolled over and slowly picked himself up off the floor. His legs wobbled, his vision was blurry. He felt as if he'd awakened with the world's worst hangover. Worse than that, though, he remembered everything he'd said and done. The thought of having betrayed and attacked Amy made him feel sicker than he already did. And the sight of her bound to the altar infuriated him. He tugged and pulled and clawed at the chains that held her tight until his fingers bled, but they held firm.

Mother, worried about her weakening power, concentrated on the incantation and hoped the net would hold the beast long enough for her to finish. The beast growled and roared and slashed at the weakly pulsing net, tearing small threads of it apart. It was now a race and Mother drew on everything she had.

"Chain ain't as strong as what live in de heart.
"A love dat is true c'n break dem apart."

Henry's chest tightened and his whole body felt as if he were standing on the third rail. His hands took on a blue glow, and when he laid his fingers on the manacles around Amy's wrists they shattered like a rose dipped in liquid nitrogen. He lifted her off the table and covered her in his shirt, squeezing her tight against his chest.

Mother turned toward Tommy, who was still lying on the floor, his hands over his face.

"Diamond or ruby or emerald or pearl,
"De mark on de boy mus' go to de girl.
"When de mind locked up come roun' t'de call,
"Fire and staff bring an end to it all."

Mother cupped her hands together and squeezed. When she opened them, a multi-faceted jewel rose from her palms. Arcs of red and green fire danced within it. It hovered for a moment and then shot forward, whizzing past the almost free demon. It struck Tommy in the upper arm and disappeared into his flesh, leaving behind what looked like a blue-white tattoo of itself.

Mother dropped to her knees, spent. The blue circles of her protection dissipated. Tommy screamed in momentary pain, and the demon beast tore through its prison. It lunged at Mother, bellowing out its rage and triumph. Razor sharp talons tore into her face, ripping the flesh from the bone. Mother screamed, but it was choked off as the beast seized her by the throat and lifted her into the air. A smile broke across mother's lips, and the beast lost its hold on her as it clapped it hands over its ears. Its head was full of her voice.

*Mot'er be but a shadow of Mot'er. You know dat. De hands be free but de rest still lie where you put her. De shadow fading, dat be true. But dat part of de shadow dat live in de light gon' send you below an' lock you up tight.*

The beast howled and its fury poured out. Slash after slash after slash ripped at the image of the old woman, passing through her as if she were air. Mother laughed and held out her hands, palms up. The fingers curled inward and then sprang open. A ball of blue-green fire rose, growing larger and larger. It enveloped the beast and drove it back. When it reached the altar, the ball bulged outward and swallowed the box and baby. The glass dissolved. A moment later, the man-beast exploded into a green powder with a screaming howl of anguish. The powder, the essence of Wickersham's and the demon's combined evil, was drawn into the baby. The floor split open and ball and baby plunged into the opening.

"Dis room gon' be sealed and de prison be made.
"Hold man-beast an' child till de las' price be paid.
"New generations full must elapse.
"Den all de evil rise to collapse.
"Mot'er an' daughter and daughter again,
"Are destined to bring all o'dis to an end.

Mother moved toward Henry, a shimmering aura of blue surrounding her. Henry took a step back and Amy rushed to his arms.

"Don' be afraid, children. Mot'er on your side. You two gon be ... an' not gon' be ... de ones to bring dis all to its end." She reached down and snapped off the little finger of her left hand and held it out. "Dis be de key dat keep dis room locked till de generation time come around. You take it, boy. It fall to you t'keep de secret o'dis place."

Henry shook his head. "No. I ... I don't want to touch that thing."

"Want got not'in' t'do wit' it. Besides..." Mother laughed. "It gon' show you de way out, so you take it. When you leave dis room, lock de wall wit' it ... you'll know how."

Henry took the bone from her with two fingers and a grimace of disgust. The old woman smiled and faded away like windblown smoke.

Behind them, the block slabs moved toward each other, sealing the opening in the floor and locking the baby-man-beast within. The whole house shook with the force of an earthquake. Windows blew out on every floor. Dust and debris rained from the cracks, and the secret passage in the wall through which they had come in opened up. Matt, Janet and Tina stood outside, their hands clasped together, their lips moving silently.

"Help me with Tommy," yelled Henry.

Amy grabbed Tommy under one arm, and Henry the other. Three seconds later, Matt was beside them. As they got him to his feet, Henry heard mother's voice in his head for the last time.

*Mot'er gon' help you, but for everyt'ing there be a price. T'lead dem all out you mus' leave dem behind. When de time com' roun' for de rejoining, your time com' t'say goodbye. A life t'give life. Agree ... an' Mot'er's finger show you de way out. It grow de flowers dat only you can see. Back t'de beginning dey will lead.*

"I agree," said Henry, and instantly a ring of honeysuckle grew around the bony finger.

"Agree to what?" asked Matt.

"Never mind. Get Tommy out into the hall." Even as he spoke, the ring of honeysuckle sent out its vine. It spread rapidly across the floor and out into the hall. The sweet scent of it swamped the house.

"Come on, everyone; we're getting out of here. Follow me." Henry followed the unseen, snaking trail of honeysuckle the others couldn't see out into the hall. The house shook again as the stone wall closed up behind him. A circle of honeysuckle flowers surrounded a small hole in one of the blocks. Henry gently slipped the tip of Mother's finger into it. A burst of light traced the outline of the secret door's opening and disappeared. He withdrew the finger, turned and followed the snaking honeysuckle that only he could see up the stairs. At the middle landing the vine turned and disappeared into the wall. Henry drew a deep breath. Everyone held hands. Matt wrapped an arm around Tommy's waist and grabbed Janet with his free hand. Janet took Tina's hand and Amy took Henry's.

"Okay," said Henry. "I know you'll think I'm crazy but we're getting out, right here. The only way it will work is if you close your eyes and follow the leader. Trust me."

"We do," said Amy, not giving anyone a chance to speak. "Lead on."

The group closed their eyes and Henry stepped toward the block. He passed through as if it were a doorway. The others followed. When they opened their eyes, they were standing outside beside the well where their journey had begun.

"I don't believe it," said Matt. "I have to ... *but I don't*"

## 4

"'... *but I don't*.'" Matt stopped reading and let Henry's letter fall to his lap. He sat back in his chair and wiped at his eyes. Emma had her hands to the sides of her face. Neither of them spoke for a long time. Finally, Matt sat forward and picked up the letter.

"There's only a little left; I guess we should finish."

Emma couldn't speak, so Matt began to read.

"That is the story as far as it goes for me. What is to come for those of you I leave behind I can't say. I cannot be with you. I wish I could, but there is a bargain to be honored. I now know, as I write this, my time is short.

"To my darling and loving daughter: I love you more than anything. Do not grieve for me. Be strong, for I have a feeling that you, too, may have a part to play. My only hope is that wherever it is one goes when he leaves this earth, they don't make you drink decaffeinated coffee, give you margarine instead of butter and there's plenty of bacon.

"To my most precious granddaughter: Annabel, you have always been the heart that beats within my heart. If you ever believed in anything, believe in this – I am (was, if you're reading this) not senile. That house is evil. Please, please let it go – for your sake, for Brian's sake and for your mother's sake. Please do not disregard the story I have told here.

"To Brian: Take care of my granddaughter the way I know you will. You are a good man, and I do not believe Annabel could have done better.

"I love you all. Henry."

Emma wiped the hot tears from her cheeks and stood up. "Whatever it takes, this ends tonight. I don't care if I have to fight the devil himself. This has taken my father from me. It will not take my daughter." She looked at the time. "We'll give Janet and Tommy fifteen more minutes. Then I'm going to that house and finish this. Are you coming with me?"

Matt rose. "I'm old. I'm tired and worn out. I'm also afraid. I've been in that place before. But I am not going to let Henry's sacrifice be dishonored. And I am *certainly not* going to let you go there alone. Besides, in my line of work I've laid more people to rest than I can count. It's high time I laid this mess to rest as well. One last adventure for Matthew Holloway."

Emma picked up the little leather pouch from the table, pulled the drawstring open and dumped the finger bone into her hand. "I don't know whether or not we'll need this, but better safe than sorry."

## Chapter 30
## UNION

**7:50 p.m. – 9:52 p.m.**

Brian held out his glass of scotch, Annabel her vodka. They clinked them together.

"Cheers/Cheers."

The spectral essence of the incubus laid its hands on Annabel's hips, slid them up her sides and cupped her breasts, imparting its lust, its need to be satisfied. Annabel shivered and then flushed, feeling suddenly warm all over. She found herself wanting Brian more than she ever had in her life. She needed him to touch her, to take her – to *use* her.

After they each downed a healthy gulp, Brian threw an arm around Annabel's waist and drew her in. His kiss, light but sensual, sent a shiver coursing through Annabel's body. Brian pulled her even closer, feeling his member stiffing against her thigh. Annabel felt it too, and smiled.

"Are you trying to get me drunk so you can take advantage of me, mister? Because if you are, I have to tell you ... it just might work. You know how horny I get when I drink."

Brian placed an index finger on the bottom of her glass and pushed it up to her lips. "Drink up, baby. I promise I'll still respect you in the morning."

Annabel put her hand on top of Brian's drink and pushed it down. "Well, if you're making promises of sexual advances, you'd better go easy on this stuff. You know what they say about the spirit being willing and the alcoholic flesh being weak. Trust me, weak flesh is not a girl's best friend. And ... it certainly doesn't improve a guy's reputation."

"Don't you worry your pretty little head about that, darling. I'll rock your world." He slowly nudged her backward toward the couch. When her calves bumped up against it, he tipped her drink up and held it to her lips until it was gone. As he took the glass from her hand, he pushed her down onto the couch with a nudge of his shoulder. "Why don't you rid yourself of some of those unnecessary clothes you're wearing and I'll freshen our drinks. You can leave the shirt but lose the bra. You always look so inviting like that."

"You're a pig; but sometimes I like that about you."

Brian began to refill their glasses and stopped in mid-pour. A bitter chill raked through his body and he shivered. It seemed to move through him from head to toe and then – it felt as if whatever it was sank right into him, as if his body had absorbed it, like water drawn into a dry sponge. His eyes fogged over. Something was pushing at his mind, shoving his consciousness into some mental storage compartment. That personal, amorphous something that makes us the individuals we are was, for him, being locked away. Something – someone – else was taking control. But it was still his body and he felt every sensation his unknown marionette forced upon him. Whatever or whoever was in control finished pouring the drinks and walked back over to Annabel. He set their glasses on the coffee table and leaned over her and took her face in his hands, inveigling her to look into his eyes, eyes that looked as if they'd been chiseled from coal and imbued with swirling motes of fire.

"You feel very hot, now. Don't you, darling? You need to be touched; your desire can not be checked. You must entertain me, mustn't you? Entertain me! You know what I want to see." His eyes bored into her, mingling with the implanted desire of the incubus, sapping her own will.

Unable to stop herself, she deftly removed her bra without taking off her shirt. She tossed it onto the floor, laid back on the couch with her back against the armrest and one arm hooked behind her head. Her body felt like it was on fire. She couldn't remember ever having been so aroused, so in need of sex. She arched her back, her nipples poking little mountains into her t-shirt. With her eyes closed, she dropped her hands to her hips and worked her jeans down to her thighs.

Brian watched helplessly from some sequestered part of his brain as his wife's fingers moved inside her panties and she toyed with herself, moaning lightly. He savored her every movement, an uncontrollable lust building within him. His penis stiffened as her hips began to move in rhythm with her fingers and her moaning grew louder. And when she climaxed and lay there panting heavily, he slipped his hand down his pants.

"Again!" he commanded. "Remove your pants and entertain me again."

Annabel sat up and wiggled her pants all the way off and placed her hand between her legs.

"Remain standing and entertain me. Tease me with your body until I can no longer resist."

Horrified, Annabel found herself standing in front of him, her fingers curled into her vagina. Words she couldn't stop poured out of her mouth. "You want this, don't you? I know you do. I can feel your lust. But you can't have me ... here. You know where you must take me. You must ... mus-must ... *make* me pleas-pleasure you-oooo." Her legs came together as she climaxed. The force of it knocked her to her knees.

Deep within herself, Annabel heard the same soft and reassuring voice that had led her to the house.

"*Dis be a hard t'ing you have to face now, girl. But it gon' all come out irey, long as you trust in Mot'er. Ain't no harm gon' com' t'you. Mot'er won' permit dat. She gon' send you someone to help. But you got t'be strong for now. What gon' happen won' be pleasant. Just remember dat ... in de end, even t'ough he ain't himself, it was only your man dat touch you.*"

Brian lunged forward. His hands flew out, one closing on Annabel's throat, the other entangling itself in her hair. He jerked her off her feet and dragged her across the living room. When she fell, he mercilessly tugged and pulled her across the floor. As they entered the turret library, the house shifted and the new construction fell away. The polished walnut spiral staircase was now a solid stone staircase. He dragged her over to the steps and started down, yanking her along, the whole time growing more and more aroused as she choked and gasped for air.

At the bottom, he let go of her throat long enough to push in the small square stone that sat among the larger ones in the wall. Nothing happened. Two voices suddenly filled his head. "Touch it, Brian. Lay your hands and heart and soul against the stone. Join us. We will make you strong. You already feel our power within you. Touch the wall and release us, and we'll release your passion in ways you've never dreamed of. You've already tasted but the edge of the desire we can give you. Look at the bitch that must serve your every sexual need. Want her! Know that she is but a toy to be used. Touch the wall and join us Brian."

Brian threw Annabel to the floor and laid his palms against the wall. The hidden stone door slid open. He pulled her to her feet with a vicious yank of her hair, and with a twist of his arm, spun her into the darkened chamber. The force of it sent her stumble-stepping sideways until she lost her balance and fell hard on her side, knocking what little breath she had out of her.

Brian screamed inside his head, trying to force his body to stop. It paid no attention. It wanted what it was about to be given. He crossed the room in two quick strides, yanked Annabel to her feet and threw her down on the bare wooden cot that stood against the left wall. The sound of the manacles clicking together on her wrists and ankles sent a shiver of pleasure coursing through his body, and a sense of revulsion through that part of him that was still his own. His mind recoiled as his hands reached out and tore Annabel's shirt open.

"When the summoning is complete and the union fulfilled, we will move you to the altar and fill your belly with the vessel of my immortality."

Annabel screamed and the sexual desire the incubus had imparted vanished, leaving behind only fear and horror. Brian's face rippled as the bones beneath reshaped themselves. The face that now gazed down upon her bore pock-marked gray flesh that dangled in strands from the bones within. Tangles of white hair hung from the head in random clusters. Bony and partially denuded fingers of blackish flesh squeezed her breasts and toyed with her nipples. Thick, yellow drool oozed from the corners of his mouth, plopping down on her chest and face.

"Please stop this, Brian," she pleaded. "Please, please, please-"

Brian slapped a hand over her mouth and pinched her nose closed.

"I like to watch your breasts rise and fall as you struggle for air. I enjoy watching your beautiful legs struggle against your bonds. Fight. Fight for your next breath and entertain me with the thrashing of your body. Draw my lust out of me until I must have you."

Things began to gray and her chest burned. Just before she lost complete consciousness, Brian released his grip. The sound of her wheezing as she gulped air brought him to a full erection.

"I so want you, my dear. I would take you this very minute ... but I must contain myself." He ran his tongue up the side of her cheek, balled up a handkerchief and gagged her with it. Satisfied, he straightened up and walked away.

Annabel could hear him mumbling something from somewhere behind her. Tears spilled from her eyes, her whole body wracked with fear. Suddenly a feeling of warmth washed over her. She closed her eyes and was no longer bound to a bed in a musty dungeon room. For a brief flicker of time, she found herself lying on her back in a field of flowers, the sun gently caressing her skin with its radiance, the flowers filling her lungs with the sweetest smell she'd ever known.

"*Mot'er send you to de nice place for a bit so she can tell you what need t'be done. De hard part comin', child. Mot'er gon' help, t'ough. Mot'er gave you a precious gift t'help. Breat' in deep ... an' let m'child come forth. She always been part o'you.*" There was a deep sadness in the voice in Annabel's head, a hurt that was palpable. "*You an' my Abigail ... you both get t'rough dis ordeal. Mot'er promise, you bot' gon' be irey. The time is comin' for dis all t'end, child. Be strong.*"

A blistering chill filled the room, accompanied by the sweet smell of honeysuckle. Frost formed on the iron cuffs and crawled along the chains. It slowly melted away and the room grew warm again. Annabel opened her eyes and she was there. A young, light-skinned black woman, who looked to be in her late teens and was no more solid than a pane of glass, stood gazing down at her. She was dressed in a long white gown that appeared to have been ripped or cut open. She raised a finger to her lips, and then floated upward.

Inside her head, Annabel heard the voiceless words of the ghost before her. "Always been wit' you since your birt', livin' in de shadow of your soul. Now is my time to come forward for what is t'com'. Time for you t'hide in de shadows till all is done." She stretched herself out as if she were lying down, drifted over top of Annabel and slowly descended. Annabel drew in a single, gasping breath and the specter sank into her. She felt herself sinking away, disappearing into the void of her own being, as Abigail rose to the forefront of her consciousness.

Brian returned carrying an array of objects of various sizes and shapes. He laid them out on the bed beside Annabel, bent down and ran his tongue across her lips. When he straightened up, he picked up something that looked like the end of a fat broom handle, studded with blunted spikes.

"We have some time to kill, my lovely, before I can have you." He leaned in close, his hot, putrid breath clogging her nostrils. "Yes, some time, indeed, before I am permitted to have you. However, that does not mean I can't enjoy myself in the interim. As you can see, I've brought us some toys to play with. I'll bet you can guess where I'm going to put this, can't you?"

The toys suddenly dropped from Brian's hand, clattering onto the floor. He threw back his head, his face flush with anger. "No! Nooooo! You fucking *bitch*!"

Wickersham stretched out his mind and found what he sought. Janet Egan and Tommy Vorland had just turned onto Route 10. They were coming; and they had to be stopped. He tried to force himself into Janet's mind and failed. The link between she and Tommy was too strong to overcome. Infuriated, he dug through Brian's mind searching for something useful. If he couldn't get to them, perhaps he could get to the unfamiliar machine that carried them. He found it. He concentrated on flames, tongues of raging fire surrounding the front of their horseless carriage. And within moments, the infernal metal beast began sputtering and hissing. In his mind, he saw a black tube split open and spew green liquid all over the mechanical heart that kept the beast moving. The thing was dying. He smiled, as he saw it slow, heard it clunk and chug and then stop.

Weak from having to send himself so far, he collapsed to his knees, exhausted.

## Chapter 31
## SECRETS REVEALED

**8:12 p.m. – 10:07 p.m.**

### 1

"No. No, no, no, no, no. It's ... it's not real. I just had too much to drink. This can't-"

Walcott reached across the table and grabbed Ralph's hand. "Easy, Ralph. It's real. It's real and it's okay. Calm y'self down."

Ralph tried to pull away but Walcott's grip was too strong. *Too strong? A few minutes ago the old man could barely lift his liquor glass. I must ... I must be hallucinating. He put something in my drink. That's it. He drugged-*

*Thawp*!

The sting of Walcott's fingers on his cheek shook Ralph from his contemplations. The man had moved faster than he'd ever seen him move in his life. One minute he had a vice grip on his hand, the next, wham! the cold sting of his fingers on his face.

"Sorry about that, Ralph." Walcott sat back in his chair, his palm flat on the table. "We ain't got the time for you to work this all out so's it makes sense to you. It ain't never gonna make sense, so just accept it and let's move on. Like I said, we ain't got a lot of time, and I'm gonna need your help. And *you* ... you got to be steady, Ralph."

Ralph rubbed lightly at the side of his face. Looking across at the young man sitting opposite him was hard; keeping from running out of there screaming was even harder. It was the look on his old (*old*?) friend's face that kept him in his chair. Sincerity. More even than that. Beneath that, in the depths of Walcott's eyes, Ralph saw the look of a man desperately pleading for help. He could almost hear his cries for help. Almost ... no. He could hear them. They ran through his head like a train through a dark tunnel, the pitiful wail of its whistle begging for deliverance from its dark journey.

*Help me, Ralph. I always been fair to you, always counted on you. You ain't never once shirked your duties. And, although this ain't technically your duty, I need you to stick with me to end all this. Can't do it without ya, Ralph. Please, I ain't never begged nothin' of nobody in my life. Never. But I'm beggin' you now. Please don't leave me to this all on my own, 'cause I ... 'cause I ain't got the strength to see it through alone.*

As much as his mind cried out for him to deny the reality of it all, to ignore the man's supplication, he couldn't. Walcott had been a friend to him for many years, and it just wasn't in Ralph to abandon a friend, no matter how absurd the situation seemed.

He drew a deep breath and folded his hands on the table in front of him, interlacing the fingers. "What do we have to do? How do we end this?"

"Sad part is," said Walcott, "I ain't exactly sure. I know we got t'go to that house, ain't no doubt about that. And believe me, I sure as hell don't wanna go there. Beyond that, I ain't got no true sense of what we gotta do when we get there." He paused, thought a moment and then added: "What I think, though, what I'm feelin' ... is that those kids, the ones that went into there all those years ago, they got some important part to play. I know, on top of everything else it sounds crazy for me t'sit here and tell you *this*, too. Somehow, somehow, I think they already know they got t'be a part of it, too.

"I think what you need t'do, Ralph is this. I want you to go pick up old lady Farley and bring her back here. Then we'll see about getting' to the house."

"Tina Farley? I thought you hated the Farleys?"

"Hate, love, like, trust, distrust ... ain't none of that matters. What matters is whether or not she'll come with ya. No matter how you do it, you got to convince her."

"But ... well, if you said that they already know they have to-"

"I did. And I think the others will come on their own. I think Farley knows she's got to come, too. I just got a feelin' that you got to go get her. There's lots of forces at play right now. There's fingers reachin' out in lots of directions from lots of sources, good and bad. You understand?"

Ralph nodded that he did. "What makes you think she'll even come with me? She knows you ... that you two aren't very friendly. Why would she come here?"

"I think she'll come, Ralph, because, like me, she knows she has to. Leastwise, I'm hopin' that's a good enough reason, 'cause I can't think of nothin' that'll persuade her if she stubborns up on us. But if she does, come hell or high water, truth or lie, you'll have to figure a way around that. You got to get here, Ralph. You got to. That's all I c'n say."

"I'll do my best, Mr. Walcott," said Ralph, pushing up out of his chair. I know it'll take me at least fifteen to twenty minutes there and the same back. Don't know how long it'll take to talk her into coming with me."

Walcott poured out two more shots. "I know I said we should be sober for this, but ain't got no way of tellin' how this is all gonna turn out." He raised his glass high. "So here's to you, Ralph. A true friend, a loyal friend and pret'near the only man I trust in this whole damned Hollow. Be swift; be smart ... and above all, come back safe."

They touched glasses, knocked back their drinks and Ralph left without another word.

## 2

Walcott let his eyes drift down to the few things that were left on the table from the box: two keys (one of bone, one of iron) and a small golden chalice. A line of sweat popped out along his hairline and a quick shiver rippled through him. Now that it had come to it, he wasn't so sure he was ready to go through with the sacrifice that would be demanded. All those years ago it had been easy to ignore the passage of time. There were so many years ahead that could be lived in ease. So many years. Yet, how fast they had flown. Now, sitting alone in the kitchen, Walcott contemplated the trick of time and what was to come. It seemed to him as if time itself were no more than a malicious prestidigitator promising true magic, but in the end delivering only a hollow illusion.

With his eyes fixed on the two keys, he found his finger closing instead on the chalice. He held it up, twisting it back and forth by its stem. His stomach knotted with the sense of revulsion he felt just holding it. He placed it on the table upside down and picked up the keys. The sense of revulsion he felt holding these was there, but not quite as strong as with the chalice.

"Christ!" he muttered, letting the keys slip from his fingers. "I don't know if I have the strength to do this."

The room abruptly filled with an overpowering smell of sweet honeysuckle. It was a smell with which he was all too familiar, as he was with its meaning. Without looking around, he said to the specter of woman he knew stood behind him: "You needn't worry; I'm scared. Very scared. Still, I know what I must do, what is expected of me ... and I will see it through."

"Mot'er ain't here t'judge you. Mot'er com' t'help. De time be comin'. De young ones ... dey gon' fulfill der role. Dey gon' bring Mot'er to herself 'gain." She moved forward and placed her ghostly hands on his shoulders.

Walcott twitched at the touch. Ice, burning ice that quickly shifted to warm softness. The sensation passed through his body and he could feel himself relax. His shoulders dropped and his head felt too heavy for his neck. The choking smell of honeysuckle thinned. His eyelids suddenly felt like lead and dropped over his eyes.

"Mot'er com' 'cause she know what you need now. You rest calm. Ask de questions dat be at de heart o'de confusion you feel ... de questions dat be at de heart o'your fear."

"Grandmother, when I do this ... when I give what must be given ... what will happen to me?"

"De universe has many levels, child. Some of dem we see wit' our eyes, touch wit' our hands and hear wit' our ears. Some of dem are woven too deep for de mortal parts of us to recognize. Even de scientists of today, de ones dat don' believe in de ways and likes of me, dey know dat energy is eternal. Dey know dat it change forms but don' never go away. De soul is eternal energy, child. You only gon' move from one world to anot'er."

"Why now? Why have we waited so long to make things right, waited so long to release my mother from her suffering?"

"All t'ings move at der own pace and follow der own pat'. When t'ings were set in motion all dem many years ago, de rhythm of time dat enfolded us, dat we moved t'rough and dat moved t'rough us began to tic out a separate time. It was like de settin' of a stopwatch. De hand dat set dat watch in motion was de hand of Obatala, de Sky Fat'er. He de one dat made you an' your brot'er twins. He de one dat give you bot' the misshapen form in which you came forth. Dat was not de curse you t'ought it was. It is what saved you. On dat Halloween night, your half of de twins came out o'your mot'er second, on de stroke of midnight ... at de time when de night change to de morning of de saints and purity. Isaac was born to dis world when de evil spirits held der most power an' was swallowed up by dat curs-ed man. It is now time for you to reclaim your brot'er."

Mother Cassandra lifted her hands from Walcott's shoulders and his eyes fluttered open. His body felt somehow rejuvenated and washed out at the same time.

When he could finally focus, he saw on the table before him a walking stick of some kind, though shorter than one would expect. Beside it, the chalice he had turned on its head sat upright.

"You will not be alone in dis. De young ones from all dem years past, de ones dat awakened Mot'er, will play out de rest of der destinies. One of dem, who is not one of dem, has de power t'use what I have given you. You must give dis *only* to de one who can use it. It must go to no ot'er ... or all will be lost."

"How will I know who-"

Before he could finish asking, the sickening sweet smell of honeysuckle choked off his words. When the room cleared, he knew she was gone. He drew a sigh and bent his attention to the stick on the table. It was black and knotty along its length. One end came to a gentle point, the other bore a thick rounded prominence. At the very center of this prominence was a hollowed out area, as if it had at one time been occupied by something that had been lost.

*"It is time for you to go to dat house, now, child. Your pat' is known to you."* The voice that filled his head came with a dark image of a thin path that ran through the woods behind his house. *"Walk quickly an' wit' a sharp eye. Like Mot'er, his power be growin', too. He tried once wit' dem foul birds t'take your soul. Mot'er stop him dat time wit' de sky fire. Dis time ... you must be de one dat keep him from gettin' what he want."*

Walcott got up and went to the bedroom. At the foot of the bed he knelt down, reached under and pulled out a rectangular wooden box. He undid the clasp and lifted the lid. Wrapped in several folds of purple velvet lay a long silver chain. At the end of the chain, a sickle-moon shaped medallion glittered brilliant white, its outer edge pulsing a thin line of blue. Walcott slipped the looped chain over his head and let the medallion drop down the front of his shirt. He closed up the box, slid it back under the bed and walked to the bathroom.

For a long time he studied the features of the man that stared back at him from the mirror, searching for any sign of his Jamaican lineage, any vestige of his mother's heritage. He found none. The eyes that gazed back at him were bright blue. Against the white of his cheeks they seemed almost to shine with some unnatural inner light. What (for a long time now) had been a balding pate was now covered in thick brown hair, smooth and fine as brown silk. A flicker of anger shot through him, and he watched the lips of the man before him curl into a snarl as his fist shattered the mirror.

"Damn you, Wickersham! *DAMN YOU!*"

He moved to the closet, pulled out an old, green canvas back pack and went back to the kitchen and laid it on the table. After tossing in the chalice and what was left of the bourbon he closed the flap. With only one hand, it took a bit of work to get the straps buckled. When he finally got the prongs seated in their respective holes, he slung the pack over his shoulder, picked up the two keys, dropped them in his pants pocket and hefted the walking stick off the table. The weight of it surprised him, and just the touch of it imparted a sense of security. He tapped the end of it on the floor a couple of times, curled it up under his arm and left the kitchen.

Walcott crossed the living room and stepped out onto the front porch. At the same time the screen door slapped shut behind him, the grandfather's clock belched out the last announcement it would ever make. A single chime called out the half hour, and at 9:30 p.m. on Halloween night, 2017, it stopped ticking.

Outside, Walcott walked the porch from one end to the other, looking out across the land that had sheltered and comforted him for neigh on three hundred and twenty years. Sadness, to a depth he'd never felt before about anything, filled his heart. What surprised him was that it was not for him, not per se. He knew he would not be coming back. But that, in itself, was not what brought the tears to his eyes. He was not afraid (or not too much) of what lay ahead. What knotted his stomach and split open his heart was having to say goodbye to such a trusted friend and seat of comfort. He turned and looked at the house once more, sighed, and strode down the porch steps. At the back of the house, he stopped. The urge to look back, just one more time, was almost overwhelming. He fought it and moved on into the dark of the woods. Overhead, the red eye of a blood moon (unexpected for this time of year) watched through the wavering tree branches.

### 3

Ralph rolled the pickup to a stop in front of Farley's store, not bothering to angle it into one of the lined space. He had to smile to himself, looking at the bales of hay he and Walcott had delivered. There were three stacks, each made up of three bails. A scarecrow in tattered clothing with a small pumpkin for a head sat on one stack. A skeleton with one arm missing sat on a second. The third stack was tiered, each tier having a different sized jack-o-lantern perched on it, the biggest, of course at the top.

He waited as a mother and two young girls (one dressed as a princess and the other a ghost) collected their treats and walked on down the street. Amos Farley stood in the doorway. When he caught sight of the pickup and Ralph, he slapped his hands onto his hips. From where he was, Ralph couldn't really see the man's eyes, but he had no doubt they were brimming over with defiance and anger.

"What the hell do you want?" Farley yelled. "Come back to gloat?" He walked forward, stopping just short of the truck. "I'll bet you think it was real funny sending all the hay I asked for on the last day, huh? You knew I wouldn't be able to sell it this late. You knew that, didn't you ... you ... you bast-"

"That'll be enough, Amos." Tina Farley's voice was surprisingly strong for her age. "You can go on back in now. I'll handle this."

Amos turned toward his aunt with a look of pure disgust (and a hint of embarrassment at being dressed down) in his eyes. "I can handle it, Auntie. In fact, I have quite a few things to say to mister high-and-mighty-I'm Walcott's-lackey Strunk, here."

"No. You don't have anything to say to Mr. Strunk. He and I have some business to take care of. And you're not a part of it. Now get yourself inside."

Amos opened his mouth to say something, thought better of it, and stomped past his aunt in a huff, slamming the door behind him. Tina walked to the truck and opened the passenger side door. "I won't apologize for him, because he's right. But that's a whole other matter, isn't it? I know why you're here, although, I must say it wasn't you I expected would be coming."

The truck's yellow cab light gave a kind of glow to Tina's face. Ralph was struck by the strength he could see in it. The face was that of an old woman, but the eyes ... the eyes were rich and strong and full of youth. He was also surprised (and perhaps a bit amused) by her clothing. It wasn't often one saw a woman in her eighties wearing a checked flannel shirt tucked into a pair of worn but serviceable Levis. Even more surprising was the fact that both the shirt and jeans seemed to fit her. Not at all hanging loosely as would be expected.

"Well?" asked Tina. "Are you going to ask me to get in, or are we just gonna stand here and stare at each other all night?"

Ralph was stunned. "Uh ... no ... I mean ... yes ... uh-"

"Which is it? No or yes."

"It's no ... we're not going to stare at each other all night ... and yes ... please get in."

"Good. Now you can help me in. I've aged pretty well but for my knees. Arthritis. You're gonna have to give me a bit of a boost."

Ralph got out and walked around. How in the world these people ... these old people ... were ever going to be able to do anything about whatever had to be done at that house was beyond him. One thing was certain, though. Walcott believed in them, or at least felt they had some part to play. And if that was good enough for Walcott, it was good enough for him.

"Boost me up," said Tina. "But keep your hands off my ass. I ain't that kinda girl, just 'cause you're loadin' me into a pick-me-up truck."

A moment of silence passed before Tina broke out laughing. "I'm joshin' you, Mr. Strunk. Just grab hold and push."

Ralph started to laugh. And as soon as he put his hands on her hips to hoist her up, it grew louder and harder. Tina Farley had a sense of humor. She was not at all what he'd thought she'd be, based on Walcott's attitude toward her all these years.

"Come on, Mr. Strunk, give me a good shove. No need to be shy, and I ain't made o'glass. Maybe not as sturdy as I once was, but a damned sight removed from comin' apart from a push on my tush."

Ralph started to push, laughed harder and had to stop. On the next try he contained himself and got her seated. "Maybe you might consider calling me Ralph."

"Okay, Ralph it is. And you can call me Miss Farley ... or ma'am." She paused again. "Or ... how about ... your ladyship?"

Ralph stared slack-jawed for a few seconds. This time he knew she was joking, and would have laughed, but he wondered how she could be making jokes with what lay ahead. As if she had read his mind, she leaned toward him. "I'm scared shitless, Ralph. If I don't keep myself from thinkin' too much about what we're doing ... well, arthritis or no, I'd jump right out of this truck and run away. So I guess the best thing is for you to plant yourself behind this wheel here and get us moving."

Ralph nodded, closed her door and got himself seated. As he pulled away from the curb, Tina laid a hand on his knee. "I've got the feelin' we're headin' right to the witch's castle. If we pass a sign that says: 'If I were you, I'd turn back now'... flyin' monkeys notwithstanding ... ignore it and drive faster."

"Tina," said Ralph, his voice devoid of all humor, "I have to be honest with you. I didn't expect you'd be willing to come with me. You know, with the way you and-"

"Whatever's between me and Walcott has nothing to do with this ... at least not in the way you're thinking. I came because I knew ... I *know* it's what I have to do. And I can tell you this, too. I'm not alone. I'm pretty sure the rest of us will show up there as well."

Ralph smiled. "Walcott said the same thing. He told me that you all have some kind of unfinished business that has to be settled."

"Ralph, I have no idea what's going to happen. No idea, even, of what it is we're supposed to do, or even be able to do. And I certainly don't know what Walcott's part in all this is, other than being somehow hooked to that house. Still, I have a feeling that whatever it is we have to do won't mean much if he doesn't do whatever it is *he* has to do."

"I don't know what it is *any* of us is supposed to do, least of all me. All I know is that I got this feelin' that ... whatever it is and whatever it's gonna take to get it done ... it's going to be expensive."

"I think, Ralph, you hit the nail on the head, as they say. I think for us ... us kids that went in there all those years ago … for us … it's payment time. I'm just hopin' it turns out to be the good kind of payment ."

"The good kind?"

"Yeah … like payin' something forward, rather than paying for a mistake. Or maybe, in this case, collecting a payment that's long overdue. I pretty much feel we all paid a heavy price already. Good friends all set adrift … apart and alone … separated for always. It really sucked. Don't know if that's true. Can't know that. But I guess we'll find out soon enough."

Ralph glanced over at her and cleared his throat. "Would you mind if I asked you a personal question?"

Tina let out a light chuckle. "Mind about a personal question? Hell, there's a good chance neither one of us have tickets for a return trip. Why would a personal question bother me at this point? Ask away."

Ralph took a moment to phrase the question. Despite what might lay ahead of them, he still didn't want to offend the woman. At last, after another nervous throat clearing he asked: "What is the beef … the contention … between you and Walcott. He's never really told me what it was all about. I've been curious."

Tina laughed out loud. When she finally stopped, her face grew tight and serious. "Before I answer that, I need you to tell me something. How much do you know, really know about Joachim Walcott?"

"A good deal, I can assure you." He thought about everything Walcott had just finished telling him. He thought about how, even though he did somehow believe what he'd been told, the whole thing still seemed impossible. Totally *un*believable. Best to err on the side of caution and not look like a fool or idiot. "Is there something specific you're talking about?"

"Oh yes, there certainly is. It's something about him that, if I told you outright, you'd think I was one hundred percent bonkers."

Ralph understood. They were both dancing to the same music, whose fiddler was incredulity. Neither of them wanted to be the first to voice the preposterous. "Whatever it is, after what he told me tonight, and he told me a lot of things that just couldn't be ... whatever it is, I won't think you're bonkers. After what I saw happen in his kitchen tonight ... I don't think there's much I couldn't accept at this point."

"Okay then," said Tina. "The trouble ... point of contention, as you put it ... between us is that I know a secret of his. I accidentally discovered it because of my nephew. Amos had come to live with me after my brother and his wife were killed. That's a whole story in itself and not at all relevant. What is relevant is that is Amos had gone off to play one day. I found him in old Walcott's yard. I arrived just in time to see old man Walcott chasing him out of his barn with a broomstick. That's when I learned his secret, a secret I've been forced to keep to myself all these years or risk being locked away. You see, the man that chased Amos looked exactly like Walcott ... except-"

"Except he was only about thirty years old, right?" finished Ralph. "I saw that trick tonight for the first time and thought I was losing my mind."

"Well then, you know what's between us. I knew ... know ... something he couldn't have anyone else learn. And even though there was nothing I could do about it

... well, I knew and that was enough. That was enough because I *knew* that what happened in that house with us kids all those years ago ... well, he was somehow behind all of it. And I hated him for it."

"Then why are you helping him now?"

"I'm not. I'm helping my friends and hoping that because you came for me, because he sent you, that maybe I've misjudged him. I'm hoping that. But I'm not trusting that. Let me be clear right now. I'm doing this for my friends and only for my friends. If you and Walcott are going to help, fine. If either of you get in the way, well, let's just say I can make things very unpleasant."

Tina closed her eyes and concentrated. In her mind she saw Henry and Matt and Janet and Amy, all sitting on the bank of the creek the day they parted company. In her mind she connected with their images and then focused that concentration toward Ralph. A moment later, Ralph felt as if his head were going to explode. For no reason and unable to stop himself, he aimed the truck to the side of the road. Just as the front tires crossed the gravel shoulder, his foot slammed down on the breaks.

"Sorry, Ralph. Just wanted to let you know that us old geezers, me, Matt, Janet and Tommy ... we ain't helpless. Least of all when we're together."

Ralph backed up and pulled back out onto the road. "I can't speak for Walcott, though I believe his intentions are good, but I'm not planning on getting in your way or anyone else's. For me, this is about what Walcott told me, trying to stop something evil from destroying everything I know and care about."

Tina patted Ralph's leg. "Then we're on the same page."

"We're almost there," said Ralph, swinging the truck onto the driveway that led up the hill to the house. "I sure wish I knew what we were going to do when we get there."

## Chapter 32
## RENEWAL

**10:00 p.m.**

Deep within the well outside the house, the black water churned and bubbled and frothed. Thin geysers shot upward and fell back. And then all went quiet. At precisely ten o'clock the waters sank away into the dirt floor. The fingers that had breached the wall stirred. They closed around the stone that encased them and began pulling. Bit by bit, the wall crumbled, and the skeletal form of a long dead woman scratched its way to freedom.

It rose to its feet and shook off the dust and decay of centuries. Slowly, ever so slowly, decayed flesh was renewed. Bone, long devoid of integument, grew sinew, muscle and skin. Hair sprouted from the yellowed and cracked skull. Mother Cassandra was whole once more (minus a single digit).

"Abiye Lespri Bondye a!" A thin strip of bright blue light formed around her neck and began to expand downward, encircling her body. When it reached the floor it burst into a blazing glow of yellow and disappeared. Mother stood there in her blue-topped gown with a floral print, floor-length skirt. She grabbed it and gave it a little shake and the well instantly filled with the smell of honeysuckle. She took in several deep breaths.

"Mot'er almost whole now, almost got her full powers ... and she comin' for you Wickersham. All dis gon' end now. Time t'pay for de t'ings dat need payin' for. You took my daughter. Now, your time com'. Mot'er gon' take your soul into de blackness it won't never escape. De young ones are comin'; I know you know dat. You t'ought dey be outa your way forever. And Mot'er let you t'ink dat. Mot'er make it so dey couldn't be t'get'er ... keep dem separate and away from you. Keep de power Mot'er give dem hidden from your soulless eyes. But now your eyes gon' be open and see de trut'. Dey all comin' for you ... and Mot'er once again ready for der help."

"Moute!" Mother held out her arms and rose, turning in slow circles, up the shaft of the well. She drifted over the rim and settled on the ground. Her eyes burned like glowing coals as she turned her gaze toward the house, seeing through the trees as if they weren't there. The house trembled. Shutters banged shut, hiding the pale yellow of its candlelit window eyes. Doors latched themselves and the chimney belched out a column of fiery fear.

## Chapter 33
## JANET and TOMMY

**8:37 p.m. – 10:18 p.m.**

**1**

Janet pulled to the curb in front of the hospital. Tommy was waiting out front. He bent over and looked in the window at her. "I don't want to talk yet. Later. When I'm ready ... I'll tell you how I knew you were coming and how I got out of ... of ... that place." Janet had simply nodded, opened the car door and waited for him to get in. Tommy watched Fairfield Institute recede in the side view mirror.

Every now and then Janet glanced at Tommy out of the corner of her eye. He had changed so much. Not that that was surprising. It's always hard to stop seeing people the way you did the last time you saw them, especially when it had been years and years. We all have a tendency not to age our long ago friends. The large gut surprised her, but it was the silvery moustache and beard she found most unexpected – and slightly disturbing. It made him look somewhat like Kenny Rogers, except his eyes looked sunken and hollow, devoid of the energy and mischief she remembered.

"I guess I should call..." Janet suddenly sat bolt upright and grabbed at her forehead with her left hand. She barely managed to maneuver the car to a skidding stop at the side of the road before she lost complete control. Tommy had both his hands over his face, which was buried in his lap.

"Christ! Did you feel that, too?" asked Janet.

Tommy groaned and finally sat back in his seat. "Yeah. It was like a tsunami of bad info crashing into my head." He looked at Janet and saw the sorrow he was feeling reflected in her eyes, too.

"Hen-Henry's dead. Oh dear God. Henry's dead. I was just going to say we should call him. Oh my God. Now what?"

Tommy sighed and laid a hand on Janet's shoulder. "Make the call anyway. Emma will answer. Tell her we're coming." He closed his eyes and slid his hand down her arm and took her hand. "The call won't really go through, but it'll be enough. We'll link with her."

"How do you know-"

"Call NOW," barked Tommy. "Before we lose our chance. Then I'll explain everything on the way over there. And we're going to have to hurry. We're all running out of time."

At 8:48 p.m., Janet dialed Emma's number. The call went through and was promptly lost, though not entirely. As Tommy had said, Janet made a mental connection with Emma. It lasted just long enough for her to tell Emma they were coming. And she learned something else. She learned that Matt Holloway was already there.

"Drive," said Tommy, "and I'll tell you what I can. It'll be the short version. No time for details of the past seventy miserable years I spent in that institution."

Janet patted Tommy's knee and stepped on the accelerator, kicking up a small tornado of dust and pebbles from the shoulder of the road.

"The truth is, there's really not a whole lot to tell. I spent most of those years in a semi-catatonic state. When I first arrived, taken there by my parents and the police, all I could do was mumble about the horror of Lucy's death. The cops ... and my parents ... believed I was responsible for her disappearance. They never believed my story about what had happened. They were convinced I'd abducted and killed her. So, the court ordered my mental incarceration. Two days after being committed, I clamed up ... went so deep within myself nobody could reach me. And I didn't really want to come out. At least, not until last night."

Tommy shifted uncomfortably in his seat and stared out the passenger window, his forehead resting against the glass. "Last night ... well, it started with what I thought was a dream. It wasn't. I have no idea what time it really was, though I had the distinct sense that it was just on the stroke of midnight. The whole room, my cell, if you will, suddenly filled with the aroma of fresh honeysuckle. I sat up and rubbed at my eyes, and over in the corner stood an old woman in a flower print dress. I could see right through her, as if she were made of smoked glass. She smiled at me and told me not to be afraid. She told me it was time to do what I was destined to do.

"As I said, at first I thought I was dreaming. Then ... then..." Tommy lifted his shirt sleeve up over his shoulder. "Then this began to glow."

Janet drew in a sharp breath of surprise. On Tommy's upper shoulder, a tattoo of what looked to be some kind of gemstone, sparkling in vivid colors. They shot through it like lightning through thin clouds.

"This ... this is what the old woman gave to me on that horrible night all those years ago. She told me then that it was to be given to someone when the time came. I still don't know to whom, or even how, I'm supposed to give someone a tattoo. But she said last night that you'd be coming for me and I was to be waiting." He lifted his head off the glass and looked at Janet. "And here you are and here I am. And ... and I'm really scared that whatever it is we have to do ... I think it's the last thing I'll ever do. Maybe the last thing any of us will ever do."

"Then why did you come?" asked Janet. "If you were safe where you were-"

"That answer is simple. Because I had to. Just like you had to pick me up. Whatever it was we got ourselves into back then, it's come full circle. And we have our parts to play whether we like it or not. Even Henry. Like me, he was given something that night, too. I know he's dead, but he's still a part of this. We all are."

Janet wiped a tear from the corner of her eye. She wasn't sure whether it was from fear or sadness. The feelings were mixed together. What she did know was that Tommy's foreboding was rolling around inside her as well. She knew something else, too, though how was a mystery. The timing of Henry's death had been no coincidence. His death, today, had been a sacrifice. She swung the car onto the onramp for I-76 W and accelerated to 80mph. With any luck, she could cut the hour and a half trip down to an hour. That is, provided they didn't get pulled over.

## 2

As it turned out, they didn't get pulled over and made better time than Janet had hoped. She wheeled the car onto Route 10 at 9:45, just a little over an hour since they'd left Philadelphia. If their luck held, they'd be at Henry's in another fifteen or so minutes.

Their luck didn't hold.

Janet suddenly felt a prickling sensation crawl across her scalp. Her ears started ringing. She felt the fingers of Wickersham's mind probing at her, digging at her. She grabbed Tommy's hand, and he too felt it instantly. Their minds locked and together they pushed the interloper out.

Three minutes later, the car coughed and wheezed. The temperature gauge zipped over to red and the car sputtered to a stop. Steam billowed out from beneath the hood and the car gave up a final death rattle.

Janet slammed her fist down on the steering wheel. "Dammit! Dammit to hell!"

"He's trying to stop us," said Tommy, his voice surprisingly calm. It won't work."

"How can you be so sure?" asked Janet, not waiting for an answer. She climbed out, walked to the front of the car and gingerly opened the hood, being careful not to get a face full of hot steam. "The fucking radiator hose is broken. There's a long gash almost all the way-"

"Let me." Tommy stood beside her, his eyes fixed on the useless hose.

"You have a roll of duct tape I don't know about?"

"I have this." He rolled up his sleeve and leaned over the engine. The tattoo on his shoulder began to glow, first red, then orange and then blue. A thin line of blue-white fire shot from the center of it and crawled along the length of the split hose. Little by little, very slowly, the gash along the length of the hose began to close.

"He'll try again," said Janet.

"I don't think so. I don't think he can afford to waste that much energy. He didn't stop us, but he sure slowed us down. I think he'll have to be satisfied with that."

"I should try calling Emma."

Tommy stopped working on the hose and laid his hand over Janet's cell phone before she could open it. "Waste of time."

She slid it back into her pocket. "Yeah. I know. Come on, get back to work, wizard. Let's get going."

Tommy smiled. It was the first real show of any emotion Janet had seen from him since she'd picked him up. She returned the smile as they got back in the car. Seventeen minutes later they rolled to a stop in front of Henry's place.

## Chapter 34
## A MEETING IN THE DARK

**9:41 p.m. – 10:24 p.m.**

Walcott made his way through the woods toward the destiny that awaited him. The eye of the moon, bathed in eerie red, seemed more to glower than peer at him through the tightly stitched canopy of trees. The swaying of their branches in the light breeze gave it the unsettling appearance of winking knowingly at him – the unwanted gaze of an enemy scout. He shook it off with a slight shudder and moved on.

He scrambled up a small slope, fighting the underbrush that had grown wild across the tiny path. The air closed in on him with unseasonable humidity. Sweat plastered the front of his shirt to his chest and he had to stop, panting, to catch his breath. The forlorn cry of a distant screech owl drifted hauntingly through the stillness. A mocking bird answered and fell silent again. Nothing else disturbed the oppressive silence. Walcott readjusted the backpack on his shoulder and fought his way through a tangle of branches. The woods closed in on him, the brush growing denser, the trail thinner. The forest – this forest, an extension of the house – was trying to stop him. Or at least slow him down. Of this he had no doubt; he could feel it deep in his bones. A sudden darkness swallowed him, the fragile light of the moon disappearing. It was as if the great red eye had closed, no longer needing to see what would come.

Unable to see more than a foot or so in front of him, he stumbled and struggled and clawed his way ahead. Branches grabbed and slapped at him. Roots and vines arched up out of the ground, grabbing at his feet. Twice he fell, the second time, face first into a patch of netted brambles. A patchwork of broken skin oozed trickles of blood down his cheeks, across his forehead and down his arm where the thick, hooked thorns caught in his flesh. Painfully, he plowed on, grunting out an *ow*! here and a *dammit*! there.

The closer he got to the house, the harder it got to maneuver through the foliage. Thick vines, woven together like wooden nets, crisscrossed his path. He was forced to bend and climb and push and pull his way through them. Once, he tried to work his way around them and was nearly crushed when a fat limb of oak suddenly cracked free of its trunk. It landed two feet in front of him, flattening a small pine and another fledgling oak. So back to the path and vines he went.

Finally, sweating, exhausted, bruised and battered, he stumbled into the clearing of the old well at a few minutes after ten o'clock. He dropped the backpack off his shoulder, leaned the walking stick against the well and then plopped down. The air was still and heavy. Not a sound disturbed the silence, not a single insect buzzed or chirped. No owls cried and no mocking birds answered. He sat with eyes closed, trying very hard (and not succeeding) not to think of what lay ahead. For him, and the others, tonight was the night of all nights, the culmination of a battle that began over three hundred years ago. It was all too surreal to comprehend – to accept. A wry smile crept across his lips as he tried to imagine the looks he'd get if he tried to sell his story, *this* story, to the newspapers. He had no trouble envisioning the reporter's index finger twirling in "he's crazy" circles behind his back. The image almost made him laugh out loud. Almost.

Drawing a deep sigh of resignation, Walcott forced himself to his feet. What, exactly, he was supposed to do now he had no idea – no real idea. Of course, the first order of business would be to get into the house. He stood for a moment looking over top of the well toward the house – at least another seventy-five yards of woods and vines to negotiate. The prospect was depressing. But at this point, what wasn't? That did make him laugh out loud. He slung the pack over his shoulder, picked up the walking stick and moved into the brush.

"I wish to Christ that, if nothing else, I could see. This is ridiculous."

Suddenly, a wavering, soft white glow bloomed beneath his shirt. He could feel the warmth of it against his chest. When he pulled it out, the pendent was no longer just a sickle moon but a full moon. Free of the confines of his shirt, it blazed with a brilliance that illuminated his surroundings in a bubble of white. More than that, when he took his first step forward, trees, brush, vines and whatever other obstruction lay across his path bent out of the way.

He moved ahead slowly, cautiously, until... A loud crack and the rustling of branches from behind him brought him to a dead stop. Another sharp pop! rang out. Someone had stepped on a fallen branch. A brief silence ensued. Then, the soft flutter of hushed voices. Walcott couldn't make out the words, but he was sure there were at least two of them. He guessed they must be at the well, probably deciding which way to go ... or maybe ... which way *he* had gone. If, of course, they were following him. The real question that had to be decided (and quickly) was: were they friend or foe? Being so close to the house, the odds did not seem to favor friend.

While Walcott took a moment to puzzle the question, the voices suddenly got louder, closer. His heart jumped into his throat as the realization struck him that, whoever it was, there was no way they could miss seeing the bright aura of his pendant. He dropped the walking stick and hurriedly closed the thing in his fist. It made no difference; its brilliance shone through his hand as if it were made of glass.

"Jesus!" He picked up the walking stick, preparing to use it as a weapon. There seemed nothing else for it but to stand and fight. He dropped the backpack to the ground and braced himself. The wait was short. The first thing he saw was the dancing beam of a flashlight. Then the bushes rustled, parted, and two figures stepped out in front of him.

"Christ, A'mighty!" barked Walcott in his old man voice. "Ya tryin' t'give me the final send off?" He paused and then grinned.

Ralph and Tina just looked at each other, Ralph with the flashlight dangling at his side and one hand pressed over his heart. Tina had her hands on her hips as if she were confronting a recalcitrant schoolboy.

"You scared the hell out of us, too," Ralph finally said.

Tina nudged him in the side with an elbow. "Speak for yourself. At my age, nothing much scares or surprises me." Her eyes drifted in the direction of the house, and Ralph and Walcott followed her gaze. "Well ... maybe a couple things still scare me. Besides, if you're trying to be all stealthy and whatnot, you should probably dim your damned chest beacon, there."

Walcott shrugged. "Would have if I could have. By the way–" He held up the walking stick. "-might this be yours, young lady?"

Tina laughed. "It's not mine; never saw it before. But thanks for the young thing."

Walcott grinned. "Remember ... compared to me..."

## Chapter 35
## THE PAST REJOINED

**10:24 p.m. – 10:59 p.m.**

**1**

Emma and Matt had decided to give Janet and Tommy fifteen minutes before she and Matt headed to the house. As it turned out, they only had to wait four. Emma had just finished cinching up the leather pouch with the finger bone key in it when a car rolled to a stop outside. She looked at Matt who held a finger to his lips and walked to the window. He moved the curtain aside just enough to peek out, let it drop back into place and sighed. "They're here."

Emma, with Matt standing slightly behind her, opened the door. Janet's hand was poised to knock. Tommy stood slightly behind and to the left of Janet. There was a brief awkward pause, then Janet threw her arms around Emma and hugged her tightly, tears spilling form the corners of her eyes.

"I'm so, so sorry about Henry. I can't believe... I can't..."

Matt and Tommy were trying to make sense of each other. All they could remember was how they'd each looked that last time they'd been together. Matt couldn't decide whether it was the beard and moustache that were so out of place or the potbelly that drooped slightly over Tommy's belt buckle. Either way, it was certainly not the same Tommy Vorland who had led them down into the tunnel all those years ago with a pack of Marlboros rolled up in his shirtsleeve. For Tommy's part, he wondered where Matt's hair had gone and marveled at how thin and frail the man looked. He smiled, remembering the kick in the butt he'd given him way back then.

"So," asked Tommy, "you still screeching like a little girl whenever you get scared?" He smiled. "Bet you thought I forgot about that, huh?"

Matt leaned sideways and looked pointedly at Tommy's shoulder. "How about you? Give up the cigarettes you used to chain smoke?"

"C'mere, dumbass!" Tommy stepped inside. His arms swallowed Matt in a big bear hug, lifting him off the floor.

"Easy, big fella," pleaded Matt in a playful voice, "you're gonna break me. And I'm fresh outta duct tape."

Tommy set him down and put his hands on his shoulders. "It's really ... really, really good to see you, my old friend."

"You, too, Tommy. You, too. I just wish-"

"I know. I do too." Tommy stepped around Matt. He offered his hand to Emma, who shook it lightly and then drew the man into a hug.

"Thank you so much for coming, Mr.-"

"It's Tommy. Always has been; always will be ... especially to you. I'm so sorry about Henry. Worse, I have to admit that his absence has me a little scared. I'm sure you know-"

The sudden joining of all their minds into a single collection of thoughts was so powerful they almost all passed out from the shock. It was as if their brains had been stung by a thousand hornets all at the same time. They each staggered back or sideways, grabbing for support. Tommy found a chair. Matt grabbed for the wall and Janet and Emma grabbed each other. When they recovered (a slow process), they no longer needed words. The group was together once again.

*I suppose we should get started*, thought Matt. The group just nodded.

"Wait." Emma walked over and picked up the small box from the table. "My father left this for you, Tommy."

Tommy took the box, turned it over and over and then slowly opened it. A smile crawled across his lips and he coughed out a laugh. "I'll be damned. I guess this means it's back to my old look." He patted his belly. "Too bad this has grown so much." He unbuttoned his shirt, pulled it off and tossed it on the chair in which Matt had been sitting. Still smiling, he pulled the (still cellophane-sealed) pack of Marlboros and matches out of the box and held them up for all to see before rolling it up in his shirtsleeve.

Matt shook his head in an *of course, why not* gesture.

## 2

At ten forty-two they turned onto the drive that led to the house. At ten forty-four they passed Ralph's truck, unseen and hidden off the road in the same spot Tommy had parked back in '47. At ten forty-seven the car came to a sudden stop. Janet cursed and slammed her palms down on the steering wheel. No one had spoken a word for the whole trip, not that they'd had to. Their thoughts were as tightly woven as a Cherokee wedding blanket. Grumbling another curse, Janet fished a flashlight from the glove compartment, flicked it on and got out. Tommy followed suit.

*Seems we're supposed to hoof-it from here.* Tommy opened the pack of cigarettes and tapped one out. In keeping with his old tradition, he flipped it toward his mouth. It struck his lower lip and dropped to his lap. *Guess I'm way out of practice.*

*I think Henry would be disappointed. Your lack of grace, however, doesn't surprise me at all. You always were a shmuck, Tommy.* Tina's voice was as strong in their heads as if she'd been standing beside them, though they all knew instantly she was on the other side of the house. And they knew she wasn't alone. Joachim Walcott and Ralph Strunk were with her.

*And you were always a pain in the ass*, answered Tommy. The emotion of reunion that passed between them had the same strength and depth as that of the greetings in Emma's living room. It held for a moment, a blanket of comfort and familiarity. It faded, swallowed by the dark reality of why they were all together again.

*I don't suppose anybody has a real plan, do they?* queried Tina. *Or maybe thought to bring something useful, like ... oh, I don't know ... an A-K-Forty-Seven ... or maybe better, a priest and some goddamned holy water?*

*It seems to me*, chimed in Janet, *that some kind of plan is already laid out for us. By whom is the million-dollar question. Looks like we're attacking the problem* on two fronts: you from the back and us ... Lord save us ... we get to march right through the front door.

*We're not alone in this*, interjected Walcott. *My grandmother-*

Mother's voice suddenly thundered in all their heads like a pounding waterfall. *Mot'er Cassandra not gon' let you stand alone. T'ough she not be de be-all-an'-end-all o'what be t'come, an' dat be fer certain, don' underestimate de force dat she bring t'bear on your side. De true end of what be comin' caint be known fer sure. De universe unfolds as it will. But der be hard power in de ones dat walk in de gift of life. Man always walk in de shadow of destruction; woman glide t'rough the light of creation. One has de strengt' o'body, de ot'er de body dat can break dat strengt'. Thoughts once clear run muddy when de heads don' work t'get'er. When de children return an' de child-man come forth ... den ... all will be decided.*

The voice died away and time hiccupped for them, a brief pause in the universe. All except Emma. What was said next, only Emma heard.

*Mot'er t'child an' child again.*
*De strengt' o'de woman is de way t'de end.*
*When all seem lost for de ones we hol' dear,*
*De wisdom's t'know when t'not interfere.*
*What's seen wit' de eyes gon' sting in de heart,*
*But out o'de pain com' de ending's real start.*
*De beast o'lust arose from de fire.*
*A slave to its purpose; a slave t'desire.*
*From de depths it was called for my an' your daughter,*
*Its undoing comes not from flames but from water.*

*When daughter an' daughter submit to its vice,*
*De joining of crystal and staff bring de ice.*
*Den out o'de flames o'de beast's heart o'lust*
*De fire an' ice bring water an' dust.*

When Mother withdrew from Emma's mind, the face of a giant clock bloomed behind her eyes. The minute hand ticked over to 11:24 with a booming *CLICK*! She stood trancelike, watching as the face of the clock melted like plastic on a hotplate. Emma watched it *drip-drip-drip* and then regrow into the face of some hideous, horned beast. The image became larger and fuller, as if some phantom cameraman had decided a wide-angle shot was called for. She watched in horror, unable to avert her eyes, as the thing beckoned a young woman, drawing her to it. When it reached her, the woman disrobed and offered herself to the beast. And when the thing laid her on the ground and climbed atop her, Emma saw Annabel's face. The scream of terror and disgust brought her forward, but not completely out of the trance. She was vaguely aware of people around her, their voices ringing in her ears as if echoes from a great distance. "Are you all right? Emma … come out of it. Are you all right? What's wrong? Emma! Emma!"

She felt as if her mind were made of Jell-O and she was drowning in her own thoughts, unable to swim to the surface of clarity. Further and further she sank, her mental lungs feeling like overinflated balloons, her brain about to rupture. And then:

*EMMA LANSING! EMMA LANSING! RISE*! A ghostly hand plunged into the gelatinous abyss of her mind and pulled her to consciousness. She opened her eyes and gulped in air as if she'd really been drowning. Tommy and Janet were crouched beside her.

"For a moment, there, we thought we lost you." Janet smiled weakly, a hand on Emma's shoulder. Tommy had both her hands in his. "Caught you just before you fell. Feeling better?"

"I-I..." Emma started to get up and Tommy pushed her gently back down.

"Just give it a couple minutes, okay?" He patted her hands once more, pulled a cigarette from its pack and flipped it into his mouth. This time he caught it perfectly. "Guess I haven't completely lost my touch."

"I-I was ... it was like drowning in myself. I couldn't seem to..." Emma shook her head in frustration.

"We know," said Janet. "We saw it too."

"Who ... did you ... Somebody pulled-"

*Rest a few minutes; we still have a long hard night ahead of us.* The voice in her head was clear and strong, yet gentle. It was the same voice (familiar, yet not) that had pulled her out of the trance.

*Thank you. Thank you,* she thought back. *I honestly believe you saved my life.*

*We're all in this together, now; we need each other. Take a few minutes, but then ..!*

Emma took a few deep breaths. The image of the beast calling her daughter to it bubbled to the surface and she pulled herself to her feet. "Come on, we're wasting time. And I don't think we have any to spare. I don't know exactly what it means, but I saw a distinct time in my mind. Eleven twenty-four. Whatever is going to happen ... it's going to happen then, I'm sure of it."

Tommy stuck his arm under the beam of Janet's flashlight. "Ten fifty-nine. If what you say is true, we'd better get a move on."

### 3

At the rear of the house, Walcott watched with a kind of childlike fascination as Ralph and Tina wound to a stop. Their movements got slower and slower, as if time around them was running out and they were being dragged with it. He reached a hand toward Ralph and, at two minutes past eleven, his mind suddenly filled with a horrible image. The face of a giant clock appeared and began melting and reforming, turning into something else. He realized he was in someone else's mind. He saw what Emma was seeing. He felt what she was feeling. It was as if she were... The pressure in his lungs suddenly flared to unbearable intensity. Emma was ... sinking, drowning in her own mind. He wrenched himself from her thoughts long enough to steel himself against what had to be done. When he was confident he would not lose himself, he crawled back in.

*EMMA LANSING! EMMA LANSING! RISE!*

In one swift mental motion, he plunged his arm into the swirling abyss of Emma's thoughts and pulled her free of them. As she came to the surface of her consciousness and the connection was broken, Walcott pitched forward into Ralph's arms, who, like Tina, had just resumed normal time.

"Mis-Mister Walcott? Are ... are you okay?" A chill ran up Ralph's spine as he eased Walcott to a sitting position. Walcott's eyes were vacant. His lips were moving lightly but the words he spoke reached neither Ralph's nor Tina's ears ... or mind. Emma Lansing was the only one to hear them.

*Rest a few minutes; we still have a long hard night ahead of us. We're all in this together, now; we need each other. Take a few minutes, but then..!*

A few moments later, Tommy's words were clear to everyone. "Ten fifty-nine. If what you say is true, we'd better get a move on."

## Chapter 36
## DASHED HOPE

**10:03 p.m. – 11:00 p.m.**

*Are we not feeling well?* The voice thundered in Brian's head, battering Wickersham like storm waves upon a weakened pier. *Feeling a bit rundown, are we?* The words were Annabel's, picked carefully from the book and volume of her vocabulary. The voice that taunted Wickersham with them belonged to Abigail.

Brian struggled to his feet. Wickersham slapped his hands over his ears; Brian fought them back down to his sides, his will rising ever higher within himself. He could feel Wickersham losing his grip, a man with a tenuous hold on a splitting branch.

Abigail laughed and Wickersham recoiled. To him, it was the sound of a thousand demons screaming in his ears for his soul. Brian heard only the voice of his beloved Annabel: *Push Brian; keep pushing. He's weak. Dislodge him. Reclaim yourself and save us. PUSH HIM, BRIAN!* Beneath Annabel's voice, like a song within a song, Abigail spoke softly and clearly: *Confuse him, Brian. Muddle him. He is too weak now to hold his grip and deal with the unfamiliar. He stretched himself too far to stop that machine. Dig into knowledge that is yours alone. Overwhelm him and you can drive him out.*

Brian could feel Wickersham clawing at his mind, struggling to push him back down into his mental prison.

He also felt something else – fear. Wickersham was afraid – afraid of losing his grip on his puppet. But there was more than that. The fear that ran through Wickersham's consciousness flowed out beyond the struggle for control. They were coming; they were coming and Wickersham was afraid of them. But who were they? Brian could not quite glean a clear sense of who it was that scared Wickersham so. He closed his eyes and tried to concentrate. He tried to claw at Wickersham's mind, to open it up and reveal his secret.

The sudden rattling of chains as Annabel/Abigail fought against their bonds broke Brian's concentration. He turned and was horrified to see two faces rapidly changing places, like the tilting of a hologram card. One was the face of his Annabel, the other an unknown woman.

"*Be not/Don't be* – afraid." The two spoke together. "We are one and not one. We are separate and joined. We always have been." The voice of the strange woman faded, leaving only Annabel's. "Forget about Wickersham's fears. He's trying to distract you. Think, Brian. Think of something unfamiliar to him that he can't comprehend. Think ... and you can be rid of him."

Brian slumped down against the wall. Everything seemed to be spinning out of control. Think. Think about what?

*Fear, boy. Think about fear ... about my dark secrets.* Wickersham's voice was stronger, more deliberate.

"NO!" yelled Brian, and threw his head back in anger. It struck the stone wall hard enough to make points of light dance across the backs of his eyes. But when they cleared, he had it. He knew what he had to think about. He thought he had a pretty good idea of what Wickersham would have no way of comprehending.

Brian sat back against the wall and closed his eyes. He tried thinking of advanced equations used in architecture: stress factors, loadbearing principles. It didn't seem to make a difference; he could feel Wickersham crawling through his mind, pushing at him, clawing at him. Obviously, mathematics, even advanced, wasn't much of a threat. He needed something with bite, something that Wickersham would have no way of understanding. But what?

He puzzled over it for several minutes. The whole time he could feel Wickersham trying to regain his foothold, could hear him whispering over and over again: *secrets, boy. Concentrate on my secrets.* It was distracting and scary. He cupped his hands over his ears, knowing that they couldn't block out the voice in his head.

"*Ahhhhhhhh!*" Brian's scream echoed around the room and came back to him in thundering volume. "This is going to make me crazy. I'm going to strip all my gears and end up in a psych..."

*Gears.* The thought, that single word, was so stunning, so fluid that the idea it inspired was almost childlike in its simplicity. "Gears," he mumbled. "The car ... the damned car. The bastard had to dig into my brain to figure out what it was and how to stop it. Technology. That's the key."

Leaning forward, Brian rested his elbows on his knees and covered his eyes with his hands. In his head, he began bringing up images of machines: a self-propelled lawn mower; a motor cycle; a dump truck, followed by a bull dozer. It seemed to be helping, but not quite as much as he needed. Wickersham was still there, weaker, but still digging away. Something more unfamiliar, more out of reach was called for.

    He stood up and began pacing, a habit of his whenever he needed to think. When he shoved his hands in his pockets and his fingers closed around his iPhone, he knew exactly which way to go. He imagined one of those fancy holographic tables he'd seen on various TV shows. His mind threw up a picture of a computer and let the mental holograph spin it in three dimensions. With each turn the image went deeper and deeper. The motherboard came into view. He imagined the circuits actively processing data. Threads of light wound their way through the minute, silver threads of its channels. He went deeper again, for what he'd seen called: *Internal Enhanced View* in one of the *Walking Dead* shows. An endless series of numbers streamed across the screen of his thoughts. A flood of ones and zeroes, branching, diverging, joining together here, separating there, rushing along in bits and bytes, carrying an unintelligible, undecipherable secret message that was truly beyond the scope of Wickersham's knowledge and understanding.

    Words rushed at Brian's mind, most weak. And was it ... did he almost hear desperation in those words? Wickersham was losing his grip; he was fighting but not winning. The battle was almost over and Brian knew it. He shifted his focus to the big screen TV that he and Annabel had splurged on only a few months ago. He let show after show unwind, play out in rapid and jumbled succession. *Walker, Texas Ranger* played into *Hercules*, which morphed into *Sea Quest*. *Sea Quest* slid back in time to *The Wild, Wild West* and merged with *Star Trek*. The face of James T. Kirk wavered and became the face of a flesh-rotted zombie. Voices overlapped in a kaleidoscopic cacophony of noise.

Pain (like none he'd ever experienced) exploded in his head and brought him to his knees. His body felt like he'd been dropped into a freezing river; his lips blued and his teeth burst into a staccato clicking, the speed of which would do any professional typist proud. A moment later he was free. He could feel Wickersham's presence leaking from him, like air from a punctured inflatable. It took more than a few minutes to recover, but Brian was once again Brian, and only Brian.

Now, fully himself, he moved to free Annabel and drew up short just in front of the cot on which she lay. The woman he looked down upon was unfamiliar. Her skin was softly dark, her hair wet and tangled. The clothes he (under Wickersham's influence) had ripped open were something from another century. A stained and yellowed bodice dangled its mold covered, frayed ties from rusted and deformed eyelets. He took a few steps back, blinking rapidly, as if doing so would make everything right again.

*You must free us, Brian.* The woman on the table, her mouth gagged, pleaded with him with her eyes, and the pleas rang inside his head. *You must free us, for we are both here, I, Abigail, and your beloved Annabel.* The next words that he heard were spoken in Annabel's voice. *Please ... please set us free while there is still time.*

Brian grabbed at the sides of his head, clutching at his hair as if he intended to tear it out. "No, no, no. This isn't right. How ... how do I know this isn't just one of his tricks?"

*Think, Brian*, came Annabel's voice. *Why would he want you to free us? Please, you must hurry; you* must.

The woman on the table still looked foreign, all but her eyes. He could not mistake his Annabel in those eyes. He removed the gag from her mouth and lightly stroked her cheek. "I don't understand any of this; I don't know who you are, and yet ... and yet I see the love of my wife in your eyes."

"We are one and separate, Brian. I am Annabel and I am Abigail. We are here together."

Brian smiled and shrugged. It was a familiar gesture to Annabel, and Abigail smiled back. "I guess that no matter who you are, you shouldn't be here like this. I'll get you out." He turned and scanned the room for any sign of keys that would unlock the shackles. Nothing. He searched himself, hoping that he had kept them in his pockets. Again nothing. The helpless feeling that swallowed him was almost too much to bear. He began yanking and pulling at the chains, as if he could tear them apart with brute strength. He tugged and pulled and yanked until sweat dripped from his forehead and his hands blistered and bled. Angry and scared, he pounded his fists in futility on the side of the cot and then slid to his knees beside it. Tears spilled from his eyes and rolled freely down his cheeks as he stroked Annabel's/Abigail's cheek with the back of his hand.

"I can't-can't get them undone. I'm sorry; I'm so, so sorry, baby."

The room suddenly echoed with a horrible, booming laughter. The voice that followed stabbed at Brian like ice picks to his ears.

*Of course you can't get them undone, boy. The girls are mine; they will remain mine. And ... and soon ... you will be mine once again, and together we will take our pleasure from them. More than that, I will take my immortality from their issue.* The laughter erupted again and filled the room with a darkness that clutched at Brian's very soul. "And by the way, that little trick you just pulled won't work again. So don't even bother trying."

## Chapter 37
## CONVERGENCE

**11:00 p.m. – 11:06 p.m.**

**1**

"Let's go," said Emma, "my daughter ... and son-in-law ... are in that damned house and I'm going to get them out." She plucked the flashlight (a bit unceremoniously) from Janet's hand and started for the house, walking straight up the middle of the drive toward the front door. It was pure defiance, as if she dared whatever powers residing within to get in her way, to try and stop her. Tommy and Janet fell in behind her. Matt stayed back a few steps, continually looking over his shoulder. The last thing they needed was to be surprised from behind.

The woods pressed in on them from either side of the road. Branches slapped and grabbed at them in the still night air. Emma remained undaunted, committed. Her mind was as sharply focused as the lens of a laser. Her jaw was set, her eyes narrowed. What lived within them belied what lay behind them. Her mind turned on the events of the day: her father's passing; Matt's arrival and his finishing of the bizarre tale of their visit to that house that her father had begun; the unexpected mental connection that linked all of them; the eerie and inexplicable journey she and Matt had taken back in time to actually witness events that had long passed into history; and finally, the threatening phone call from the house, telling her it had her daughter. Fire burned behind her eyes. It was a fire of nuclear proportions, born in the ferocity of a mother's determination to protect her child.

A thin smile of self-satisfaction broke across her face as she thought, *Whatever damned powers you think you have, whoever or whatever you are in there, I'm coming to show you that you haven't got a clue about power. Never ... never ever get between a mother and her daughter, you bastard.* The thought was so strong, so powerful it made the rest of the group pull up short and sway in their places until the thunder of it subsided.

"What the hell?" stammered Matt.

"I think mama bear is pissed," said Tommy. "And ... to be honest with you, now that I think about it ... so am I. I spent the majority of my life in a loony bin because of that place. I do believe it's retribution time."

*I still think we should have brought some grenades or rocket launchers.* From the other side of the house, Tina's tongue-in-cheek thought made everyone smile.

"What do we need with those?" asked Walcott. "We have a stick." He held it up and laughed. He laughed hard and deeply. Not because the joke was that funny, but because he couldn't remember the last time he'd made a witticism, or for that matter, with the exception of Ralph, that he'd had friends. He'd lived the majority of his life as what others would describe as a surly old man. And now, here he was about to go head to head with his destiny, and finally, at last, he felt he was not alone. He felt as if were part of a group, a group that cared about each other. He laughed again. "Guess we all have to walk softly, huh? We have a big stick.

Guaranteed to scare the b'jeebies right out of the devil himself."

In the front of the house, Emma came to a dead stop. She couldn't believe what her mind was seeing. Joachim Walcott, a man whom she knew by reputation but never had any dealings with, was holding the shillelagh her father had gotten rid of all those years ago. It wasn't possible. But there it was; and there was no mistaking or denying it was the very same one. She knew that as surely as she knew her own name, for it was outlined with overlapping, intertwining auras that were unmistakable imprints of her parents.

Walcott stopped laughing and turned his head toward the house, toward the driveway in front of it, as if he could see right through the building to the woman on the other side. He stretched out his arm, holding up the shillelagh. The words spoken to him in his kitchen by Mother Cassandra flooded his thoughts, and in turn flooded Emma's. *"You will not be alone in dis. De young ones from all dem years past, de ones dat awakened Mot'er, will play out de rest of der destinies. One of dem, who is not one of dem, has de power t'use what I have given you. You must give dis only to de one who can use it. It must go to no ot'er ... or all will be lost."*

"What's wrong/What's the matter?" asked Tommy of Emma at the same time Ralph asked Walcott. Each, Emma and Walcott, appeared frozen in time to those around them. Walcott stood motionless, unblinking, barely breathing, his arm outstretched with the shillelagh clutched vertically in his fist like a wizard's staff.

Emma, save for her arms hanging limply at her sides, mirrored Walcott.

"Wait," said Janet, as Tommy reached a hand toward Emma's shoulder. "There's something going on, a connection of some kind, one which we haven't been invited into. I can feel a light thread of it. Tommy closed his eyes and concentrated and finally felt what Janet was feeling. It was no more than a glimmer of a thought, a warm feeling of comfort, like an oil lamp casting its soft yellow glow across a cottage living room.

Suddenly, Emma reeled backwards. The flashlight dropped from her hands as her arms pin-wheeled in search of balance. It didn't work. Tommy caught her before she fell and eased her to the ground. Behind the house, Walcott imitated Emma but unlike her, he fell flat on his back before Ralph could grab him. When his fist hit the ground, the shillelagh bounced out of his hand. The two of them, Emma and Walcott, lay stretched out, their eyes fixed and open, staring upward at nothing.

Janet picked up the flashlight and its beam died away. The glowing moon necklace around Walcott's neck spit out a burst of dazzling brilliance and faded away to nothing. Overhead, the moon cloaked itself in a patchwork of dark cloud leaving everyone in a darkness so deep they couldn't even see each other while standing next to one another.

"Jumpin' Christ on a pogo stick! What now?" Janet shook the flashlight, banged it several times against the heel of her hand and grumbled another curse. She looked skyward to where the moon had disappeared, let out an exasperated sigh and shook her head in disgust.

"This can't be a damned accident, and I'm not much caring for the implications."

"It's gone," said Tommy. "It's gone and I think we're in big trouble here."

"What's gone?" Janet moved toward the sound of Tommy's voice, her hand feeling the empty air in front of her. A minor sense of relief swept over her when she finally touched his arm. "What's gone, Tommy?"

"Our connection. Can't you feel it? I can't hear your thoughts anymore."

A shiver ran through Janet's whole body. Tommy was right, but that wasn't what spurred her fear. Tommy's voice was coming from somewhere in front of her and off to her right. Whose arm was she touching? She drew her arm back and something clamped down around her wrist, something cold and hard, yet insubstantial. There was a moment, a flicker of a fly's wing, where her mind touched the entity that was touching her. In that touch she found hatred, anger, greed, revenge and a lust beyond all imaginings. She screamed, but only silence spilled from her open mouth. Whatever had her by the wrist had her by the throat as well. And then she was moving, being dragged backwards through the brush. Her legs kicked frantically; her heels dug grooves in the dirt and forest detritus. The sound of Tommy's voice faded into the distance.

***

Wickersham had retreated to his bubble prison when he'd been driven from Brian's mind. Merged once more with the totality of his consciousness and that of the incubus demon that shared his thoughts and prison, he rejuvenated himself. It was a kind of battery recharging, driven by the anger of expulsion, the demonic lust of the incubus and his need to conquer mortality. But most of all it was driven by his need to, once and for all, eradicate the locusts of his plague: Mother Cassandra and her simpleminded octogenarian minions. Soon, very soon now, it would be time to teach them all a lesson.

As his strength grew, he sent it forth once more. This time, the strength of his thoughts became palpable. The invisible form of his conscious essence flew up the steps, passed through walls and doors and burst into the night. It moved in the shroud of evil that sustained it, a cloak of blackest malice, and darkened everything around it. The moon closed its great bloodshot eye and hid behind a cover of cloud.

Wickersham, in a pure rage, railed at the gauntlet of defiance that that woman, Emma, had thrown down. How dare she lay a challenge at his feet. How dare she think herself capable of intimidating him. She had deluded herself, believing that the strength of her love for her child could be a match for his centuries of accrued hatred and the power that hatred bestowed upon him. She would soon learn of her folly. But not yet. She would be almost the last to suffer. And oh, what a suffering that would be. An evil joy filled his mind as he thought of the one that would incur his greatest wrath, the progeny that had been stolen from him and delivered into light and salvation by the old witch. The boy that he had sired. The boy that had been lost to him and had come to see him destroyed.

His spirit moved toward the ones in the road that dared march right up to his front door. They would be first. He extended the minatory specter of his purpose and snuffed out the light of the metallic torch. He did the same to that cursed pendent on the lost one. Now, bathed in the black of night, he would test their aged hearts. He would take them one by one.

Seizing the first by the wrist and throat, he dragged her away into the night, back to the house, his house – the bones of his very being. There she would die, her spirit doomed to roam the halls for all eternity in search of a solace that would never be found.

## 2
**11:07 p.m. – 11:13 p.m.**

"Janet? Tommy? Where are you? I can't see a damned thing, nothing." Matt moved cautiously from side to side, inching forward, both arms outstretched and searching the air for anything tangible.

"I'm over here," said Tommy. "I can't see anything, either. How could it be this damned dark?"

Tommy's voice came from ahead and to Matt's right. "Keep talk-" A light thump sounded, followed by a heavier one. "Oh shit! I just fell over Emma."

Tommy moved slowly toward the sound, sweeping his foot lightly in front of him until it bumped up against Matt's leg. "Ah, there you are."

Matt felt for Emma's hand, took it and reached up his arm. "I have Emma's hand. Take mine, Tommy, and grab Janet's too." Tommy found Matt's hand and clutched it in his own.

"Janet? Where are you?" Tommy swept the air with his free hand hoping to connect with Janet somewhere. After a few moments of trying and no response to his or Matt's calls he gave up and knelt down beside Matt, who was kneeling beside Emma.

"A little light would be nice. Any idea where the flashlight got to?" asked Matt.

Tommy shook his head, realized that Matt couldn't see it and just said: "No."

"Wait. Tommy ... your smokes. You have matches, right?"

"Oh hell, you're right. I guess I am going senile." Tommy dug out the matches and struck one. Its feeble light was swallowed in the darkness, leaving it to cast a pale glow barely strong enough to allow Tommy to see to the end of his arm.

"Well, that was useful," quipped Matt.

Tommy gritted his teeth and bawled out a scream of frustration. "Fuckin' hell, you dumb son-of-a-bitch matches. We need LIGHT!!!! FUUUUCCCCKKKK!"

*If you need de light ... den make de light. Mot'er give you dat power long ago.* The woman's voice ran through their heads like a soft, trickling brook on a summer's day. *T'ink o'de light ... den summon de light. It be a glow de old evil one can't put out.*

What light? thought Tommy. *What damned...* He suddenly remembered the car. He could hear Janet asking: *You have a roll of duct tape I don't know about.* He mumbled his answer to her aloud. "I have this."

"What? What do you have?" asked Matt.

Tommy let go of Matt's hand and raised his arm. A single word, spelled out in brilliant letters popped into his mind: L-I-G-H-T. The tattoo of the crystal on his shoulder began to glow softy, dim at first, and then brighter and brighter until it flooded their surroundings in blazing white.

"That's a pretty damned neat trick, if you'd ask me," said Matt, smiling. "But ... where-"

"Where's Janet?" Tommy finished.

"Yeah, where's Janet, indeed? And what's wrong with Emma?"

"What's wrong with Emma, and where Janet got to aren't the only things that bother me, Matt. What happened to our mental connection? It should be there ... here ... whatever. Where the hell is it? And why did we lose it now, when we need it the most?"

***

Inside their minds, Emma and Walcott found themselves in a sphere of dazzling blue light. Before them, in her flowered dress stood Mother Cassandra. As always, the smell was rich honeysuckle. A feeling of complete tranquility pervaded the space. There was something else, as well: connected knowledge between Emma and Walcott. Each knew everything the other knew.

Mother grinned and spread her arms wide. "Mot'er bring you here dat you meet now, in de place where de evil one's mind can't go."

"What ... where ... is this place?" asked Emma. "I feel like my whole body's floating."

Mother laughed. She laughed hard, her voice deep, her hands pressed against her shaking belly. When she finally stopped, she drew a deep sigh. She laid a knowing index finger aside her nose and then pointed it at Emma. "Ain't no bodies here, chil' ... only de mind ... de spirit ... de soul. Dis is de place between worlds, a place where de shadow has substance and substance is but a shadow. It is de place where all t'ings begin and all t'ings end, where everyt'ing exist and not'ing exist. Some call it de Void; some call it Limbo. It is a place dat is and is not."

"But ... but if we're here-" began Emma.

Mother laughed again. "You ain't here, chil'. Nobody here. An' der ain't no more time t'worry 'bout dis place and what is and what isn't. De evil one's powers be growin'. Come his hour, when de numbers make t'irteen, he will free himself along wit' dat part of him dat belong to de demon beast, de incubus. Years ago, your friends play der part. Now, der part is done, t'ough dey still share a power you need. To end all dis fall to you." Mother turned an eye on Walcott. "An' to you. But you bot' must beware de house. De house belong to *him*. Wit'out him, de house can *not* be. Wit'out de house, *he* can not be. Dey one an' de same an' full o'de same evil."

"What must we do?" asked Emma. "How do we stop him?"

"You must learn dat for yourself, chil'. Mot'er give de two of you de shared knowledge. Each of you must learn what de ot'er need an' help dem get it. What de evil one want is a child born of himself an' de demon incubus. Dis he will take for himself to once again move among the living. He will take it from our daughters if de two of you do not find de way to stop it. His mind ...

de specter of his mind already strong enough to pass t'rough de walls. No matter what ... his body must never be allowed to leave de house."

"You're going to help us, right?" Emma asked the question almost defiantly. "To do what you've done so far you must have great power. You are going to use it to help us, yes?"

"De time for questions be at de end now. Now you must bot' find your own way ... toget'er. What Mot'er can do now is give you de light back."

Emma started to say something and an odd feeling washed over her. She felt as if her body were coming apart, like a sand sculpture being blown apart in a high wind. The next thing she knew, she was staring up into Matt's concerned face, lit by Tommy's tattoo.

Walcott had the same feeling, awakening to find Tina hovering over him, and Ralph shaking him lightly by the shoulders. Their faces were illuminated by the moon necklace that once again burned brightly.

***

The specter of Wickersham's will dragged Janet to the house. Her body was wracked with numbing cold. Unvoiced screams spilled out of her in endless wails of unheard agony. At the side of the house, her shadowy captor dropped her to the ground. She lay there in a frigid rigor, her arms angled out to her sides and her eyes wide and staring up into the cold darkness that hovered over her.

*Now*, came the ghostly voice in her head, *you shall be the first to pay for your insolence and for the undue suffering you and your young friends caused me all those years ago. You awakened me before my time; you allowed ... helped ... that witch confine my spirit in endless torment. From that day unto this, you lived but a handful of years. For me, each hour, each minute was a hundred thousand lifetimes of anguish and agony. Now I will show you ... show you all ... how that feels.*

Janet's body was lifted from the ground. The sensation of cold she felt suddenly changed. Her body felt as if it were burning from the inside. A moment later she was freezing again. Her stomach felt the same way it did when she was a child on her first roller coaster ride. And then came blackness. It engulfed her, shrouded her, suffocated her with primordial desolation.

She had a discomforting feeling of floating in a vast emptiness. Her heart sank and her mind filled with despair. Slowly, the shroud dissipated. She awoke to find herself in a small, round, stone-walled windowless room with a single door. A full-length mirror hung on one wall, flanked by two flaming sconces. She stood before it staring at her own disheveled reflection.

Janet bolted for the door and reached for the small brass knob in its center. The door disappeared and reappeared on the wall eight feet to her right. When she reached it, it disappeared and reappeared on the wall behind her, next to the mirror. The house shook with Wickersham's booming laughter.

"Welcome to your eternal prison, stuck forever chasing an unobtainable exit."

Janet wanted to cry; she could feel the emptiness of eternal isolation overwhelming her. Instead, she refused to give in. Anger grew within her. "I *will* find a way out of here, you bastard. I don't think you're as strong as you think you are. I will never give up. Do you hear me? I will NEVER give up."

## 3
**11:14 p.m. – 11:23 p.m.**

Matt and Tommy helped Emma to her feet. The tattoo of the crystal on Tommy's arm grew in brightness when he touched Emma and dimmed a bit when he let go. Behind the house, Tina had to shield her eyes from the glow coming off Walcott's necklace, as Ralph helped him to his feet.

Tommy started to ask if Emma was alright but she held up a hand to silence him. "Janet's been taken," she said, but the voice coming from her mouth was male. "*He* has taken her spirit, her soul, into the house. We have to help her. But first, we must join up with those at the back of the house."

Behind the house, Walcott was suggesting the same meet-up to Ralph and Tina. They both exchanged glances and took a couple of steps backward. The voice issuing from Walcott's mouth was distinctly female. Walcott waved their questions away and handed Ralph two keys he dug from his pocket. This time when he spoke, the voice was his again. "Hold on to these for me, will you, Ralph? We'll need 'em soon enough. We have to get to the side of the house. There's an old door there hidden behind a tangle of thorny shrubs. It leads down into the basement. That's our way in. Unfortunately, getting to it won't be easy, and the thorny shrubs are the least of our problems. The house itself will work, at the very least, to keep us out ... at worst ... well, you know the worst."

On the other side, Emma briefly explained the merging of minds she and Walcott had experienced with Mother Cassandra. "I guess the voice thing was a leftover or something. Anyway, Walcott has a way into the house. We'll have to make our way around to the side. That leaves us with a conundrum: I'm pretty sure walking straight up the drive isn't the best plan. On the other hand, the damned bushes and trees surrounding the house seem to be in collusion with the loathsome place. They've been slapping and pawing and grabbing at us the whole way. I'm afraid to think about what the ones closer to the house are capable of."

Matt let out a hiccup of a nervous laugh. "I don't think it matters which way we go. I'm pretty damned sure that the closer we get to the house, by this way or that, we're in for a tough time. And that's being optimistic."

"What about Janet?" asked Tommy. "We can't just abandon her; that ain't right and it ain't in *my* game plan. The last time we were in this damned place I fell apart and left it to Henry and Amy to do what I should have done. Not this time." He turned toward the house and raised his arm. The glow of the tattoo spread in a large cone down the driveway and fell upon the front door. The house seemed to shudder. The doorframe bowed inward; the windows bowed outward and the shades dropped almost to the bottom. It was as if the house had to squint its eyes shut against the light. "We're coming, ready or not. We're coming for Janet; we're coming for you ... and we're coming right at you."

Tommy started forward. Emma fell in beside and Matt a few paces behind. A few yards from the front of the house, a gale force wind blew out of nowhere and ripped down the drive right for them. It passed them on either side, flattening the shrubs, trees and bushes that lined the road and grabbed and tore at them.

"What the hell was that? Matt turned, appraising the ten foot wide swath of destruction on either side of them.

"What the hell is that is a better question?" said Tommy, pointing at a small tornado of dust that rose out of the ground in front of them. It remained stationary, dead in the middle of their path. Matt thought it reminded him of the old *Taz* cartoon whirlwind.

Emma took a couple of steps toward it. Tommy reached for her but she shook him off. When she was standing directly in front of it, its rotation began to slow and the air was filled with the scent of honeysuckle. Just before it stopped completely it exploded outward from the center, revealing Mother Cassandra.

"De time has come for all my children t'play der parts. Being toget'er has brought Mot'er to her full powers. De way ahead is now clear, but de dark time comin'. *His* time, de time o'de number t'irteen will see de beginning o'de end ... for good or bad."

"Thirteen?" said Tommy. "I don't understand. It's well after eleven at night. Thirteen would be tomorrow afternoon."

Mother laughed. "T'irteen is but a number. At eleven twenty-four, de evil one will be free an' de final battle begin'."

Emma smiled. "I get it. Thirteen. Eleven twenty-four."

"Christ," said Matt. "I get it too."

Tommy looked at both of them as if they were crazy.

"Twenty-four minus eleven. See?" Matt nudged Tommy in the ribs with his elbow.

"That makes no sense at all," said Tommy.

Mother smiled an empty smile, devoid of pleasure or mirth or even reassurance. "It makes sense to him, an' dat's important. From de time of his number, all t'ings be in play. He need to complete his plan before de stroke o'midnight. You need to see he don't."

"Why can't you stop him?" asked Matt. "If you're at the height of-"

"Mot'er got to use her powers in anot'er way. What Mot'er got to do will cost her everyt'ing." She smiled again, and this time it was full of warmth. "Mot'er be wit' you, but not in de way dat you would hope. Dis be de last time you gon' see Mot'er. As Mot'er talk to you here, she talk to de ones on de ot'er side as well. Right now ... we all be toget'er. An' what Mot'er got t'do gon' take almost all her power. You all got good hearts. Dat's de bond dat have de strengt' to undo de evil. But strong and good hearts ain't enough now. What you need, Mot'er have t'give you."

"What do we need that will cost you so much, Mother? Wouldn't having you with us be just as powerful as whatever it is?" asked Emma

Mother let out a belly laugh. "No chil'. What you need ... what Mot'er must give you ... is what de young ones dat come here all dem years ago had. An' de time has come. Now, you must meet wit' de ot'ers. De way is clear. Hurry, for *his* number be almost upon us."

Emma started to say something but Mother held up her hand. "Time for Mot'er t'go, chil'. Time t'give what must be given." Before any of them could do or say anything else, Mother exploded. Fine particles, like shimmering confetti enveloped the group, whirling around each of them like a miniature cyclone. Their skin began to tingle as the particles adhered and then soaked in.

*Now be what you must be and do what must be done.* Mother's voice in their heads was no more than an echo of an echo.

"Come on," said Emma, "we can't waste any more time. Let's join up with the others and get this whole thing over with." She broke into a dead run and the others followed. They skirted the front porch and made their way around the left side of the house. Walcott, Tina and Ralph were waiting for them. The bramble bushes Walcott had told them blocked the door were gone, flattened like the trees and shrubs along the sides of the driveway. But there was no door, just a stone block wall.

"I feel funny all of a sudden," said Tommy, leaning over and supporting himself with a hand on the wall.

"Me too," said Matt. "I feel like ... like my insides ... I don't know. It just feels-"

"Like you're on the wildest rollercoaster ride you've ever been on," finished Tina.

"It'll pass," said Walcott. "Trust me, you'll feel better in a few minutes. Right now, we have to get started. But first, I believe this belongs to you." He handed the shillelagh to Emma and asked Ralph for the keys. He picked one and clamped it between his teeth, stepped up to the wall and laid the palm of his hand on the block. "Moutre m'."

The wall flexed in a wave from bottom to top and back down again. Windows flew open and slammed shut. Great plumes of black smoke belched from the chimneys. For a moment the wall seemed to thin, become transparent. It quickly re-solidified with a final rumbling shudder.

Walcott grumbled a curse, took the key from between his teeth and handed it back to Ralph. More determined than ever, he strode to the wall, pressed his hand against it as firmly as he could and repeated the command for the house to *show* him: "Moutre m'." This time, a small square of block under his index finger melted away, revealing a brass keyhole. "Would you care to do the honors, Ralph?"

Ralph slipped the key into the lock and twisted it. The house screamed out its anger. The sound of it was like barbed wire scraped across glass. Windows exploded; doorframes bowed and splintered and the foundation rumbled. When it finally settled down, a section of wall to the left of the keyhole opened onto a descending stone stairway.

Emma pushed past Walcott but was yanked back abruptly by Tommy. "Un-unh! Not this time. This time I'm leading ... like I should have done back then. The light from his shoulder tattoo grew in intensity and Matt gasped, unable to believe what he was seeing. Tina stood slack jawed staring at Tommy's face. The three of them, Matt, Tina and Tommy, looked as if they'd stepped into a time machine. If Matt didn't know better, he would guess Tommy and Tina to be in their early to mid-fifties. Tommy and Tina thought the same about Matt.

"What in the world?" Matt rubbed a hand across his face, his fingers unable to find the familiar wrinkles that stared back at him daily from his mirror. "I swear ... I even *feel* younger."

"Of course you do," said Walcott. "You are. Mother has split what was left of her power, her life force, so to speak, between you. It is the gift she spoke of. The task ahead requires a vigor your true age would not allow. It was her final sacrifice to help ensure we succeeded."

"Then let's quit wasting time," said Tommy. "Time to meet this fucker head on." He turned slightly sideways so that the tattoo shone down the steps and started down. Emma was right on his heels, slapping the end of the shillelagh into the palm of her hand. The sight and sound of it reminded Tina of an old beat-cop with a nightstick. Matt followed Tina, and Ralph, Matt.

Walcott closed the opening behind them and sealed it. With the incantation, "Objè nan je yo," the door became invisible once more. Outside, the key (still in the lock) disintegrated into a powdery dust and blew away. The keyhole faded from sight. Satisfied the exit was sealed, he hitched the backpack up onto his shoulder and turned to follow the others. He paused a moment, thinking about what lay ahead for him. A shiver ran up his spine and he shook it off. Drawing a deep sigh of resignation, he hurried down the steps. One at a time, the steps disintegrated behind him as he passed down.

\*\*\*

Below the altar, Wickersham's imprisoned spirit could almost feel the ticking of the clock edging toward eleven twenty-four – edging toward his number, his re-assumption of power and corporeal existence. He could feel the strength of his consciousness grow. Still conjoined to the incubus, he felt its demonic powers growing as well. Soon, very soon now, they would be free. Soon they would have what they wanted, what they needed.

## Chapter 38
## THE THIRTEENTH HOUR

**11:24 p.m.**

At precisely eleven twenty-four p.m. time stopped. The great house rocked on its foundation as it slid all the way back in time. Wooden shutters sprang from the walls beside widows that slammed and bolted themselves shut. Furniture, long gone to rot and decay, sprang into place. The sunken living room leveled itself. The Brazilian Oak flooring was swallowed by the reformed original planks, still rutted, gauged and oil-stained from centuries past. The stone walls of the turret room gobbled up the bookshelves. Caught in the backwash of time, the mahogany spiral staircase disintegrated, fell to the floor as dust and disappeared. At the top of the house, abutments reshaped themselves into the stone gargoyle guardians of yesteryear. All that once was three hundred and twenty years ago was again.

In the dungeon room, the stone blocks at the foot of the alter shook, cracked and split apart. Bright orange and red flames shot from the opening and licked at the ceiling. The whole room – the whole house – reverberated with the mixed thunder of a baby's cry, a beast's growl and a man's laughter.

Brian, scared beyond belief, threw himself atop Annabel/Abigail to shield her/them from the horror he knew was coming. Not wanting to see but unable to turn his gaze away, he watched as a creature, the likes of which did not belong in this world or any other, crawled out of the hole. Its body was aflame. Tongues of fire danced on its shoulders and ran up and down its arms. It stood almost eight feet tall, a single bat-like wing jutting from its back on the left side. Its chest was divided right down the center, the right half human: the left, thick and gray, studded with round nodules that reminded Brian of wood burl. Half of an infant appeared to be growing out of the things right shoulder. One tiny leg and one tiny arm kicked and paddled wildly at the air. Its head rested against a neck that supported two other heads. The head on the right was human. Silvery-gray hair, greasy, knotted and tangled, framed its sallow cheeks. Its eyes were sunken and burned a fiery red. The head on the left was larger. Its skull was plated with scales and sharp, serrated spikes of varying lengths and thickness. A thick drool leaked from the corners of its mouth and its eyes, locked on the female body that Brian shielded, burned with lust.

The creature strode from the fire and stopped at the head of the cot. The baby wailed; the demon shrieked and Wickersham laughed. The beast reached down with its clawed hand and plucked Brian off the girls. It hurled him against the wall like so much refuse. Wickersham turned his attention toward Brian, the beast toward Annabel/Abigail.

"Now has my time come," bellowed Wickersham. "Three hundred and more years have I been held prisoner here. Three hundred and more years has my spirit grown entwined with this house. We are one and the same, as I am one and the same with the incubus. But now the time of redemption has come. Now, the separation and rejoining can begin. Now, together, beast and man and man, I shall take back that which was stolen from me. I shall take back the woman, and through her ... through our issue, our offspring ... shall I attain my immortality. And you–" He pointed a finger at Brian. "You shall be the instrument through which I satisfy my lust and desire. You shall help me fulfill my destiny. I will take you. And you shall watch and feel from the prison of your own mind as I use your body to violate the woman."

The baby stopped wailing; the demon closed its eyes and fell silent. As the unit they were, they moved to the altar and stood amidst the flames that still poured from the gaping floor.

"Oh Great One of the Eternal Darkness," called Wickersham, "Now is the time of my redemption. Grant unto me, your humble suppliant, the power of separate union. Grant that I may be man and beast, both and none, separate yet linked."

The flames died away, leaving behind a swirling mass of thick black smoke. The room filled with the stench of a sewer. Rats, hundreds of them, scurried out from cracks in the walls and floors. They formed a circle around the smoke, chittering and squeaking and squealing. Some stood atop of others; some stood on hind legs. All watched, paying their rat homage to the smoke-being that slowly settled into a dark, indistinct form. Three thick arms of smoke trailed outward, their ends forming huge clawed appendages. Each grabbed a part of the Wickersham/demon/baby amalgam and with a single twisting pull, rent the three apart. When it finished its task the smoke swirled away, disappearing into the hole from which it had sprung. The rats ceased their chittering and squealing and darted back into the cracks from which they had come. The air cleared of the foul scent and Wickersham stood next to the demon that hovered over Annabel/Abigail. On the floor beside Wickersham and the demon lay the baby, still kicking it sole leg and waving its sole arm. Teeth, like fags, protruded from its pallid infant lips. Its black marble eyes stared upward, darting from side to side.

"We are separate and one," Wickersham said, closing the distance between him and Brian. "Now ... *we* shall merge to become beast and man and man. And our lust shall be slaked and our offspring begotten through the taking of the woman by the incubus that shares our consciousness and has been summoned to do our bidding."

## Chapter 39
## INSIDE – OUTSIDE – BOTH SIDES

**11:24 p.m. – 11:42 p.m.**

**1**

Janet stood in the center of the room before the full-length mirror. All around her, doors appeared and disappeared, first on this wall, then on that. She refused to play the game any longer. So she stood there doing the only thing she could think to do. Concentrating with all her might, she tried to reestablish her mental connection with the others.

When the house shook and reformed itself at eleven twenty-four, the mirror cracked. The sound broke her concentration and the image of Tommy she had managed to summon disappeared.

Suddenly, one of the doors appeared on the wall behind her, reflected clearly in the mirror. "I'm not playing anymore. Do you understand? I'll figure a way out of here, but I'm not about to waste my energy entertaining you." She remained facing the mirror, unmoving. The door vanished abruptly, leaving only the jamb and an open doorway. Janet just shook her head and folded her arms across her chest.

*Dat's right, chil'.* Mother's voice was strong in her head. *T'ink, girl. Dis house do not'in' but play tricks on a body. You know dat. In here, only one illusion is not an illusion. Dat be de way out.*

Janet puzzled over this for a while. At last, a wry smile twisted Janet's lips. She knew full well what was going to happen when she moved toward the open doorway, but she had a different idea in mind. And she hoped with all her might that she was right. The only real illusion was her image in the mirror. It was real, yet not real, no more than a reflection of reality. Just as she anticipated, a few steps away from the open doorway, the wooden door suddenly appeared on its hinges and slammed shut. At the same time, she turned and dashed toward the mirror, keeping her fingers crossed and hoping she wouldn't be sliced to ribbons.

As her body made contact with the glass, it shattered and disappeared. She passed through. A rush of sensations assaulted her. She felt as if she were floating; she felt as if she were drowning. She felt tired and dizzy, weak yet strong and revitalized. For a moment, there was no sensation at all. Then, a sharp pain as she burst through the front door and went tumbling down the porch steps, her spirit reintegrating with her body.

A gentle laughter filled her mind. *Raise y'self, chil, for de time has come t'see de end o't'ings.*

Janet sat up slowly, everything a mental and physical blur. Things cleared slowly and she realized, with a slight sense of panic, that she was alone. The others were already inside. She was going to have to find her own way in. But certainly not the way she had just exited.

*Ain't for you t'be part of de inside goin's on, girl. Your part got t'be played out here an' alone. You com' t'Mot'er. You know where. But you got t'hurry, before de crumblin' time begin.*

Janet looked at the house, shot it the finger, and headed off into the woods. In total darkness, the going was slow and difficult. And somehow, her feet seemed to know where she was going – even if she didn't. She just let her feet carry her forward. Sweat stood out on her brow, matted the ends of her hair and dripped down her cheeks. With every step forward, the undergrowth in the back (which had not been flattened) grew thicker and denser. The sudden and unseasonable humidity was almost too much. Twice she got tangled up. The second time she didn't think she was getting out. Brambles had wrapped themselves around her left arm and right leg. The thorns dug in like the biting hold of a bulldog. The harder she struggled, the tighter they got, the deeper they bit. She finally managed to extricate her leg at the cost of her pants leg and a significant amount of flesh. Gritting her teeth against the pain, she wrapped both hands around the branch that held her arm and worked it up and down until it snapped. She reached the clearing and the well, the remnants of her attacker still clinging to her forearm. It took quite a bit of patience to unwrap it and even more to pull out the thorns, one at a time. But at least she could see what she was doing. A blue glow spilled from the well, enveloping the entire clearing. All around the perimeter, any branches or foliage that crossed into the light withered and died. The only living plant within the circle of light was the honeysuckle that covered the well.

Why she was here she had no idea. All she knew was that this was exactly where she was supposed to be. Whatever her part was to be in all of this was to be played out here.

"Well," she said, looking around and hoping that Mother was there somewhere, "here I am. I can't say that it makes me feel very secure or comfortable being on my own. I'd much prefer to be with the others. Guess I have no choice but to trust that I'm here for a good reason. I sure hope you know what you're doing." Then, under her breath she added, "'Cause I sure don't."

## 2

The stairs seemed to go on forever, twisting ever so slightly to the right every now and then. With Tommy still in the lead, they went down and down and down. At least, so they thought. It was Emma that finally noticed that something was wrong – very wrong. She grabbed Tommy by the shoulder and pulled him up short.

"Look at this." Emma pointed to a crusty patch of mold on the wall. Its shape was reminiscent of a starfish that had been cut in half. "We've passed this before. In fact, I think we've passed it several times but I can't be certain."

"That's impossible," said Tina, "we've been moving steadily down. How could we–"

"It's not impossible," said Walcott, who had caught up to them. "This house is alive. It's alive with Wickersham's soul and will."

"But how can we go down, then be up to go down again over and over again? Stairs can't move, change. And even if they could, wouldn't we have to feel like we were climbing to get up enough to go down again? It doesn't make any sense." Tina shook her head.

"An Escher painting," said Matt. "Kind of like a Mobius loop. Or Klein bottle. Nothing goes in the direction it looks like it goes if you follow it. The inside is the outside and vice versa."

"Okay," said Emma. "How it looks or works doesn't matter. How do we get off the merry-go-round is the question."

"Up!" Tommy turned and worked his way past the others on the steps. "If down is up, then up must be down."

"Normally," said Ralph, who for the most part preferred to remain silent and see how things played out, "I'd say that was the stupidest thing I'd ever heard. But in this case ... I think it sounds so wrong it might be right. Or, at least ... it's worth a try." He shrugged his shoulders.

"Wait a minute. We can't afford to waste any more time," cautioned Emma. "That's exactly what he ... and this damned place ... wants. Let's just take a minute to think about this."

Walcott said, "Emma's right. We have to stop playing his game." He moved to the front of the line and started down the stairs again. After the seventh step he stopped. His necklace moon pendant began to spark off a rainbow of colors. It finally settled into an electric green. He closed his eyes and said, "Moutre m'!" Like a slinky, a green pencil of light fell to the steps and tumbled down one after the other. "Here we go."

They followed the light down and down until they came to the bottom at last. This time, without any twists or turns. The slinky guide-light faded out. Tommy, who had once more taken the lead, found himself and his group hemmed in by three solid block walls and the untrustworthy staircase.

"Guess you're up again," said Tommy to Walcott.

Walcott stepped forward. "Moutre m'!"

Nothing happened. He repeated it, his eyes closed and his mind focused on an image of a doorway. "SHOW ME!" he screamed, his frustration getting the better of him.

Nothing happened.

"I guess it's *not* me this time."

Tommy leaned against the wall, unrolled the pack of smokes from his sleeve, fished one out and stuck it in the corner of his mouth. He didn't bother tossing it there this time. It took three matches to get it lit, the first two blown out by a breeze that came from nowhere. He took a deep drag, held it a moment and then let it out slowly in a long line. It drifted lazily across the room, suddenly made a right turn and passed rapidly through the wall as if it had been sucked into a vacuum.

"Oh my God," cried Tina. "That's it. That's it. You know what, Tommy? I think your bad habit just became useful." She turned to Matt. "Do you remember how we got out of here the last time?"

Matt shrugged. "Herny. Henry got us out before. I don't think he's going to be able to help much now."

"Yes, Henry got us out. But how?" Tina gave Matt a *could-of-had-a-V-8* slap on the forehead. "Right through the fucking wall, remember? Somehow, he took us right through the fucking walls of the house." She turned back to Tommy. "Blow out some more smoke."

Tommy complied. They all watched the smoke drift across the room, make the same sharp right and rip right through the wall. Tina walked over and put her hand where the smoke had gone through. Her arm disappeared up to the elbow. "Everything in here is an illusion, a trick. I'm going through."

Emma grabbed her before she could move. "Maybe we should do a little probing first. Just to be sure it's safe, what do you think?"

Tommy stepped around them, tossed his cigarette through the wall and walked through. He called back to the others. "Come on. Looks like Tina was right. It's the way through."

Tina winked at Emma and went through. Emma went next, followed by Walcott and Ralph. Matt went last, as usual. They found themselves in a long, narrow hallway that stretched to their left and right into the darkness beyond the radius of Tommy's tattoo light. Behind them the open doorway through which they had come was clearly visible, in front of them, an apparently solid block wall.

"Tricks," said Tina. "Tricks and illusions ... all of it."

"Perhaps," said Ralph, speaking his mind for the first time, "but can we know which tricks and illusions are safe to ignore. If we ignore the wrong one..."

"He's definitely right," said Matt. "Remember Lucy? That was one hell of a nasty trick."

"Which way?" asked Tina, looking down the hall to either side of her.

"Some people do go both ways," Matt said, crossing his arms and pointing in opposite directions. No one laughed. No one even smiled.

"This is where we must split up," said Walcott. "Although our destinies are tied together, mine is mine alone. I'll take the right. The rest of you ... that way. I have no doubt that we will eventually meet in the same place, but we're out of time and we can't take the chance of going the wrong way as a group."

"If that's the way you're going, that's the way I'm going," Ralph said.

"No, Ralph. You should go with the others. I will be all right alone."

Ralph shook his head. "Sorry, Missss-ter Walcott, but I've been with you for a long time now and that ain't about to change. Like it or not, I'm with you."

"I don't like the idea of splitting up at all," Emma said, her eyes darting between Walcott and Ralph. "But I agree that we can't waste any more time. So if you're going, then I have to agree with Ralph. You're not going alone. I just wish there were some way we could keep in touch."

Matt shot out an arm and grabbed Tina's hand. "Keep in touch. Come on everyone, hold hands. Let's see if we can reestablish that mental link we always used to have. I can't believe such a thing was given to us just to fail us when we needed it the most. Come on."

They all linked hands, Emma resting her free hand on Walcott's armless shoulder. The glow of Tommy's crystal tattoo dimmed to almost nothing. Walcott's moon pendent did the same. They stood there in the dark but for a small, pale circle of light, eyes closed and minds reaching for one another.

It took some time but it was Emma and Walcott who touched first. It didn't hold; it dissolved almost as quickly as it had formed. They both understood why. It was a remnant of the joining Mother had had them share. And they also knew that it would be the others, the ones who had been here seventy years ago, that would have to make the connection. Emma drew her hands away from Ralph and Walcott, and Walcott pulled Ralph gently out of the circle.

"It's up to you/it's all you," said Emma and Walcott almost simultaneously. "If you can't do it, it can't be done."

The circle of old friends closed in. Ralph gasped at what he saw and Walcott nudged him and motioned him to be quiet. Like some bizarre double-exposure photo, Tommy, Tina and Matt were old and young at the same time. Their teenage bodies shimmered within the worn out shells they had become.

It was Henry's voice who spoke to them first. *You've been deceived. You have always had the gift of connection.* He *cannot take from you that which is beyond his grasp. Believe in yourselves as you always have. For so long we've been apart ... yet...* Amy's voice picked up the thread. *...yet we have never truly been apart. Our strength ... your strength ... lies solely in your belief. Believe now as you did then.*

Their minds suddenly merged all at once with the power of colliding freight trains. They all staggered backward a few paces and their circle was broken. Almost. Still visible where they had been standing was the afterimage of the three of them as teenagers, still holding hands. Their translucent bodies shimmered and wavered in a rainbow of colors and then faded.

*Have you got me?* thought Tommy. The question was unnecessary; he knew they had. They were connected again.

*I've got you,* answered Janet, and Matt and Tina heard it in their heads as clearly as did Tommy. *I've got you, and I think it's about time we start causing some trouble. Remember how bad things always happened when we were together all those years ago? Well, let's put that to use. Let's make some really bad things happen.*

Tommy smiled. *Leave it to you to play Alice through the looking glass. What the hell are you doing at the old well?*

*I'm not really sure. I just know this is where I'm supposed to be. Looks like it's an I-do-my-thing-you-do-yours deal. Whatever the hell our* things *are supposed to be.*

"Guess we'll see you on the other side, then, Janet." Tommy vocalized this, mostly for Ralph's, Emma's and Walcott's benefit.

"If you're all good to go ... mentally ... then it's definitely time to take the fight home," said Emma. "I suggest that you go with Walcott and Ralph, Tina. That's our line of communication. Whoever finds him ... or my daughter and son-in-law first, tell the others."

There was no need for any further conversation, except for wishes of luck.

### 3

Wickersham loomed over Brian, who lay up against the wall where he'd been thrown. The impact had knocked the breath out of him and his chest burned. Wickersham reached down and yanked him up and off his feet. "Now shall three become one, boy. This time, it will not be just your mind I take."

From over Wickersham's shoulder Brian could see the demon slavering over his Annabel. Its eyes roved over her body, its talon-fingered hands opening and closing with the frustration of impatience. Brian's stomach turned as he watched the beast reach out and stroke its curved claws up the inside of Annabel's thigh. And his heart broke to see her struggling helplessly and to hear her cries of fear and desperation and disgust.

"I'm gonna kill you, you motherfucker!" Brian practically spat it in Wickersham's face. "I'm gonna-"

"ENOUGH!" roared Wickersham. "I will brook no further delay."

Brian slammed the heels of his hands down on Wickersham's elbows in an unsuccessful effort to break the hold. Wickersham laughed and set Brian down. "Now we join."

Wickersham's body thinned into a fine yellow mist. It drifted forward until it completely enveloped Brian. Brian screamed as it sank into his pores, and he found himself looking out through his eyes and the demon incubus's at the same time. He could feel the lustful desire that coursed through the beast's body, could feel the cool soft flesh of Annabel's thigh through the thing's touch. Then he felt himself sinking away, like being sucked down by some mental undertow. He was once again a prisoner within himself, witness and unwilling participant to all that would happen, unable to affect any of it – able to feel all of it. His soul screamed silently in torment, for he knew what Wickersham knew, what the incubus knew. They were one, the tree of them, and he would partake in the defiling of his wife.

Under Wickersham's control, Brian moved over past the beast and undid the chains that bound Annabel to the cot. Taking an iron collar with a short chain attached to it from the wall above the cot, he latched it around her throat and yanked her to her feet. He fastened her arms behind her back with a small pair of wrist cuffs. "Take her to the altar and put her on her knees," he said, and handed the end of the chain to the beast.

The thing gave a violent tug on the chain and the collar bit into Annabel's throat as she was jerked forward. The force of it stung her balance and she fell hard. The demon paid no mind and dragged her across the floor. When they reached the altar, it bent down, ran its blue, forked tongue up and down the side of her face and pulled her up onto her knees by her hair.

Terrified, Annabel knelt there, helpless as the beast tore the shirt from her body.

"Through my friend here," said Brian in Wickersham's voice, "I shall impart my seed to you. But don't worry about me, my dear, I ... we, your inept husband, shall feel the pleasure of your body as you are taken and inseminated. But first, your husband must share in your torment. He shall feel and see my violation of you." Brian undid his pants and let them drop to the floor. "Before you are taken, I ... *we* ... shall make good use of your pretty mouth."

Annabel started to scream but suddenly fell silent. Her eyes glazed over as her lungs were filled with the aroma of honeysuckle and a melodic voice filled her mind: It is time for me to stand, Abigail told Annabel. *I must rise; it is my part to play. Submerge yourself in the deepest recesses and sleep ... dream ... be unaware of your body. Float within yourself. Your time is yet to come. What is now to come is for me and me alone. It is I, not you, that must face the beast.*

Annabel felt her *self* sinking away, as if a powerful narcotic had suddenly flooded her brain. She floated down, deeper and deeper into a feathery darkness of comfort.

Brian took a step back in shocked surprise as the features of the woman before him changed. Wickersham felt a surge of panic, wondering how what he was seeing was possible.

"As you have waited, so have I," said Abigail. A knowing grin curled the edges of her lips. "And as I have waited, so has my mother ... and my son. They will be your undoing. And it is I you must face, not the woman within. Do what you will with me, as you had done in the before time. But you shall not touch this woman."

Wickersham quickly regained his composure and stepped forward. "I will have you ... and in so doing shall I also have the woman whose body you now possess. Are you not one and the same, as I am one and the same with her husband and the incubus? To have you is to have her."

***

Emma and Tommy discovered the hallway that had been linear two minutes ago began to bend to the right.

Walcott and his group found it bending to the left. Eventually the two groups met up on what had to be the opposite side of the house from where they'd started. Fastened into the wall with iron hardware was a single, round-topped oaken door about three feet in height. It had a large iron ring as a door pull.

"This can't be," said Tommy. "Unless I'm wrong, and I hope to God I am, this is the damned door-"

"You're not wrong," finished Matt. "It's the very same door. I'm sure of it. I can feel it in my gut."

"Me too," added Tina. "It's the door that killed Lucy. But it can't be. That door was down in the tunnel, and it led to a large room, not a hallway."

"It's the house again," said Walcott.

"So what are we supposed to do now?" asked Tina, keeping her eyes averted from the door. The memory of Lucy being stuck, squashed in the jamb, turned her stomach over.

"We go through." Emma grabbed the ring. "I told you, I've had it with this place." She gave a sharp tug and the door swung open easily. Whatever was on the other side of it was shrouded in complete darkness.

"Getting it open is one thing," said Matt. "Getting through it alive is another. Last time we had a cooler to keep it from closing all the way."

"I'm with Emma. I've had enough of this shit, too." Tommy walked straight past everyone, ducked down and went through the open door. "It's another hallway."

Emma followed Tommy. Once through, she could feel they were closer now. She could actually feel *his* presence. She looked to her left and then her right. "It's another trick ... another corridor that leads nowhere. The door is here, right here. We just have to find it."

"That must be me, then." Walcott pushed the door open a little farther and stepped through. Ralph went next and then Tina. The door never shifted.

Matt started toward the opening and then stopped. The image of a worm on the end of a hook popped into his mind. He let out a nervous chuckle. "I think you guys are all worms."

"What?" Tina moved toward the door and Matt held up his hands to stop her.

"You're the bait. I think you were all allowed safe passage to invoke the proverbial false sense of security. I'll bet that if I tried to walk through right now I'd end up a door jamb sandwich."

The house suddenly shuddered. The sound of stone grating on stone echoed down the corridor like a gunshot in a barrel. A door appeared on the wall opposite the door through which they had come. Tina screamed, as she watched in horror as the hall with Matt in it rearranged itself. Instead of a hallway, Matt stood at the top of the incline that had led down into the tunnel way back when. The house gave another shake, this time only on Matt's side. He staggered backwards, lost his balance, and tumbled heels over head down the incline. Everyone heard the sharp crack of breaking bone, Matt's scream of pain and a final splash.

"He's in that deep pool at the bottom of the ramp," yelled Tina.

Ralph started forward and the door slammed itself shut. No matter how hard they tried, even with everyone pushing at once, they couldn't get it open. Finally,

Emma straightened up and turned to face the new door that had appeared on the opposite wall.

"Another trick ... another delay," Emma said. "It's trying to make us waste our time saving Matt."

Walcott was already studying the door that had materialized. It was a single plate of iron, six feet in height. Its face was completely smooth. He ran his hand across it slowly, feeling for any sign of a hidden keyhole of latch. He felt nothing but the cold flat of the iron. "Dammit!" Frustrated, he gave the door a solid thump with the heel of his fist. "Moutre m'! Moutre m', dammit!"

The soft glow of white light from the moon pendant around Walcott's neck began to grow brighter and change colors. Red became orange, which became green and then yellow. The yellow became blue and when the blue deepened to purple, a narrow beam erupted from its surface. It cut a sharp angle downward toward the bottom left corner of the door. There, illuminated in its glow was a keyhole.

"I believe you might be holding the key for this, Ralph," said Walcott. "Mind doing the honors once more?"

"Are we just gonna leave Matt?" asked Tina. What if he's stuck in that pool and can't get out? Are we just gonna let him drown. Or worse, what if he's not alone over there. We have to do something."

"We are," said Emma, her voice soft and calm. "What we're doing is what's going to solve the problem. The only way for Matt ... and *us* ... to possibly survive all this is meet that bastard Wickersham head on. And that's what we're doing." She nodded toward the door.

"He's on the other side of that. I know it. And if you stop and think ... stop and feel it ... you know it, too."

At the same time that Ralph slipped the key into its hole, Wickersham was undoing his pants in front of Annabel, and Annabel's features were becoming Abigail's.

## Chapter 40
## ALL OR NOTHING

**11:42 p.m. – 11:59 p. m.**

Ralph twisted the key but the door didn't open, it just disappeared. Tommy pushed his way through first and Emma was right on his heels. The sight that greeted her froze her heart. Though everyone else saw Mother Cassandra's daughter, Emma saw both Abigail and her Annabel. She was held down on her knees and manacled like a slave. Brian stood before them, his pants around his ankles and one hand holding his member in front of her daughter's face. The demon was holding her head steady with one hand and squeezing her breast with the other. Beneath the façade of Brian's appearance, Emma saw Wickersham clearly.

When Tommy and Emma burst into the room, the demon let out a howl of rage. Wickersham planted a foot on Annabel's chest and pushed her over onto her back. He fumbled to get his pants all the way off, as he commanded the beast to defend him.

"Destroy them," bellowed Wickersham. "Tear them apart. They must not be allowed to prevent us from succeeding." He hauled Annabel/Abigail up onto the altar, slammed her down on her back hard enough to knock the wind from her and chained her there.

The demon closed the distance in several large strides. It swiped it thick claws at Emma, who ducked easily under its arm. Tommy barreled forward, driving the top of his head into the thing's chest. He bounced off and went sprawling across the floor. As the beast wheeled on him, Tommy rolled to one side. At the same moment, Tina jumped on its back. She wrapped her legs around its abdomen and her arms around its throat and tried her best to choke it. The feel of its slimy, leathery-like skin made her own skin crawl. The thing paid no attention to the woman on its back. It reached down and lifted Tommy from the floor by his shoulder with a single hand. Delighting in the man's scream of pain, it squeezed as tightly as it could, sinking its thick talons into Tommy's flesh.

Ralph started toward the demon and Walcott pulled him back. "Not yet. Be patient."

"Be patient?" Ralph looked at the man as if his head had fallen off. "I think they need help *now*, don't you?"

"You have to wait, Ralph. I'm going to need your help." He pointed a finger across the room. "See that infant lying there? That's what I have to get to, and if we try now, I don't think we'll make it."

Ralph's mouth dropped open when he saw the half-infant lying on the floor at the base of the altar. Even from the doorway he could see the thing's heart pulsing in and out of an open chest, its legs kicking wildly and its black eyes rolling form side to side.

Above the baby, Wickersham had climbed atop the altar and perched himself over Annabel. Naked from the waist down, he forced her legs apart and threw back his head like a howling wolf. "Now shall my seed be planted. And from that seed shall spring the vehicle of my corporeal immortality." His hips thrust forward as his member took on the appearance and size of the incubus's. It angled toward the sweet spot of his ... of *its* ... desire.

*CraaaaaKKK*! Emma swung the shillelagh like a baseball bat, catching Wickersham in the side of his head. The blow sent him tumbling off the altar – off Annabel. That it was Brian's body that just took the blow made Emma queasy. Nevertheless, whatever had to be done to save Annabel, she'd sure as hell do. She started around the other side of the altar to catch Wickersham before he could regain his feet. With her mind fixed on stopping Wickersham, she never noticed the baby at her feet until she inadvertently kicked it across the floor. She watched it as the thing went spinning across the room like an out of control top and landed up against the block wall with a soft thud and deafening wail of pain and anger.

Ralph couldn't stand it anymore. It just wasn't in him to watch his friends battling for their lives while he stood in a doorway. He shook himself out of Walcott's grip. "You need the baby? You got the baby." He charged toward the infant and almost made it. But something heavy slammed into his back and sent him to the floor. He went down hard, his forehead striking the block and the blackness closed in.

It was Tina's body that had driven Ralph to the floor. Wanting to concentrate on Tommy, the beast had reached back over his shoulder, snatched Tina around the neck and plucked her off. The next thing she knew she was flying through the air, arms and legs pinwheeling uselessly. She was sure that if she hadn't smacked into Ralph, her neck would have been broken when she hit the wall. Ralph had been driven face down and she rolled off him onto the unforgiving stone like a kid rolling off a runaway sled. A pair of loud pops, followed by a louder snapping sound and a lightning bolt of pain, told her she'd just lost a couple of ribs and her left arm.

With Tina gone, the demon's full attention fell on Tommy. The fire that burned in Tommy's shoulder began to dissipate. He could feel that whole side of his body going numb. The beast's other hand was closed around his throat. Its gray, leathery lips pulled back, revealing teeth that looked as if they belonged to a giant wolf. Thick yellow liquid dripped from the incisors, and Tommy had no doubt that it was more than just saliva, it was venom. The whole thing almost made him laugh. To come all this way, through everything that had happened, just to die before being of any real use. It seemed to be the story of his life.

On the other side of the room, Emma had moved around the altar to find Brian lying motionless face down. Blood oozed from the side of his head and puddled on the floor. She raised the shillelagh over her head and stopped just short of brining it down. Something didn't feel right to her. Taking a big chance, she knelt down to see if Brain, or Wickersham, still had a pulse. It was there but very weak and his breathing, very shallow. The million dollar question was: was this Brian, Wickersham, or still both. Who would she be killing if she killed him?

\*\*\*

At the same time that Walcott's pendent was showing them the keyhole, Matt was fighting his way to the surface of the pool. The plunge into the cold water had momentarily stolen his breath. He'd broken the surface just in time. He was thankful that the worst that had happened on his bounce down the stone ramp was a separated right shoulder. At his age, he was sure he'd find himself with at least a broken hip, if not a broken everything.

Using his good arm, he inched his way across the pool toward the well side. He figured that if he was going to have a chance of getting out, that would be the only way. As Tina was being hurled into Ralph, Matt pulled himself up out of the water and fell back against the wall to catch his breath. He sat there in dark wondering what was going on with the others. It seemed his fall down into the pool had somehow severed his mental connection. He hoped it was just temporary.

Knowing time was of the essence, Matt forced himself up. The pain in his shoulder was substantial but manageable. Unable to see anything in the pitch black, he felt his way along the tunnel. He hadn't gone very far before he banged his forehead on a low outcropping of rock.

"Shit, I forgot. This is gonna feel good on the arm." He hunched himself over. After only two steps, he realized he was still too tall. The only thing he could do was to get down and crawl. It wasn't a very pleasant prospect. On top of that, what the hell did he expect to do once he reached the well? Scaling a stone wall was definitely out of the question. "Guess I'll worry about that when I get there, right?"

***

As the others were gaining access to the dungeon and Matt was nursing a separated shoulder and bruised forehead, Janet paced restlessly back and forth in front of the old well. She came to a dead stop when the others entered the room and the battle began. Her heart swelled with anger at being left out, and with shame for not being there with her friends.

"This is fucking ridiculous," she cursed. *I need to get in there. What damned good am I doing here, walking in circles around an empty well?* She turned toward the house and headed for the little path that would lead her back. She'd only gone a few paces before a vine wrapped itself around her leg and dragged her back to the well.

*You don' want t'be leavin' jus' yet, chil. Mot'er tol' you ... de part you have to play have to be played here.*

The vine unwrapped itself, spread out across the ground and grew into the image of Mother Cassandra. She gave Janet a sly wink and rustled her dress, sending waves and waves of honeysuckle through the air and down into the well.

"But I can't just leave my friends on their own," protested Janet. "I can't!"

"You ain't leavin' nobody, girl. Mot'er tol' you ... your part is here. An' it's comin' soon. An' more important ... you gon' help Mot'er ... an' all your friends ... t'end dis." She gave Janet another sly wink. "You see, chil, *he* an' de house be connected ... one an' de same. What he don't know is dat it be de same for Mot'er and de grounds. Toget'er ... you an' me an' de one you're waitin' for gon' pull him down. So you be patient an' know you got a purpose here." She paused a moment and then added: "Mot'er give you all a gift a long time ago ... but you ain't usin' it. If you want dis all t'end ... de ones from before got t'do what dey done before. Toget'er you c'n hold de beast until de crystal and staff become one."

Janet started to open her mouth, but Mother vanished, leaving behind only a tangle of honeysuckle vine. "What we did before. What we did..." She thought back seventy years and one single image came to mind. She walked over to the well and sat down with her back against it. Then, closing her eyes, she stretched her arms out on either side of her. *Come on guys, link up. Grab my hands and mind and let's put a stop to all this now, just like we did when Henry and Amy needed us way back then.*

\*\*\*

Tommy was sinking fast when Janet burst into his mind. The power of it shot through him like an electric charge. It's intensity was so great it traveled up the beast's arms and slammed into his head. He let Tommy drop and slapped his hands to the sides of his head as he staggered back. Tommy closed his eyes and saw himself taking Janet's hand. As he did, he reached out to Tina, who was just getting to her feet and preparing to charge the beast again. She stood absolutely still and held out her hands. Her mind instantly joined Tommy's and Janet's.

Down in the tunnel, Tommy's voice slammed into Matt's head. It was so loud and strong he thought he actually heard it with his ears. And then it was joined by Tina's and Janet's voices. Their thoughts merged, locked, became a single thought. *Time to make the bad things happen. Only this time, they're going to be focused.*

Tommy suddenly knew what had to be done. The problem was, Emma was not part of their connection, and he didn't dare break his with the others to tell her. For now, he needed to keep the demon at bay. He imagined a high voltage wire, bristling with charge. It sparked and danced around, whipping this way, then that. When the beast moved toward him, the wire lashed out. When it tried to move toward Tina it struck at him like a snake.

Emma stood up, looked at Brian one more time and then over at the demon, who seemed to be dancing in place. What the group had created with their minds was invisible to Emma. To her, it looked as if the demon were auditioning for some trained monkey act – except for its guttural screams and growls of anger. Whatever it was doing, it was totally occupied. If she could just find something sharp, she might be able to end this right now. Of course, walloping it good with the shillelagh occurred to her, but she didn't really think it would do all that much good. *Nevertheless*, she thought.

She moved quietly toward it skirting the wall. She waited, the shillelagh held at the ready, baseball bat style, as before. Her moment arrived, it bellowed out another loud roar, its head thrown far back. She stepped forward and started her swing.

Ralph grabbed her wrist just before she could bring the blow home. He threw his other arm around her neck and started squeezing. The shillelagh dropped from her hand as she tried to pry Ralph off of her. Her throat was beginning to burn and tiny stars were shooting willy-nilly across the backs of her eyes. He was just too strong for her and his touch was that of ice. She suddenly realized why Brian had been so still. Wickersham had left him; he had taken Ralph.

Now it was all or nothing. Tommy realized what he had to do and told the others. Nobody liked it, but they all agreed on its necessity. Temporarily letting the image of the live wire slip from his mind ... their minds ... Tommy broke his mental connection with them. He threw himself across the floor past the still dancing demon and snatched up the shillelagh. Wickersham was dragging Emma's failing body toward the altar, whispering softly in her ear.

"Okay, Mother," yelled Tommy, "I sure hope I got this right." He held the shillelagh up against his arm underneath his tattoo. The tattoo began to glow and then spark. Tommy had to grit his teeth against the pain. With an explosive flash of blinding white light, the tattoo disappeared from his arm, and seated itself atop the shillelagh.

***

When Ralph grabbed Emma, Walcott realized that the moment he awaited had come. He slipped the back pack off, pulled out the small chalice and a short dagger, which he shoved into his belt. The time for games was over. Walcott walked right across the middle of the floor. When the demon turned for him he stopped, held the chalice in front of it and demanded it retreat. Smoke, like dry ice, rose from the chalice and spilled over the edge. "What was my grandmother's is now mine. To me has she given the last of the best, as she with flora and earth now may rest. Burn in the fire and freeze in the ice. For all that you've done must you now pay the price."

The smoke from the chalice encircled the demon's feet and they were instantly frozen to the floor. Walcott continued across the room toward the baby, his attention centered on Wickersham and Emma. On his way past, he gripped the chalice in his teeth and lifted the shillelagh from Tommy's hands and kept walking, his eyes fixed solely on Wickersham. "We are all bound together ... house, infant, you, me, Abigail, Grandmother. One heart beats for all of us, without it ... none survive."

Behind him, the demon let out a thundering roar and struggled to free itself. The freezing smoke around its ankles began to thin. Walcott ignored it and kept going until he stood beside the abomination that was his brother. He knelt beside it, setting the chalice on the floor next to its head and the shillelagh beside it. "Born together as one, ripped into two ... one to serve the darkness ... one to serve the light. Half each, whole together, good and bad, darkness and light. Now has come the time to purge this house of life, of its evil."

Tommy and Tina were fixed in place, awestruck, not knowing what they should do. And then Janet's voice blasted into their heads. *Reconnect! Reform the circle.*

Tina moved over, knelt by Tommy and took his hand. At that moment, the demon freed itself and lumbered toward them, growling and snarling.

"NO!" yelled Ralph in Wickersham's voice, as he backed toward the altar, dragging Emma with him. "NO! You shall not prevail. *My* time has come." When he reached the altar, he tightened his arm around her throat, and with one last violent squeeze, let her drop, choking and gagging, barely conscious, to the floor. Tearing at his pants, he quickly stripped them off and climbed up on top of Annabel/Abigail. "IT IS MY TIME!" he thundered, and drove his penis into the woman.

***

Matt had made it almost to the opening at the base of the well when the overpowering aroma of honeysuckle flooded the tunnel. The air was so heavy with it he thought he could almost see it. In fact, he could see it. Intertwining strands of yellow, no thicker than balloon strings, swirled in beautiful patterns within a gossamer cloud of white. Within the cloud, pinpoint flashes of light danced around the yellow strands. Matt sat back against the wall, hypnotized by the effect, unable to draw his eyes away. He was unconscious of the fact that the pain in his shoulder had suddenly abated. And then her voice, sweeter than candied sugar, filled the tunnel.

"Mot'er got two last tricks before all dat she is is no more. One I saved for you 'cause you got de heart dat beats only wit' love an' kindness. Mot'er feel bad dat dat heart gon' break ... but t'ings dat must be must be. When you get to de well, you gon' sleep. It ain't for you to see de end o'all dis. Dat's why Mot'er keep you out of de connection wit' de ot'ers. Your part come after ... an' it gon' be awful hard on de good heart dat beat wit'in you. What Mot'er tell you now ... dat you gon' forget when you wake." Now wake from your dream o'de beautiful lights and continue on de journey dat is yours."

Matt's body gave a little shiver and he found himself still on his hands and knees. He felt funny, like something was different, or maybe missing. When he started forward, he realized that he was using both hands to crawl along and the pain in his shoulder was gone. In fact, it was no longer separated. Picking up his pace, he made his way to the opening and into the bottom of the well. For a few minutes he stood there, gazing up at and wondering how the hell he was going to climb out. Then, without warning, a wave of dizziness struck him and he dropped to his knees. A moment later, his eyes too heavy to hold open any longer, he laid down and fell asleep.

***

Ralph fought against the control Wickersham exerted, disgusted at what his body was doing. Wickersham railed at the interruption, pushing harder against Ralph's will. *Stop resisting. Let your body feel what it has never felt before.* Wickersham laughed. *Yes, we are one, I know all your thoughts; you have never had a woman before. Let this new sensation wash over you like a flood. Let it drown you in pleasure and be swept away from all interference.*

Wickersham refocused on what he was doing. He drew himself out of his struggling victim, raised his hips and slammed himself back inside her, letting all the feel of it sweep through Ralph's nerves. He felt Ralph's body shudder with the feeling of it. *Taste*, he told Ralph. *Taste the sweet pleasures of a woman's body.* He bent his head down and ran his tongue up Abigail's throat and across her lips. *Now shall we, together, Ralph, implant the seed of my future.* He drew himself out of her again and raised his hips as high as he could. Before he could drive himself back into her, a hand closed on the collar of his shirt and pulled him off the altar onto the floor.

"Get off my wife, you sick son-of-a-bitch." Brian threw himself on top of Ralph and closed his hands around his throat. Blood still ran from the head wound. It had clotted one eye closed. The other glared down at Ralph, reflecting nothing but pure hatred. "I'm gonna kill you, you motherfucker."

Ralph's years of faming made him anything but weak. In a single, quick motion, he twisted himself free. One minute Brian was on top, the next, the bottom with Ralph's hands on his throat. "I shall not waste time strangling you, boy," said Wickersham. He grabbed Brian by the back of the head and the chin. In one quick twist to the right, Brian's neck snapped. The sound of it turned Emma's stomach. And Annabel's wail of disbelief and grief poured from Abigail's mouth.

"Now I shall finish what must be finished."

"I don't think so," said Walcott, drawing Wickersham's attention. "Your time is done!"

"Nooooooo!" Wickersham watched in anguished horror as Walcott plunged the dagger into the infant's heart and filled the chalice with its blood. "Separated at birth, ripped into two, I now rejoin with Isaac, my brother. As we become whole, all that has been within this house becomes undone."

Wickersham charged for Walcott. As he came around the end of the altar, Emma shoved a leg out in front of him. He went down on his belly and slid forward, almost within reach of Walcott – close enough to watch him upend the chalice. When he had drained the last of it, Walcott tossed the chalice aside. "It is done!"

\*\*\*

As Wickersham tossed Emma's body to the floor and mounted Annabel/Abigail, Tommy, Tina and Janet linked minds once again. The demon, free of its freezing bonds, shambled toward them. Its eyes burned red, its fangs dripping venom and its clawed hands cutting the air in great swiping arcs. Flames danced across the thing's shoulders, licking at the ceiling. Tina started to reform the image of the live wire but Tommy shifted her focus ... their focus. In his mind he saw the shillelagh and crystal moving across the floor toward Emma.

At the same moment Walcott plunged the dagger into the growling infant's heart, the shillelagh shot across the room and stood upright in front of Emma. Red lines of fire circled the edges of the crystal, intensifying the electric-blue blaze of its core. Emma grabbed the staff with both hands. The minute her fingers closed around it, her mind joined with the conscious echo Mother had left within the crystal and the two became one. She worked herself off the floor just as the demon sank its thick talons into Tina's chest. It closed its fist around her heart and delighted in watching the light go out of her eyes.

The shock of it broke the connection between Tommy and Janet. Each of them felt the pain in their chest that Tina felt. Janet grabbed at her chest and fell to her knees, panting. It was worse for Tommy. He had been holding Tina's hand. The pain in his chest shot upward through his neck and into his head. He had no doubt he was about to have the stroke of all strokes. He leaned back against the wall and fumbled for his cigarettes. *Guess they can't hurt at this point*, he thought as he put one in his mouth. He dug in his pocket for the matches and the cigarette dropped from his mouth as he slid to the floor.

The demon roared and turned on Emma.

## Chapter 41
## THE HOUR CHIMES

**12:00 a. m.**

When he had drained the last of the infant's blood, Walcott tossed the chalice aside. It struck the floor at the same time as the ancient clock in the upstairs hallway struck twelve.

"It is done! And it is undone! We are one ... and we are none." He pitched forward and lay beside the baby, his whole body convulsing. Wickersham also began to convulse, as did the baby. On the last chime of the hour Wickersham's consciousness exploded from Ralph's body and Ralph dropped to the floor. Wickersham's consciousness solidified and immediately began to decay. His flesh yellowed and then grayed. It sloughed from his bones like dripping wax. His hair fell from his head in tangled tufts and his teeth deserted his mouth. He threw his bony hands up over his skeletal face ... and then there was nothing. Dust swirled in a small whirlwind and then dropped to the floor.

*\*\*\**

Twirling the shillelagh in front of her in figure-eight patterns, Emma advanced on the demon that was advancing on her. When they came face to face, the beast shot out its clawed hand. It froze, and ice began to crawl up its arm, covering it, encapsulating it. It spread up and over its shoulders in wave after wave, where the flames that danced there quickly melted it. But the flames couldn't keep up. Slowly, the fire was extinguished, and with it, the flames of lust that sustained the beast. No longer subject to the will of the one who had summoned it, it dissolved into swirling cloud of black. Like smoke being drawn through a keyhole, it retreated into the darkness of the world from which it had been conjured, disappearing through the floor.

Emma dropped the shillelagh and went to Annabel. As Brian had been, so was she stopped by the chains. There was no key to be found and there was nothing with which she could break them. She tried touching them with the crystal on the shillelagh, but its fire and light had died away the moment the incubus vanished.

"Don't worry, baby," she said. And it was Annabel she was looking at. "I'll get you out of here; I promise."

"Let ... let me help," said Ralph, struggling to get up. He felt as if he'd just gone five rounds with the world MMA champion. He grabbed one of the chains and started tugging, but it was useless.

"You got de key, you just forgot."

Emma turned to see the wispy figure of Abigail.

"Key? I..." She stopped and dug in her pocket, suddenly remembering the key that had been in Henry's box.

"Mot'er give dat to your fat'er long ago. It served him then ... now it serves you. You set us free, de way Mot'er always believed you would. Now you got to hurry, 'cause Mot'er she gon' finish de rest." Abigail smiled. "What she call her last trick. Wickersham ... he owned de house. Mot'er ... she own all de green dat live in de eart'." Abigail's image flickered and then faded, leaving behind only the echo of her voice. "You all done what needed t'be done, an' dat set me an' Mot'er free. But now you mus' go; you mus' hurry. T'ank you all."

Emma quickly undid the shackles and helped Annabel to her feet. When she turned around, Walcott and the baby were gone. In their place was the body of a single, conjoined infant.

The house shook and cracks began to spread across the floor and walls. Branching vines grew through every crack that formed, thickening and spreading. There was no time to do anything about the others. Leaving their bodies behind was abhorrent, but there was nothing else they could do. Still, Annabel was unwilling to leave her husband. Emma and Ralph had to drag her out of the house and away from Brian. They made their way up the steps, having to climb and fumble their way over vines the size of oak roots. By the time they made it out the front door, across the porch and onto the front lawn, the house was totally covered. Stone began to crumble and break apart as the vines squeezed and tugged and pulled. Finally, with a great, thundering crunch, the house was pulled into the ground, leaving behind only a crater-sized hole.

***

Ralph led Emma, with Annabel in tow, back to his truck. He found a blanket to cover Annabel and got her seated and wrapped up. "I have to go to the well. Don't ask me why, I just do."

Emma didn't argue. There was no point. She had the same feeling. "Go, I'll stay here with Belle." A thought struck her and she grabbed Ralph's arm before he could leave. "I think you should take some rope with you, too."

Ralph just nodded, fished around in the back of the truck, slipped the coil of rope over his shoulder and left. Five minutes later he found Janet leaning over the edge of the well. "Need some help?"

Janet turned with a start and then let out a sigh of relief. "Am I ever glad to see you ... but if you ever sneak up on me like that again..." She cocked her head over her shoulder. "Matt's stuck. Help me get him out."

As Ralph uncoiled the rope and lowered it down, Janet brought herself to ask the question she didn't want to ask. "What about the others? I know for sure Tommy and Tina are dead ... but..."

"Emma and Annabel are back at the truck," was all he would say. And as he worked at hauling Matt up and out, Janet knew there *was* nothing else to say.

# EPILOGUE

**11:35 a.m. November 7, 2017**

As he'd been told it would be, Matt's heart was broken. He had his arm wrapped around Janet's waist and his head resting on her shoulder as they walked back to the limo. He couldn't stop himself from crying, not that he wanted to. Emma's tears were shared, some for those she'd lost, but most for the daughter that still hadn't returned. The shrinks said PTSD was a tricky thing to deal with, and that only time would tell if Annabel would have the strength to bounce back or not. As Emma led Annabel back to the car, she wondered if any of them would really ever be the same.

Henry and Brian had been buried the day before. Today they laid Tommy and Tina to rest. As he had wanted from the start, Timothy, Matt's grandson, provided the services. No one really spoke. There wasn't anything to say. All that remained was an emptiness that would have no filling.

***

**12:14 p.m. November 18, 2017**

Ralph tapped the side of his spoon on the glass to get everyone's attention. In this case, everyone was

Emma, Annabel and Timothy. "I'd like to propose a toast to the newlyweds, but first I have a suggestion. I suggest that we re-celebrate this occasion this coming summer when the weather is a hell of a lot nicer than now. I think this farmhouse has seen too many dark days and had way too many ghosts haunting it. We need to make it a happier place." He cleared his throat and continued. "At any rate, I wish all the best to Janet and Matt. From what I understand, this wedding has been percolating for more than seventy years. May a love that has survived this long continue to flourish."

They all raised their glasses in salute. And then, slowly, very slowly, Annabel's hand reached out. Her fingers closed around the stem of her glass and lifted it off the table.

*THE END*

## ALSO BY THOMAS A. BRADLEY
(Under the pen name T.A. Bradley)

---

*RELIC of the DAMNED*

When an ancient relic of enormous power inadvertently falls into the hands of a weak and desperate antiques dealer, hell on earth becomes more than just a cliché to the small town of Banderman Falls, Pennsylvania. Seduced into believing that the relic is his to command, Carlton Wedgemore is manipulated into serving the demonic incarnation of all evil, Zachariah Witherstone. And Banderman Falls is plunged into a nightmare of darkness from which it may never awaken. In his quest to acquire the icon, Witherstone usurps the minds of the townspeople through dreams of lust and torment. He divides the town, pitting men against women, husbands against wives and brothers against sisters. And the people soon find themselves no more than puppets dancing on the strings of destruction.

It begins with the murder of a young convenience store clerk. At first, Sheriff Jack Dougherty is convinced it's a robbery gone awry. But when two men go missing and his deputy turns up dead, Jack begins to sense that there may be more powerful forces at work in his town – a sense that is confirmed when he is brutally attacked by insects in defense of their master.

At the same time that Jack is discovering that the peace and harmony of Banderman Falls is unwinding,

Father Gabriel Jacobs receives a visit from an old friend. Geoffrey Dunsmore, a man with unusual abilities, enlists his friend's aid in a struggle that will claim more than lives.

As the terror unwinds, ordinary people must rise to a challenge that will test their faith, test their courage and demand the ultimate sacrifice for a *chance* at victory. Hell has come to devour all, and has chosen Banderman Falls as its first entrée.

## *PRIMORDIA*

Col. Ross Clayton is a dedicated scientist, devoted to his wife Irene, his ten year old son, Tommy, and his four year old daughter, Amanda. He is also a dead-ringer for Blake Arletti, a hit man trying to escape his past and outrun an assassin. When their paths cross, Ross's life comes apart in horrific fashion. Having fallen ill with a mutated virus, Ross is implanted with ERIC-D, an experimental, radio-isotope fueled pacemaker. And when he is mistaken for Blake, murdered and buried in the park, it isn't long before the damaged pacemaker enhances the mutation of the virus and Ross is reanimated in a near primordial state. Now, neither living nor dead, he is faced with the loss of everything he ever cared about. And when the assassin crosses paths with his family and murders Amanda, Ross must force himself to find one last strand of humanity. In a desperate act to bring back the daughter he loves, Ross sets in motion something more chilling than anything anyone could have imagined.

Fiction/Horror

## 13 ECHOES

A collection of 13 short stories of the macabre.

Journey with a young boy suffering with Down's Syndrome as he is confronted by bullies. Lost and alone, he finds a protector he never knew existed.

Meet a lonely man who is the butt of everyone's jokes, a man who finally finds love, comfort and acceptance in a way he could never have imagined.

They say the waiting is the hardest part. It's not!

Winning isn't always what it's cracked up to be, especially when relatives are involved.

A long overdue vacation takes a man to a place that few people ever see.

A band learns that some gigs are just never ending.

An abusive husband learns that the secret he keeps within the walls of his house has a life of its own

AND six other tales of the weird.

Fiction/Horror

**SUNDOWN RISING**

When he loses his wife to a drunk driver, Richard Anthony Millay believes there will be no more brightness in his future. He may be right, for it is the darkness of an unrecalled past that pulls him away from everything he thought was real. Moving into the house that his wife had wanted so badly before she died, he soon comes to discover that it holds dark secrets, secrets that will haunt him in ways he couldn't imagine. It will awaken in him something that had lain dormant in his being. But will he remember what he needs to know in time to deal with the evil that walks within? A terrible discovery awaits him. More than that, he will learn that when the past and present collide ... all bets are off.

Fiction/Horror/Vampire

## ABOUT THE AUTHOR

Born in Philadelphia, Pennsylvania, Thomas lives in Drexel Hill, PA with his two German shepherds. He served with the Army Medical Corps during Vietnam as a Clinical Specialist. He holds a Bachelor's Degree in Microbiology, his Master's work done in Virology He has worked for a number of biotech companies as a virologist and has co-authored several scientific papers and given presentations for The American Society for Virology and The American Society for Microbiology. From time-to-time he consults on virology laboratory safety issues.

Recently diagnosed with adult-onset myotonic muscular dystrophy, Thomas continues to put in full days at the keyboard, getting the bizarre stories that haunt his mind onto the pages.

Contact him at
tabradley55@gmail.com

**Author's Note: A gentle request.**

Please, be kind to *all* your authors. Reviews are helpful, both positive and negative. If you've enjoyed a book, the author would like to know that. If you didn't, he'd want to know that, too. Please take a moment to leave a review. Thank you.

Manufactured by Amazon.ca
Bolton, ON